D0985904

Anatomy. Monotony.

Edy Poppy

ANATOMY.
MONOTONY.

Translated from the Norwegian by May-Brit Akerholt

DALKEY ARCHIVE PRESS

Originally published in Norwegian by Gyldendal Norsk Forlag as *Anatomi. Monotoni.* in 2005.

Copyright © 2005 by Edy Poppy
Translation copyright © 2018 by May-Brit Akerholt
Cover photo copyright © by Cyril Albert-Gondrand
First Dalkey Archive edition, 2018.

Library of Congress Cataloging-in-Publication Data
Names: Poppy, Edy, 1975- author. | Akerholt, May-Brit translator.
Title: Anatomy, monotony / by Edy Poppy ; translated from the Norwegian by May-Brit Akerholt.
Other titles: Anatomi, monotoni. English
Description: First Dalkey Archive edition. | Victoria, TX: Dalkey Archive Press, 2018.
Identifiers: LCCN 2017057608 | ISBN 9781628972290 (pbk. : alk. paper)
Subjects: LCSH: Married people--Fiction.
Classification: LCC PT8952.26.O64 A6513 2018 | DDC 839.823/8--dc23
LC record available at https://lccn.loc.gov/2017057608

www.dalkeyarchive.com
Victoria, TX / McLean, IL / Dublin

Dalkey Archive Press publications are, in part, made possible through the support of the University of Houston-Victoria and its programs in creative writing, publishing, and translation.

Printed on permanent/durable acid-free paper

For
my husband,
who has given me everything,
even what I didn't want.

(He is now my ex-husband)

0:

FADE IN

I sit on a bench in St. James' Park, next to the little water pool where ducks swim. It's a warm day. A man sits down next to me.

After a while he says:

"You're Swedish, you live in England, and you're reading a French book."

"Yes, that's exactly right," I say.

He continues to talk to me, uninterestingly. I continue to read, uninterested. He asks if he can see me again. I doubt it. Still, he gives me his phone number.

"You never know, do you?"

"That's true."

Then he says:

"I don't even know your name."

I say that's how I prefer it. It's almost like being in a book by Marguerite Duras: a woman, a man, her and him, that's what I'd like us to be, anonymous people. He accepts this, but wants to continue our conversation. I don't. I prefer to continue reading my book. I think: Loneliness. And believe that is what I want.

Later I happen upon the stranger in the middle of the city, in one of the many second-hand bookshops on Charing Cross Road. When he sees me, he calls out enthusiastically. Alarmed, I run into the crowd of people. He follows me. I run from the street and down to the underground. I hesitate. Pretend I haven't seen him. Run back up to the street again. Hesitate again. Stop. Change my mind. Think that it's important to test myself, how far I can go. I give him a chance to catch up. He doesn't stop until he stands right next to me. I notice he has a strong pulse, that his heart is pounding under his skin. He insists that it would be an advantage to know my name. He looks into my eyes, for a long time. I don't blink. I smile.

"*The Lover* is a fantastic literary work, don't you think?" he asks and shows me the book he has just bought.

"Yes, but I'm not reading that one now," I hint. "There have been many stories since *The Lover* . . ."

He doesn't take the hint. Suggests instead that we should sit down together. Have a coffee maybe. Something that takes five minutes. Because he's pressed for time. I accept this reluctantly. He has aroused my interest after all.

"How did you know I was Swedish?" I ask.

"I didn't know, I just guessed."

I smile. I like to be the product of a strange man's fantasy. Outside Scandinavia, Norway doesn't exist. Outside Scandinavia, we're all Swedish. Liv Ullmann is Swedish, too, out there in the big world, I think.

We order two caffe lattes. I light a cigarette. The stranger doesn't smoke. I smoke two. I have idiotic, childish thoughts that make me horny. The coffee is hot. I burn my tongue. I look the stranger in the eyes: large brown eyes, long eyelashes. I blush, I laugh. I think: If I meet him again, we're going to make love. I try to imagine his body, naked. He asks why I'm blushing. I tell him I'm shy. It's easier to be shy, then it's up to him to find the chemistry. I talk only a little, mostly listen. He talks a lot, doesn't listen at all. Tries instead to impress. Tells me that when he's in love, he paints. No, he doesn't paint, he mixes colors. He asks what my favorite colors are. I answer at random, reel off a list of those surrounding me, look at the large clock on the wall behind his back.

"Those five minutes went really fast," he says and throws on his jacket. For once he reads my thoughts. "Do you want to meet me again tomorrow?" he asks.

"Maybe . . . " I answer.

He doesn't give up, I think. I like that. That he insists.

"I'll ring you," I add.

He smiles and hurries out the door. I know I'll keep my word. He turns several times and waves. I wave back. He almost bumps into an old woman. I like that he gets clumsy that way, that feelings can make him lose his balance. My tummy tingles, lust, that's all it is, butterflies.

I sit there and look out of the dirty cafe window for a long time after the stranger has disappeared. A light rain is beginning to fall. It's lovely with rain on a day like this, when it's hot. It's really idiotic to sit in a cafe, I think and light a new cigarette, a Vogue: long, thin lady's cigarettes with a kitschy case, cigarettes men wouldn't smoke under any circumstances. I usually get to keep them to myself. I'm about to order another caffe latte, when I discover that the stranger's cup is only half-empty. I take a sip from it, then another, place my lips where his once were, amuse myself until there's nothing left. Then I sneak his cup into my bag and take out a notebook. I write down one sentence. No more.

A LITTLE PIECE OF NORWAY . . .

I JUMP OFF THE bus and walk home. For the first time in a long time I look around. Look at the red bricks decorating all the houses in the neighborhood. Think about how this depressing working-class suburb has been changed by young people and given a new life. I find my keys, open the door in three places, and put on the security chain. It's nice to live here, I think, even if it isn't all that safe.

It's quiet. The house is empty. I feel alone without my husband. I kick off my shoes and walk over to the kitchen to make tea, English tea that I put milk in. I'm still fascinated by everything English. Then I walk up to the first floor, drink my tea in the recently stolen coffee cup, and eat a piece of Freia milk chocolate. I'm still nostalgic about everything Norwegian. I close my eyes and shut out England for a while. Then I turn on the computer and get ready to write. I try to remember Norway—a feeling, a mood, a sound.

Ragnhild hides behind a tree. She is not scared, just curious. She watches it the way she watches a movie: their large black house: yellow, now. She watches the flames. She thinks it's beautiful how they destroy everything they've had with such brutality, such ruthlessness. Her father asks her if she wants to go in and get something. He wonders why she doesn't want her toys. She wants nothing.

"The fire can take everything!" Ragnhild shouts.

She looks at the others running in and out, saving what they can, before they have to save themselves. Only Ronja stands next to her with her tail between her legs. Ragnhild pats her coolly on her head. She doesn't like the smell of dogs. "Come here!" Ravn calls, but then Ragnhild lifts the dog up into her arms. She's reindeer-gray and almost ugly with her short fur, Ragnhild thinks, and studies the little bitch with critical eyes. No one knows what breed Ronja is: just that she is a kind of bird dog. But she's certain to turn out like her master, Ragnhild thinks: devoted, loyal, cooperative, brave, moody, and self-centered. Ragnhild's judgment is biased, because she doesn't like dogs: their faithfulness, that they always follow their master, that they're so clingy. She dreams of the day when Ronja doesn't lick Ravn gratefully all over his face with her long, disgusting, dripping tongue, but gobbles him all up in one mouthful.

Ronja whimpers, she wants to be set down. It's a terrible thing to lose one's naivety, but not to lose it is even worse . . . Ragnhild thinks, and lets the dog run around in her childish way: the game a joy, even though she's afraid . . . Ronja belongs to Ravn, her big brother, and has been given an R-name, just like them. Ragnhild finds it strange that she and her brother have such similar names when they're so different. As if their parents had wanted something else. And out of spite they've just grown more and more different, almost polar opposites. Now and then Ragnhild dreams that Ravn comes in to her at night and stabs out her eyes. The strange thing is that she enjoys the thought of this pain, the blood. As if the inner tension between big brother and little sister could get some release that way.

Ragnhild looks at the flames. Is pulled into them. But from a long way away. Fire sirens are heard in the distance. Soon the firemen will come and destroy everything, she thinks and looks gloomily at her father. He too has stopped running now. He is like his daughter: fascinated. He is taking photos. He likes the distance the camera lens gives him. He gathers the family and puts the camera on self-timer. Little sister and big brother stand next to each other looking grumpy. Ragnhild wishes Ravn looked like the milkman—that would've explained a lot—but everyone knows Ravn looks like his father.

"Cheese," her mother says, off beat, and Ronja comes running into the picture.

She's like the stroke of a felt pen across their faces, preserved for posterity. Ragnhild takes a picture, too, with the past half there and half gone, burnt and mysterious. She will put it in the family album: a large, grand, black house on the edge of collapse.

It's been a while since I saw them now, my family. I get sad when I think about it, how little we talked. It just turned out like that, this lack of communication, of coordination. It's not our fault, bad luck, good luck, call it what you want.

Once I went home, it was several years ago now, they traveled to another place, the whole family except me. I didn't get cranky because they went away, and they didn't get cranky because I arrived. I remember listening to the wind. Yes, imagine, that I had time for things like that. That I listened to the fear and the loneliness as well. That I spent a few days in this new house nursing my melancholy, this strange phenomenon that strangles you slowly but surely, but that such a large, new wooden house, surrounded by forest, in the middle of the night, can be a good friend. I tried to understand which sounds silence is made of. You always find the sound of something hoarse in wooden houses, of course, like someone who's lost their voice and can now only produce a few feeble sounds. Sounds that seem soothing during the day get strangely distorted at night. I think about my big brother, who'll never move away from home: out of irresponsibility and puberty. I wonder if he still hears these sounds, or if he's become deaf to them, if he still feels alone.

When I'm alone there, I can't help looking out the window into the forest. I hear the owls' deep growling, small animals creeping around, the intoxicating roar of the waterfall . . . Natural sounds that frighten me at night. And so I try to remember the fire, remember when I stood there in the dark and watched the flames lighting up the landscape, from our farm and from many farms further up the hill. Then I was no longer afraid. I like to think about it. About this light. About this heat. And the freedom that follows.

*

Ragnhild walks around and examines the sick house like a doctor. Taking its pulse, checking its lungs, its heart . . . No response. Suddenly she feels the pain and the loss as strongly as if she'd lost a good friend. Ragnhild cries. Runs into the forest. Looks for the oppressive, almost unbearable silence.

I stop again. Think about the old, creaking house with slanting ceiling, walls, and floor. The cold house full of drafts and ghosts.

Time passes, doesn't heal any wounds, but green grass and flowers begin to grow between the walls. The remnants of a house. "Don't be angry," Ragnhild says to herself. "It has stood there for more than a hundred years, two hundred . . . It must be allowed to rest now."
Rainer Fassbinder said: "I can sleep when I'm dead." Ragnhild doesn't know yet who Fassbinder is. She doesn't know about Virginia Woolf, Sylvia Plath, Anne Sexton, Chet Baker, Nick Drake, Kurt Cobain, Yukio Mishima, Gilles Deleuze, Paul Celan, Mark Rothko, Jens Bjørneboe, Ragnhild Jølsen, Amalie Skram, Stig Dagerman, Ernest Hemingway, Sid Vicious, Adolf and Eva Hitler, Joseph and Magda Goebbels . . . Suicide, murder. The only thing she knows is the loss. And that she must learn to live with it.

SIDNEY IS A WHITE RABBIT

I THINK ABOUT THINGS that have happened and things that haven't happened. I look out the window. I miss my husband. I want to tell him about the stranger. Because my husband likes such stories about me and casual encounters, and I like that he likes them.

But my husband is out with Sidney again. Sidney Searles, aged eighteen. An easy proposition, I think. An inexperienced girl looking for experience, easy to impress. I imagine Sidney as a white rabbit: naive, young and happy. I imagine my husband as the trap she's going to fall into. I laugh to myself. I'm malicious, jealous, but also arrogant . . . Because there's something about Sidney. From the little I've seen of her, I agree with my husband that she is sensuous, that she has an erotic charm she's not aware of herself. Because Sidney is young. She still lives with her parents. But next year she wants to get her own place. She has said as much to my husband. That that's why she works in the gallery. To save money to get a studio apartment.

I don't want to think about it, about Sidney and my husband. Jealousy is something I have nothing but contempt for, but it still gnaws away inside me. I refuse to be broken. I light a cigarette and think about Sidney all the same. There's something extremely English about Sidney. The kind of Englishness you found in the 1960s and '70s. Because she doesn't look like the girls you see in the streets these days. She reminds you more of a Jane Birkin from the Melody Nelson period. The same thinness, the same small breasts. I know that my husband likes the kind of breasts that are not proper breasts. He likes women who look unfinished.

I feel the lump in my throat is growing. It's getting dark. Soon. He is still not home. I am still imagining Sidney and my husband: how they touch each other, what they are doing. I'm pathetic. Look at myself in the mirror. A tear is running down from my left eye into my mouth. I like the salty taste. I lick my mouth, I want more. But there are no more tears. My husband doesn't like women who cry. Hysteria. There was too much of that around the dinner table when he was a little boy.

FROM THE UNCONSCIOUS LIFE
OF THE SOUL

I SUDDENLY WAKE UP without memories. But with the nasty aftertaste of a dream that came and went in the night, like a thief in my thoughts. I don't know what is missing. Which part of the unconscious life of the soul has been plundered. I fell asleep in front of the computer again. Now I let myself fall. It hurts, and that's what's so good. Outside it's blowing, the trees are singing, screaming . . . Suddenly I remember what I wrote in the cafe yesterday. I get up, find my notebook, and read, anxiously:

Orgasm isn't a small death, but life.

I read it again and again. I wonder where I can place this simple sentence. Because it certainly doesn't fit in with what I'm telling about my childhood. I write it down anyway. For later. Then I have a bath, wash my white hair, pluck my white eyebrows, shave my bikini line, next to my white genitals. Afterwards I make two braids and put them up in two pretzels on my head, perfecting my milkmaid look. I hear all sounds, all steps, but not my husband's. He didn't come home. And now he'll probably be off to work soon. I lie down in bed, alone, empty. I'll lie here like this until I pluck up the courage to call the stranger.

LONDON BY NIGHT

THE STRANGER IS VERY direct, asks:

"Are you one of those women who only want to make love in a bed, indoors?"

"No, of course not."

I laugh. The question caught me offhand. I like it, I soften. I say:

"What an absurd idea to limit your sex life to a bed."

The stranger admits that he enjoys making love outside, in the most bizarre places. Claims that he's very inventive, attentive. He knows all the nooks and crannies in this town, London by night. He takes it for granted that I want to.

We drink Pimm's in every possible combination, with ginger ale, strawberries, mint, cucumber . . . yes, with anything, almost. I light a cigarette. The stranger describes his tongue, what he wants to do with it, where he wants to put it. He slides it back and forth between his front teeth, bragging about his past sexual achievements, oh yes, he knows what it is, how to do it, how he can get a woman beside herself. With lust. He talks about how wet I'm going to be when he has finished with me. Admits he has tried many things, even a whore. He tries to shock me, I think, hoping I lack experience, that I'm modest.

He explains:

"In sex there's no hygiene. Nothing's dirty." He says he loves the smell of sex, the taste. Then he asks: "Cunnilingus?" If I enjoy it when someone penetrates me with their tongue.

"Yes."

He talks about his old conquests, about their reactions, especially about a Swedish girl who had never been so horny in all her life. He is attracted to Swedish girls, he admits, because we're so different from him, exotic. I smile, but don't comment. I long for The Lover, my very own. I'm not very impressed by the stranger. Feel instead somewhat condescending, perhaps. Curious, too, of course. I think: Show me what you can do, but I doubt you're better than The Lover, than the man who was my lover for a year and a half. And then I get an unpleasant feeling in my stomach. Because he is only a means to obtain something. I want sex. It has been a long time since I've had sex with someone I don't know, an outsider, with someone other than my husband . . .

The stranger looks me in the eyes, for a long time. I can feel that he's noticing something I'm trying to hide: an uncertainty, which springs from my bad conscience. Because he suddenly says that most women disappoint him, that they always want something, to profit. I already know by then that I'm one of the women who are going to disappoint him.

He asks:

"How did you meet your husband?"

"He kissed me."

"Was that all?"

"Yes."

Suddenly he doesn't have any more questions. Wants to talk about something else. Hopes my husband is a bad lover at least. I say no and light a cigarette, make large clouds and blow them at the stranger. He doesn't get annoyed, doesn't say anything negative, tells me instead that he feels we have a great deal in common, how striking that is. I say that I haven't noticed, on the contrary I think we're very different, almost opposites. I drink the rest of the Pimm's in one swallow. Because the more I drink, the more chance of having fun with the stranger, making something or other happen between us. But it doesn't help. The alcohol goes straight through me. I don't feel intoxicated at all. I'm bored. There's a vase of flowers on the table.

I pick up a daisy and tear off the white petals one by one:

"He loves me, he loves me not, he loves me not, he loves me . . . he loves me not."

The stranger bursts into laughter. His gestures are clingy and clumsy. When he talks, he is so close to me that I feel each breath on my face.

He takes my hand and then we run off somewhere in Shoreditch between Old Street and Hoxton Square. I wonder if the clarity I feel is just a trick of the alcohol. I squat behind a car and pee.

"Here it is!" he shouts.

"Here?"

We have to close a door and walk down a flight of stairs before we find ourselves in a small gateway. We're outside, we're hidden, we're right next to the back door of a restaurant. Cars often drive past. We hear people talking and what they're talking about. It's embarrassing. The banality of their conversation. As if the content had no meaning, just served a social function. I wonder if the stranger and I, if we . . . He asks me to just forget about them. There's a rusty stove in the stairwell that's making it very hot. I'm sweating. His skin is dark, black almost. I can only just see him. Together we are black and white, like in an old film. I'm naked except for a jacket.

"Have you made love to a black man before?" he suddenly asks, a little too loudly.

"Yes," I whisper back.

I try to balance his loud voice with my weak one. Neutralizing them. He gropes me, puts his fingers deep inside me, licks them. And then he wants me to lick them too. When we kiss, it feels like I'm kissing my own sex, I recognize that bittersweet, unfathomable taste: like the sea; salty, like sweat; sweet. He likes it, can't get enough, licks me dry, swallows. I'm impressed by the size of his member, it's one of the biggest I've seen. He sticks his tongue into my ear and whispers that it's my turn to make him wet, use my mouth. I try, but his member is too big, I think it'll choke me. Like me, he sweats a lot, he turns me in all directions, front and back, says loudly that he likes my ass, kisses it, wants to know if someone has kissed my ass before, licked it.

"Yes, often," I whisper and ask him to keep his voice down.

But when he enters me, I'm the one to scream. He stops, surprised, and asks if it hurts.

"No, men are never brutal enough with me," I insist.

He is almost tender.

After the stranger has taken me three times, I want a cigarette. But the stranger doesn't smoke, and I have none left. It's time to go home. I look around, look for my things, feel nauseous. It's light outside, almost morning. People are on their way home or to a *nachspiel*. The birds are chirping. The stranger asks what I'm looking for.

"My husband's trousers," I whisper.

They're lying on the top of the stairs: a man's blue striped trousers, flea-market trousers. The stranger gives them to me, stands quite still, still naked, horny, asks:

"Do you often meet men while wearing your husband's trousers?"

"Yes, it makes me feel safe," I answer honestly.

I can see that the stranger doesn't like it. I put my foot into one trouser leg, but when I'm about to put the other one in, the stranger stops me, insists that he hasn't had enough, wants me to come home with him, wants us to keep going, everywhere in his flat, down a staircase, on top of a table, the kitchen table. Tempts me by telling me he's a good cook, that we can eat and then go on making love after. Repeats again and again that he hasn't had enough. I answer that I'm like most women, that I always want something—a profit. I put on the rest of my clothes. Quickly. Socks and shoes. And then I leave, I run, run, run . . .

SICKNESS AND SLEEP

I RUN THROUGH THE city, my legs like the second hand on a watch. I don't stop until I'm home.

I've tried to run the alcohol out of my body, but it still has a good grip around my throat.

I rest for a couple of minutes in front of my door. My head is spinning. Now that I'm going to bed, the alcohol takes full effect. One of life's little ironies, I think, and find my keys.

My husband's jacket hangs in the hall. I smile and just manage to kick off my shoes before I stumble up to the bathroom, throw myself over the toilet, and vomit. The sight of my stomach contents makes me vomit again. I wash my mouth, brush my teeth thoroughly, my tongue as well. Then I rub soap all over my body and shower myself with cold water. I still feel dirty. I put on an old sweater inside out: the Pollock sweater, as I call it, because it is The Lover's shabby painting sweater. I almost have to laugh. The faded smell of a lover on a piece of cloth, The Lover, it's really absurd. My husband doesn't like this sweater, and I can understand that. But I can't bring myself to part with it. I'm stupid and sentimental.

I'm longing for my husband. I walk over to our bedroom, which is also where I write. I open the door cautiously and tiptoe carefully into the silence. I want my sounds to become part of his dreams. I whisper a sweet nothing. He turns over on his side, but doesn't wake up. I give him a kiss on his cheek. He gives me a sigh. He's innocent and ignorant. There's a wine bottle on the floor, and a full ashtray. I take a pack of Vogues from my desk drawer, sit down, and then I can finally light the post-coital cigarette. I breathe out, blow out . . . I watch him in the darkness between puffs. Listen to the faint humming that comes out of his nose, feel the heat from his body, and kiss his sleeping lips. This is my husband, I think happily, for better or worse, until death do us part.

I feel a breeze entering the room, the sound of the wind, but also of cars. My husband likes to sleep with the window open, and I respect that, even if it's crazy in a big, noisy city like London.

I crawl into bed. My head is still buzzing. I move closer, hug him so tight that I can hardly breathe. Tomorrow is Sunday and we can spend the whole day together, I think, and close my eyes. But the light forces its way in through a gap in the curtains and irritates me. I get up and shut them properly, I want it as dark as possible. Then I snuggle close to my husband again. It's lovely to have him here in our bed.

I think: I'm about to dirty myself voluntarily. I also think: I have to separate sex from love. I want my husband to be the only one to get both. I believe I don't need to love anyone else, that he can take care of that side, that as well as the intellectual. Because the only thing he needs help to is the erotic, orgies, men who take me from all sides and are sexually almost bestial. I think I should be satisfied with that, because I get more than most women. Of freedom.

I stroke his stomach, pull his nipples . . . I don't want to be alone, separated by sleep.

1:

THE INCOMPREHENSIBLE

I WANT MY HUSBAND to wake up so I can tell him. Everything. About the stranger. So he can tell me everything about Sidney. So we can share experiences . . . and maybe jealousy . . . I kiss his neck, brush away his dark brown curls. My husband looks as French as I look Norwegian. I'm envious of wavy hair, of his having curls. My hair hangs straight down. I get up. I still feel nauseous after the screwed-up bender with the stranger. I pull off the Pollock sweater, put on a white singlet and a tight pair of denim jeans. Denim really means *de Nîmes*, from Nîmes, which is the town in the South of France that my husband comes from. That's where jeans were invented. But that's not where we met. That was in another town, in the rival city of Montpellier.

When Ragnhild arrives in Montpellier, it's the middle of the afternoon. She checks into a cheap motel. Later she walks through the narrow streets. Stops. Listens. Takes a bus to the Mediterranean. She enjoys the solitude: wandering around aimlessly, because she's new, because everything is new. She calls her parents from a phone booth. She talks just to say something, to be polite. Money disappears fast in foreign countries. It turns into a quick conversation, almost just an exchange of sounds. Her parents ask how long she has been there now. She looks at her watch and declares: eight hours.

Montpellier, France, my husband, men, The Lover . . . that was where it all began, in the middle of the French mentality, in the middle of the triangle. I enjoyed that life, so different from

Norwegian life, so immoral in a way, in everything down to the language. At the same time I hated it, the pain we inflicted on each other.

I look lovingly at my husband. He is still asleep. I let him sleep. I go down to the kitchen, swallow an aspirin, and begin making breakfast, English breakfast: egg, bacon, and baked beans. Junk is the best medicine, I think, better than a thousand aspirins. I fry it all in and add mushrooms. This is going to be so good, I'm humming to myself, looking at the clock: twelve.

I run up to the bedroom and only just manage not to fall. I put the breakfast tray down and open the curtains. The light spills into the room, the sun is blinding me. It's good to stay inside on a day you should be outside, I think, and look at my husband, so much in love. He is sleeping so heavily, so safely, but now my patience is gone, now I'm getting brutal.

"Lou!"

I shake him. No luck. I run into the bathroom, wet a wash-cloth, and put it over his face. He's desperately trying to open his eyes. He rubs and rubs, until they turn red.

"Vår, mon amour, my love, my wonderful . . . wife," he says, and stares at me with tired green-brown eyes.

"Breakfast!" I call, in a happy voice.

"Oh, thanks . . ."

He edges himself sleepily up in bed, while I put the tray on his lap and lie down again.

"You're not annoyed because I woke you up?"

"No." He looks at his watch. "I hate to sleep away my days, our days . . ."

"How sweet of you," I say, and put the plate on my lap. The egg yokes are runny, exactly the way they should be. I dip my bacon and mushroom in it. I want to grill him about Sidney, but instead I tell him about the stranger.

I say:

"Love," because that's what I need.

Lou looks at me.

I answer:

"Sex," because that's what I got. "It's not easy to make love to a man you don't love," I add.

"No."

I describe what we did together, everything from the size of his member and how deeply he penetrated me, to my body temperature and how wet I got. I talk about his tongue, cunnilingus. I admit that I'm left with a bittersweet aftertaste, that I feel dirty. I explain that it makes me uncertain, the lack of love between the stranger and me.

I say:

"Tenderness, that's what I need."

Lou understands, takes my hand, holds it hard, until my blood circulation stops and my fingers feel paralyzed.

"You were sleeping on the first floor," I say. "On the table there was a wine bottle. The ashtray was full. I lay down next to you, very close." I thought: I'm about to dirty myself. Voluntarily.

"Ooh."

"I don't want to separate love from sex any longer, I want to have both, I want them both to be the same. I'm tired of lying."

"I understand."

"Do you?"

"Yes. I can live with someone else, but I can't live without you . . ."

"What's that got to do with it?"

"Everything is connected to everything else . . . Can't you see that?"

"No."

Lou tries to explain something inexplicable. He asks me to understand the incomprehensible. He thinks it's important that things can lose their original meaning and not signify anything at all. I ask what it is that doesn't mean anything. He's alluding to her, that she's insignificant.

"Sidney?"

His answer is that I shouldn't go around worrying about something that doesn't exist. He talks without understanding what he's saying himself, like a philosopher.

Then he picks up *Thus Spake Zarathustra* and reads out loud: "'The true man wants two things: danger and play. For that reason he wants woman, as the most dangerous plaything. Let woman be a plaything, pure and fine, like a precious stone, illumined with the virtues of a world that hasn't yet come.'" He closes the book and asks: "Do you want to play a game? Something that can challenge, provoke . . . "

I open my mouth.

"Don't say anything. Listen first."

I close it again.

"These are my conditions: If you manage to fall in love with a new man, the way you once fell in love with The Lover, well, then I promise to end it with Sid. Then it'll be finished between the two of us."

"Are you serious?"

"Everyday life, habits, I'm not good at that. So . . . ?"

"Falling in love, again?"

"Yes . . . "

I think: a game . . . What does he mean by a game? Games are something you do to amuse yourself, and I like to amuse myself, especially with my husband. Besides, that he will leave Sidney, that I will meet someone else, fall in love, treachery and depravation, these are attractive thoughts. Because I want to look at life with a sense of humor. I want to be a brave little player.

"I don't understand your motivation, darling. What do you have to gain?" I ask.

"I want to conquer my jealousy, Vår. When you were with The Lover, I wasn't ready, I was too young and inexperienced. This time I'll react differently. Now I'll cope better with a situation like that."

"But you suffered terribly, Lou!"

"That's exactly why I want to do it," he says and consults *Thus Spake Zarathustra* again. "'I love him who wants to surpass himself and therefore is destroyed,'" he reads.

"I don't understand . . . " I say.

"I hate it when biology takes control, Vår. I'd rather have a bad experience than no experience," he adds. "Then I learn something at least."

"What about Sidney, don't you think about her?"

"Sid is my problem . . . "

"But you love her, don't you . . . ?"

"Yes. But there has to be something at stake, or it's meaningless . . ."

SICK LOVE

RAGNHILD OPENS THE WINDOW and admires the palms, the cactuses, the olive trees, and stone pines . . . She pricks up her ears and wants to hear cicadas sing. She takes pleasure in everything French. Her husband puts his arms around her waist and kisses her neck. He claims that she is sick. He wants to own her. Because it's difficult to be two when one is three, they both know that. Her husband is afraid of the loneliness, the waiting, it's never possible to know if she's coming back or not. He doesn't like that Ragnhild is away, that she isn't with him. He would prefer that they were together all the time: she, he, and the Painter: the trinity, ménage à trois . . . He claims that he can live with that: a friendship between two adult men.

"You want me to say hello?" is all Ragnhild says.

She doesn't have the energy for the discussion. Not now. Not ever.

"Well . . ."

Cyril takes out his tobacco and cigarette paper. When he has finished his roll-up, he makes himself a pastis, an anise liqueur, typical of the French Midi.

"Now and then I want to see the Painter alone, surely you can understand that," she says.

"No."

"Yes."

"I don't have to understand it, mon amour, there are lots of men who can't understand it, but you're lucky to have chosen me, Cyril the sympathetic . . . "

"Yes."

Ragnhild kisses him and takes her bike. It's old, but new to her. It's black and rusty, but charming and elegant. It belongs to the Painter. He wants her to be able to commute between Cyril and him as fast as possible, without wasting any time, spending it all on her two men instead.

Cyril sees her out, draws nervously on his cigarette, and exhales. Then he sets the alarm on his watch and decides when Ragnhild should be back, at what time. She accepts this. Because it's important, a principle in the lack of principles, order in chaos . . . She agrees.

Cyril closes the door, while Ragnhild goes off on her bike. It's summer in the south. The mistral caresses her between her legs while her newly dyed black hair flutters in the wind like an anarchist flag. She's humming to herself, making little soft meowing sounds like a cat. There aren't many people around on a day like this. Most have gone to the seaside to feed their bodies with vitamin D, their brains with endorphins. Heat. Sweat. Everything is perfect, wonderful . . . And there, finally: 13, rue de Suez. She throws down the bike, knocks on the door with a hammering heart. Hears steps, music, and the dark, hoarse, and sexy voice of a man who has lived . . .

"Coming, darling!"

Ragnhild is naked beneath her skirt. Her favorite outfit when she's with the Painter, so he can feel her up discreetly.

He opens the door, his arms. She throws herself against him. He holds her, runs around and around until they get dizzy and fall down.

Every time Ragnhild visits this decadent garage-atelier-dwelling, there's a new picture of her hanging on the wall. She is everywhere. The Painter shows her what he has painted during the night: a huge drawing of how she takes off a dress, from beginning to end. That's how he, possessed by details, gets entranced.

Ragnhild wishes she could think of the Painter without thinking of her husband, but she doesn't think it's possible.

She says:

"My feelings for you are limitless. Therefore they're both good and evil." The Painter shakes his head. He doesn't understand. Ragnhild explains: "When I'm with you, then I'm truly with you. Even if my husband is always lurking in the background, watching us, making sure things don't get too intense, that there's still a way back, a way out, that there can still be just him and me, as if you never existed . . . "

". . . or you and me as if he never existed," the Painter adds.

"Perhaps . . . "

"I love you," he says then, lifting Ragnhild up and placing her on the kitchen bench like a doll. He is so strong, so big, so different. He also says: "I'll do anything just to get a glimpse of your face when you come, the dull expression in your eyes then, your brittle voice . . . "

Ragnhild is in love with the Painter and with his own feelings for her. He feels no shame, no restrictions, and she adores that. She thinks a lot about the expression in his eyes, his strange way of looking at things, the world: beautiful, repulsive moments. She likes that part of him, the unaesthetic part, the part that doesn't give a fuck because everything is beautiful when you make love.

The Painter sneaks his fingers in where he knows they're welcome. With the other hand he mixes a cocktail, gets some ice cubes, and puts them in the drink.

"Talk," he says. "I want to know how it is for you. Make sounds. Show me what you feel. Be inventive."

Ragnhild gets comfortable among dirty plates and old newspapers. She's hungry. Finds some olives and eats them.

"OK."

She closes her eyes. Takes a blind sip of the cocktail. It spills over, runs down her front. She does it deliberately. Longs for his tongue: long, repellent, and wonderful.

In the beginning she didn't say anything, but came silently, like someone mute. Once, twice, for a long time. She laughs when she thinks about it now. Makes herself more comfortable. The sounds will come when she comes, that's how it is. She looks around, looks up into the ceiling, sees herself: muse. Now she's one, too: Gala, Lee Miller, Alma Mahler, Lotte Lenya, Oda Krohg, Ruth Berlau, Edie Sedgwick, Hanna Schygulla . . . It's important to inspire, to leave a mark, to have proof of your existence. Ragnhild dreams about being like Anaïs Nin, muse and creator, mother and child, the one who gives birth and the one who is born. The way Nin used Henry Miller, she, too, wants to make use of her men.

The Painter is a good lover, the best. He takes Ragnhild down from the bench and puts her on the floor. He does what he likes with her. She is willing. The stone floor is cold, shivers run through her body, tickles. She turns on her side, looks straight at the painting: La pisseuse. The Painter likes to watch when Ragnhild pulls up her skirt, spreads her legs, and lets it flow.

"Talk," he repeats, "I can't hear you!"

Ragnhild is so wet that she's lost for words, mute like in the old days. She isn't listening: tick tock tick tock . . . The Painter's garage-atelier is full of clocks. When he was young, he studied to become a watchmaker, like his family before him for generations: father, grandfather, great-great-grandfather . . . Yes, as far back as he can remember.

"Are they on time?" Ragnhild asks worriedly. "Is that really the time?"

"Yes."

"That's impossible, it can't be, impossible . . ."

"Time flies when you're making love," he answers.

Ragnhild stands up. Her heart is beating, fast, too fast perhaps, a mixture of arousal and fear.

"I have to go."

"No. You've got to come first!"

The Painter is almost brutal in his pleasure. He doesn't give her a choice. She likes it, that he takes control. They keep going, standing. She moans loudly. He does the same.

Then he lights a cigarette and gives it to her. The Painter only smokes Gitanes, so she does too when she's with him. The cigarettes are strong and surrounded by myths. They hurt your throat when you pull on it. She takes a drag, several drags. He lights one for himself as well.

"The post-coital cigarette . . . " Ragnhild mumbles. "Even if I stopped smoking, I could never give it up."

She's exhausted, but doesn't sit down, instead she runs into the makeshift bathroom and has a quick wash. When she's finished, she gives the Painter a quick kiss, launches herself on the bicycle, and races off. Tick tock tick tock . . . From one man to the next.

DARKNESS IN THE MIDDLE OF THE DAY

Lou goes to the bathroom. When he comes back, I watch him as if I see him for the first time, without recognizing, without knowing: a different language, a different culture, a different body. What I see is this: that he's mad; stark raving mad. His eyes big, green-brown: They change from green to brown and back to green again. Mad, no doubt about it. I tell Lou this, how it suddenly hit me, his madness. He is interested. Likes the idea of being seen that way, by his own wife.

"You look crazy too," he says. "If it hadn't been for the fact that I already knew you, you'd have driven me insane. Then it would've been genuine passion, even if I hate that kind of thing." Then he adds: "I want to get drunk, smashed, I want to fall down the stairs without hurting myself, behave irresponsibly."

I make revolting grimaces, like I'm about to spew. Just the thought of it makes me feel nauseous.

"I feel like Munch's 'the morning after' painting," I hint.

"Do you have any better suggestions?"

I think about it, pick up *The Guardian* and discover that the National Film Theatre is showing a movie by Béla Tarr at three p.m.: *Damnation*. Lou has seen the movie several times, but never with me.

"Look!" I call out with enthusiasm, and I show him the program.

Lou gets very eager. Now he'll finally have the chance to show me the legendary rain scene with the lugubrious bar and the worn-out cabaret woman.

"The woman is sad, everyone's sad, it's all so beautiful and melancholy," he tells me. "It's such a powerful image, simple, like a washed-out Eric Fischl picture in Hungarian."

The weather outside is gorgeous, the sun is shining. Of course, we could've taken a trip to Brighton, I think, been lying on the beach, read books, and gone to a restaurant. But Lou has been talking about this film for many years now. Besides, I dream of being in a dark, cold room with my husband, because there's nothing better than the sky without stars, our sky, a film. There's nothing better than the dark in the middle of the day, when you have a choice. Because in the city you always have a choice. In the country, on the other hand, things just happen, and it gets so dark there, so very dark. In the city it never gets that dark.

SUBLIMATION AND THE ABOMINABLE

IT WAS A GOOD movie, a good rain, better than reality, Tarkovsky and Tarr, no one does it better than those two, only Ceylan, perhaps, I think, and look at my watch. It's still quite early.

"If we hurry, perhaps we can get in an exhibition too," I say.

Lou suggests one he's wanted to see for a long time, by David Salle. We run along the Thames, all the way to the Hayward Gallery. There my husband shows his membership card and we get in for free, both of us.

We wander around silently, like in a library. We take our time, study the pictures carefully. Time goes faster when we do everything so slowly. When we're about to go up to the second floor, the gallery closes and we're told to come back another time.

"What now?" Lou asks when we're back on the street.

"Let's keep on wandering," I suggest. "I want to hold your arm and go for a walk with you, the way you and Sidney do. Could we play a game and pretend that I'm her, your lover? Just for tonight? Just on Sundays?"

"That's a stupid idea, Vår. You and Sid, you . . . You're so different. You wouldn't like yourself, in her. We're a very old-fashioned couple, the way we hold each other, like from another time. We go for long walks together. It would only bore you, Vår. No, let's think of something else."

"Tell me about these walks," I insist.

"We don't have a goal, we just look at landscapes, buildings, parks."

"Anything nice? Anything you can recommend?"

"No. Sid likes the ugly side of London best. Stuff that's falling apart. Brittle bits and pieces she can identify with. She feels that, in time, horrible things get more attractive, more liberating, that they keep getting better. She feels sick in cities that are too beautiful, she gets nauseous and short of breath."

"Is it physical or something psychosomatic . . . ?"

"Sid suffers from breathing problems. She can't walk too fast and she can't run either. She has asthma. So it'll have to take the time it needs. To get to know her. That's what I've decided. There's no rush. *Chi va piano, va sano . . .*"

"Jeez."

I'm about to say something more, but he doesn't give me time.

"Everything erotic's sublimated, in a way, between Sid and me," Lou adds eagerly. "We're like two dogs sniffing each other, and I know she's beautiful, because I rarely want her sexually. I'd rather have her just sleeping in my arms."

I wonder if that's really all he would have done if she was with him now? I'm sure he's lying. But he assures me it's true, that he would have put her in a jam jar and observed her, looked at her for hours.

"And me?"

"Had wild sex with you till I was spent."

YET ANOTHER GAME

WE CAN'T SLEEP, EITHER of us.

"Take your healing hands off my broken sentences . . . " Lou says suddenly.

What can that mean? My husband often talks about the art world, or about authors who are not considered to be authors. I think hard. I'm tempted to say Marguerite Duras, but I know her too well not to recognize her.

"Think the opposite of The Lover," Lou says.

He realizes that I need a little help. So I think The Lover, the opposite of The Lover . . .

"Marlene . . . ?" I suggest.

The name of The Lover's new lover.

"Getting warm."

"Marlene, Marlene . . . Author or painter?"

"Painter."

"Marlene Dumas . . . ?"

"Wow, Vår. I'd never have thought you'd get that one."

"Broken chords can sing, a little . . ." I go on.

"Painter or author?"

"Music."

"A Silver Mount Zion."

"I'm speechless, Lou, speechless."

We lie in the dark and admire each other in silence.

Then one of us begins to talk again. I don't remember which of us it was.

THE FREEDOM TO DESTROY

The bed is empty, apart from me. A sleepy body that refuses to let go of sleep altogether. Sundays. Another one. Gone. I hate Mondays. They remind me that it's a whole week until next Sunday. Actually, I don't like Sundays. It's a non-day. The day God rested. I think: Without death life would have no meaning. Without death time wouldn't have meaning either. And without the week, Sundays too would have been meaningless. Death is a necessity, while life is a choice. I choose life. To get up. Get out of bed.

It's late. I open the wardrobe and take out a big old shoebox with The Lover's letters and photographs. Inside the shoebox there's a small black box with a hole in it. I put my eye against the tiny hole and see: The Lover naked, on his knees, a cigarette in his hand. I love this peepshow. I sit down at the computer. I want to continue to commemorate him as the Painter, as a character in a novel, immortal. But what comes out of me is almost ugly. The repercussion of him. What is left of beauty is what Ragnhild and Cyril have to struggle with.

Cyril is waiting for Ragnhild. She is late. Anxiously she runs up the stairs, her heart pounding. She leaves the bike in the hallway. Cyril is still smoking and drinking. The music is on full volume. He asks her about intimate details, about everything they have done: if they have made love, how many times they did it, if she liked it, if she came, if she forgot him, her husband, the man she married. She gets nervous, almost hysterical. Cyril threatens to call her parents and send her back to Bø. He thinks she looks tired, claims she needs to put her feet up, get away from things, him, the Painter, think clearly, decide what she wants, whom she wants. Ragnhild throws her phone on the floor. She refuses to let him call. Because she doesn't want to go home. She wants to be where things are happening, where they are. She doesn't want to be alone, confined to peace and quiet.

Cyril hits her. It doesn't hurt, but it's the first time he has hit her, that's what hurts, that he uses violence to communicate. Ragnhild begins to laugh, unreservedly. Cyril isn't laughing. Not at all. He speaks calmly, edgily, in a controlled and domineering manner, sad. He claims that she's changed, that she's beginning to resemble the Painter, talk like him, using the same words, French slang. Cyril doesn't like it, this new vulgarity. His eyes are wet, he is almost in tears. Ragnhild becomes both happy and angry. Screams that he's a puritan, at least verbally, that he must be treated with kid gloves, with respect, that she's getting bored.

I hear the key in the door, steps, and a voice calling:

"Vår, mon amour, I'm home!"

It's a voice I know well. It's lighter and softer than The Lover's voice. Younger, but not young. It belongs to my husband . . . I smile to myself at the sound of small, quick steps up the stairs. How each person has their unique way of moving one foot in front of the other fascinates me. Lou opens the door, runs over to me and kisses my neck.

Asks:

"What are you writing? Something nice, something about me?"

"Well . . ." He begins to read. I don't have time to stop him. "Lou, I . . ."

"Yes?"

I blush. Because I'm afraid of what I'm writing, of the consequences. I wait for a little while and study his expression. It doesn't change.

"Are you angry?"

"Angry?"

"Offended?"

He looks at me, resigned.

"The only thing I care about is how you write, what you write, whether it's interesting or not."

"How do you manage to . . ."

". . . to distance myself?"

I nod.

"I have enough self-knowledge to understand that it's fiction, Vår, even if it sounds like reality, to distance myself from Cyril, even if he reminds me of myself, has the same hair, the same nose, and a similar nature. Because he'll never become as complex as me . . . And I'll never hit you . . ."

"I hope. I believe. But you never know . . ."

"That's true, and that goes for all of us."

I nod.

"Cyril is frustrated," Lou continues. "That's how I see him. Words are inadequate, he's inadequate. That doesn't excuse anything, but it makes it easier to understand."

"Violence is inexplicable, indefensible, irresponsible . . . irrespective of what causes it."

"Of course."

"Something has to change. Don't you think? Like a before-and-after he hits her? Because nothing is more demeaning that being hit by the one you love. And the worst thing is that it can bring you closer together, although in a very destructive way."

"I don't think you should attach too much importance to it, Vår. Because I believe that in this case, in Cyril's case, it's a one-off. I don't think Cyril's going to hit her again."

He hits her again. Tells her he, too, has changed, that he is dreaming of a quiet life. He wants to stop smoking and drinking. Why not? If that's what he wants. But without Ragnhild. She's going to drink herself senseless, she's going to lose control, be passionate, unpredictable. Cyril is scared, scared that every time Ragnhild leaves, she will slowly but surely change, until she's become unrecognizable, until she becomes like the Painter. He tries to refuse to let her see him, but it's too stupid, too humiliating. His heart moves, it beats in the middle of his body, he can hardly breathe. This is the first time he has experienced it, being scared of losing her, actually losing her. Before the Painter, it was Ragnhild who sat at home with clammy fingers, crying, before the Painter she was the depressed one, who kept asking questions, who got on his nerves. Now the situation is turned on its head. But Ragnhild is scared as well, afraid to be wrong.

"I've lost two years of my life," Lou says suddenly.

"I know, I'm sorry mon amour. It went too far with The Lover."

"No, Vår, no, not that. In the beginning when I was an unfaithful student, when I was flirting with your friends, when you cried. That gave me no memories. The time with The Lover, however, was painful, although not crucial. That made me look to the future, to developing myself. I actually miss the times the three of us had together."

"Miss?"

"Yes."

"Explain."

"When we made love together, then it was perfect."

"Yes, but . . ."

"If it hadn't been for me feeling such pain when we were not together, and also sometimes when we were together, it would've been a good memory, the one with The Lover."

I look skeptically at my husband, but don't interrupt.

He pulls out *Thus Spake Zarathustra*, the way he does when he wants to emphasize something he believes.

He reads out loud:

"'Never have I been so happy as in the sickest and most painful times in my life.'"

I'm about to say something but am interrupted.

"I want to have a relationship like that again, Vår. Finally I'm ready to take a chance like that, the chance of losing everything I love—you."

I hold my breath.

"I need it," he says. "This freedom to destroy."

LES TROIS GRÂCES

1 RUE DURAND IS about five minutes from boulevard Jeu de Paume, named after an old game no one remembers anymore, and Place de La Comédie, the heart of the city with the opera and the sculpture Les Trois Grâces *as the center and meeting place. It was here Ragnhild had a rendezvous with her husband the day after the fatal kiss that brought them together and made them discreet and indiscreet like all other people in love. The square is full of acrobats, street musicians, homeless people . . . The buildings are white or tainted gray, and some of them even have huge globes.*

"Salut!" People recognize the Painter. He walks slowly, greets them: kiss, kiss, kiss. Three kisses on the cheek in Montpellier. That's what it's like to be a familiar figure, a local celebrity. "Salut!" Again and again. All the way to 1 rue Durand. Finally. The most banal name in all of France, like Smith in England or Olsen in Norway. This is where they live: Ragnhild and Cyril. On the first floor, next to the writers Medhi Belhaj Kacem and Chloé Delaume, although Chloé is like Ragnhild, just a dreaming, budding author at this stage, calling herself Nathalie-Anne. Ragnhild doesn't know if this is her real name, because almost nothing she says is true. She is a good liar, with good potential for good stories, just like Ragnhild.

From the window she can see the big, modernistic parking station in the form of a snail-like spiral, and hear the local whores ranting when their customers try to haggle. It's not a special street, but it has the essentials: La boulangerie, Le tabac, La brasserie, *and* une cabine téléphonique. *Ragnhild pricks up her ears. The doorbell chimes. She runs downstairs.*

It is Thursday. Time of day? No time of day. Organized at ran-
dom: The whole day, the whole evening, until they have no more
energy left. It was Cyril's idea and initiative. That they should be
together. Sexually. Mentally. A threesome. Over and over again. He
wants Ragnhild to forget the beating, the anger, that he lost control.
He wants to make everything good again. For her. For him. For
them. For he likes this story: of happiness, of pain, the humanity
of it all. And feelings: strong, incontrollable feelings. But not the
egotism. The aloneness. Not hurting the other, oneself. For it is up
to Ragnhild to act or not to act. Regardless of what she does, it's
a choice. Passivity is also a form of activity. Something you do. A
burden.

She opens the door. He is nervous, but agreeably so.

"Welcome!" she cries and jumps into the Painter's arms.

He carries her. All the way to the bedroom. Cyril is already
lying there, under the duvet. The Painter likes that. This openness,
impertinence . . . He takes his clothes off and lies down next to him.
Ragnhild does the same.

THE NAKED TRUTH

EVERYTHING HAPPENED. MUCH TOO much. Between Lou and me. It still happens that nothing occurs. And this emptiness, the lack of action, suffocates me. Because I'm no longer the same. Because now I always want to be different. Faithfulness, even with the man I love, no longer interests me. Therefore this often happens: frustration, lack of tenderness, of love. Sex. I admit it to myself: The only form of sexual stimulation I get these days is via my work. By modeling for various painters and trying to make a bit of money. I think of The Lover. Unconsciously that's probably what I do. Take my clothes off as usual, from old habit. But The Lover has a new habit, someone new to paint: Marlene.

"The more I model, stand naked in front of a whole class as on display . . . the more I love my clothes. The privilege is to be able to have control over what's being shown. Choose small parts to expose, only to cover up the rest," I suddenly say.

Lou wakes up from my voice and wants to know what it feels like, this nakedness. In public. He wants me to close my eyes and be there. In the classroom. I close my eyes. I feel my head spinning. My thoughts whirring.

"What are you thinking about?" he asks, his curiosity roused.

"I'm thinking all the time that I want to pee. That if they don't finish soon, it'll flow everywhere. Down on the chair. On the floor."

"Are you really thinking about that while they're drawing you?"

"Yes. I feel so vulnerable when I'm on my feet. As if I can't control my own bladder. I hope that every position is over as soon as possible so I can go to the loo. But afterwards, when I come back, I'm nervous because I don't know if I've dried myself properly. Everything shows. My private life."

"Tell me more!"

"At the end of the day, after many hours, I can lie down on a mattress."

"That sounds lovely."

"Doesn't it. I close my eyes. I don't care anymore who I am, as long as I'm left . . . in peace."

SCOPTOPHILIA

CYRIL LOOKS AT HIS *wife and her lover. Then he jumps out of bed fully dressed. He tricked them. He sits down on a chair, takes out his tobacco and rolls a cigarette. Both Ragnhild and the Painter lie there watching how he puts the tobacco in the paper, smooths it out with his index finger, licks . . . How he tosses the finished roll-up into his mouth like a real cowboy and picks up the lighter. The roll-up is almost perfect: thin and elegant, like a lady's cigarette, but in a very manly way, Ragnhild thinks, who has never noticed it before. But today her eyes are sharp. Today she's interested in details. In how her two men observe each other.*

"I want to watch," Cyril says suddenly and puts away the roll-up. It has already gone out. He lights it again. He is nervous. He notices that the Painter is older and more experienced, this gives him a complex . . .

"What?" The Painter is confused. He doesn't want that. "No . . . "

"Yes!"

They both look pleadingly at her. A song can be heard in the background:

". . . Severin, Severin, speak so slightly. Severin, down on your bended knee. Taste the whip, in love not given lightly. Taste the whip, now plead for me . . . "

"OK."

"Do you want to?" the Painter asks.

"Yes."

"Why?"

"I like to be seen, Cyril likes to watch, and you like to do. There's nothing wrong in that, is there? Rather the opposite, it titillates me."

"But . . ."

"Don't you agree?"

"Yes. Have you done it before?"

"No, we waited for you."

"For me?"

Ragnhild looks over at Cyril. He nods.

"It's true. From the moment Ragnhild discovered you, we stopped looking for others, trying another body, trying another mouth, letting another man treat her in a degrading manner. We were satisfied, both Ragnhild and I, with you."

SAD TRIO

THREE WEEKS HAVE PASSED since I met the stranger and I still haven't got any new numbers in my bag. I haven't seen anyone I want, and those who have seen me haven't wanted me either. I loiter on the way home: drop into a shopping center and read books I don't buy, listen to music I can't stand, try clothes that don't fit, drink coffee that burns my tongue, get bored. I take my pocket knife out of my bag and make a tiny cut on my upper arm, admire the zebra pattern. Then I try to come up with as many words as possible to describe this condition, and in alphabetical order. I find: boring, dull, insipid, monotonous, ordinary, routine, slow, stagnant, stereotypical, tedious, trivial, uninteresting, uneventful, unimaginative, vulgar . . . Some days are like this: suffocating time, a kind of oppressiveness in the body. That's why I become pleased when it starts to rain outside, it takes the attention away from how I feel inside.

To be bored is important, I reflect. If you don't allow yourself that, you'll never think of something new either. If you're entertained, you become lazy, passive, and spoilt.

A few hours later I walk down to the tube. Continue with Plan B. Boring. Read a paper lying on the seat, a crappy newspaper. Look at the TV program: nothing of interest. Turn the page. Horoscope. Read mine, Lou's, The Lover's, Dad's . . . Read anything, until I arrive. Dawdle out of the station, dawdle home.

As I open the door, the phone rings. I run inside, kick off my shoes, whirl around and around, run up and down and finally find it under some notes on my desk.

"Hello," I say and fling myself down on the bed.

"*Salut.*"

I smile. All of me.

"What do you want?"

"Your body, Vår. I only wanted to say that . . ."

"That what?"

"That it's very different, that I've had to realize its advantages: how your vulva is placed, so extremely provokingly, and the lips, their forms, the way they stand out and point forward."

"Thanks."

"I love the fact that you can go all the way, let yourself be totally annihilated and just be . . ."

"How strange that you should call just now," I interrupt. "I was feeling so . . . disheartened."

"Why?"

"Because no one else . . . It's still you who . . ."

"Who what?"

"Love, being in love . . . it's no game," I joke.

"What do you mean?"

"It was so lovely, my two men, my life. Lou enjoyed it as well," I answer without answering.

"It was you who destroyed everything, Vår."

"No, it was us. Together. It became too much."

"I miss you, Vår."

"It was impossible. It couldn't . . ."

"Do you think . . . ?"

"Yes." The Lover is silent. I add: "I remember the best and the worst. Because they were equally intense. But I don't remember anything mediocre."

"Neither do I."

We are both silent.

He repeats:

"I miss you, Vår."

"You've got to stop that."

"Why?"

I answer that to miss me is wrong. That to miss me is the same as wasting time. I want to know if he thinks about me. A lot. If he can't forget me. I close my eyes and I suppose that deep down, that's what I hope. That I'm unforgettable.

He mumbles:

"Of course." Is self-conscious, embarrassed. But continues: "From the moment you left, my eyes became mournful and deep, almost unrecognizable." He says that he has changed, physically, that he has been depressed, that he wasn't aware of it himself, that that's what he was, but Marlene saw it, this unfinished, this unfair part of him, she saw that something was missing, and then she asked him to fix it. "I love Marlene. I love her name," he adds.

"How nice."

He admits that to see me again is an effort to be with her, only Marlene.

He commands:

"Go to the window, open the curtains. It's a nice day, blue sky and sun!"

I open the window fully. A warm breeze caresses my face.

"Does this remind you of something, Vår?" he then asks.

I sit down on the floor. Regain my breath. Light a cigarette. It's impossible, I don't believe it . . . I look out the window again. The Lover waves at me from the other side of the street, in a red phone booth next to a tree.

"Marlene asked me to go to London," he explains.

I remember that in Montpellier he would call me from the other side of the street so I could see him, and once he slept outside our door.

I find Mom's yellow shoes. She gave them to me when I moved away from home. It was a nice thought, but my feet get swollen so easily: wounds, blisters, and swellings. I wish she'd never given them to me, I think, but put them on anyway. Then

I put on my cock-fighter t-shirt and a blasé miniskirt, wearing nothing underneath. I take a quick look in the mirror. I hope I grow old and respected like a Simone: Signoret or de Beauvoir, because that's what The Lover has always wanted for me. I pick up my bag from the floor and run out into his arms. We hold each other for a long time. My whole body loves the moment.

"How long are you staying?" I ask.

"I'm leaving again tomorrow."

THE PAIN OVER LILI BRIK

I TRY TO REMEMBER the restaurant. The meal we had. If we had a meal. I only remember afterwards. I make a note of all sorts of things. Feelings. I don't look around, forget that we are in Hotel Mateo. I just lie down on the king-size bed. Sink, as if on a cloud, roll down into the duvet. The down duvet. I fantasize that it has to be like lying in a bird's nest. Because the down in the duvet is so feathery, like porous powdery snow. I imagine that the down must come from the exclusive *Somateria mollissima* species, that is, the common eider. Because it almost feels like having no duvet, that's how light it is. I hold it firmly and dream that the down becomes feathers, which become birds that fly me to Iceland, Greenland or Siberia . . .

As I soar away, The Lover falls down on the bed. There is such a springiness in the mattress. Such a tension. In the air. Between us. We are silent, as if the torrent of words was caught in floodgates, regulated, locked. Therefore we need the words of others until they are opened again. In the night-table drawer I find a cheap edition of the Bible. I open it to The Old Testament and read the section from Solomon's *Song of Songs* which the priest read when Lou and I got married.

I read:

"'How beautiful are thy steps in sandals, O prince's daughter! Thy rounded thighs are like the links of a chain, the work of the hands of a skilled workman. Thy navel is like a round goblet, wherein no mingled wine is wanting; thy belly is like a heap of wheat set about with lilies. Thy two breasts are like two fawns that are twins of a gazelle. Thy neck is like a tower of ivory; thine eyes like the pools in Heshbon, by the gate of Bath-Rabbim; thy nose is like the tower of Lebanon which looketh toward Damascus. Thy head upon thee is like Carmel, and the hair of thy head like purple; the king is held captive in the tresses thereof. How fair and how pleasant art thou, O love, for delights!'"

The Lover gets up, fetches a couple of glasses and a few small bottles of whiskey, vodka, and gin from the minibar. I point to the gin bottle. He chooses vodka for himself. I light a cigarette while he is filling our glasses, getting tonic, cola, and ice cubes. I take a deep swallow.

"Is everything all right, Vår?" he asks and lies down on the bed again. Sinks down . . .

"Yes, no . . ."

I pull on my cigarette several times and blow a large smoke cloud. Then I read another paragraph. Something the priest didn't read.

It says:

"'Whither is thy beloved gone, O thou fairest among women? Whither hath thy beloved turned him, that we may seek him with thee?' Occasionally I feel lonely, even when I'm with Lou," I explain, "but when we're apart, I never feel lonely. Because deep down, we're always together, always, even when we're away from each other."

"I don't quite understand . . ."

"Lou is mostly with Sidney, I suppose that's what I'm trying to say."

My voice is brittle.

"I see . . ."

"And he wants me to fall in love again, the way I fell in love with you, once. He has promised that if I do, he'll break up with her."

"Is that what you want?"

"Don't know."

"What don't you know, Vår?"

"If I want to meet another man so Lou can break up with Sidney, or if I actually want to fall in love again."

"I see, the agonies of making a choice."

"The truth is that we both struggle with jealousy, at the same time as we don't believe in being faithful, not in our case, not since we were so young when we met."

"What do you believe in then?"

"We believe in freedom."

"I don't understand . . ."

"The only way we can keep together is to be with others. We really believe that."

"I was hoping it could be the three of us."

"Me too."

"But as that didn't work, I want it to be you and your husband, just you and him, and then me and Marlene."

I don't know what to answer, so I say nothing. I feel heavy. Outside we hear cars driving past, people randomly talking. I wonder if it's raining. I lie still and fiddle with my white hair, make little plaits and undo them again. I want to talk about rain, thunder, and lightning. About driving too fast. Dangerously fast. On a motorway near Montpellier. In the direction of the beach. The Lover and I in the backseat. Picnic baskets and swimsuits. Music full blast. And Lou so calm. Unnaturally calm.

Lou who says:

"If this is the end, if we die now, it's nice, beautiful."

Almost as if he wanted it. This accident. The drama. The tragedy. As if he doesn't want to come back. He is handsome. Happy. Waiting for fate. Fateful. I wonder if he has pills in his bag, or perhaps a pistol. I can't stop thinking of Mayakovsky. The Russian poet who shot himself in the heart, where the pain was, the pain over Lilya Brik. Lou has told me the story many times. With alarming admiration. I ask him to slow down. The weather has calmed. The thunder has stopped.

"Do you remember . . ."

"What, darling?"

"Don't call me darling, dear."

"Don't call me dear, darling."

"Do you remember . . ."

"I remember everything, Vår. I've forgotten nothing. That's your gift to me. For better or for worse."

I turn on the radio. Move closer. We hold hands. The Lover's hands are clammy. He strokes my hair.

"You've changed," he says.

"In what way?"

"In every way."

"Good or bad?"

He turns silent. I don't disturb him.

"I miss you the way you were, Vår, because then we were together. I miss your black hair. The Anna Karina look. The way she looked in Godard's films. The fact that you keep changing reminds me of all the time we've spent away from each other, of all that's happened. I really believed I could never love anyone again after you. But Marlene . . ."

"Marlene . . ."

"I didn't mean to talk about her, Vår. That was silly. Finally we're together, and all we can talk about are Lou and Marlene."

"Yuck."

I kick off the uncomfortable shoes. I have blisters. I can feel them hurting a bit. I take a match and a needle from my bag, and prick holes in the blisters. The radio is buzzing. News. Nothing new. The Lover lies still. Doesn't move. I wonder what we mean to each other. If we still mean anything to each other. Not just for what we have been, but also for what we are. A tear runs from my eye.

"Are you crying, Vår?"

"No."

I wipe the tear from my cheek and walk to the window, open

the curtains. It's still dark outside, city-dark. Neon lights and headlamps create a special universe, a sphere. The night isn't like the morning. That's what I like. The transition between night and day. The Lover comes over to me, sits on the windowsill, and lights a cigarette. I, too, take a couple of puffs. It tastes awful, but I like it. We study Bayswater, the area around the hotel. People who come and go.

"What was her name again?" he suddenly asks.

"Who?"

"The one the Russian poet . . ."

". . . shot himself in the heart for?"

"Yes."

"Lilya Brik."

HELLO, GOODBYE

I turn around in the soft king-size bed and wake up to find it empty. In London Town the birdsong has been exchanged for people's voices, buses, cars, a long time ago . . . It's late, but early for me. I turn on the radio.

I hear:

"I am tired, I am weary. I could sleep for a thousand years. A thousand dreams, that would awake me. Different colors made of tears . . ."

I stare into nothingness. I think of the time Mom and Dad came to visit Lou and me in Montpellier, and that we weren't alone. Mom looked at The Lover and understood immediately that he was no ordinary friend. She understood it and felt an intense sorrow for my husband, a sort of compassion. She understood it, and felt an intense contempt for her daughter, a kind of hate. But Dad didn't notice that we were play-acting: that the laughter wasn't genuine and the smiles were stiff. After the fire he lost the kind of interest for people that makes you notice things that aren't said, that enables you to read between the lines.

I look around. Exhausted. Everything is tidied and ready. On the table there's a plastic bag from a grocery store. I'm hungry and thirsty. Look for The Lover with my eyes. Can't find him, but hear singing in the shower: high, false, and full of self-confidence. My eyes glide toward the loose electrical cords. It's damp in here, muggy, it steals beneath the skin all the way to the bones. I shiver when I notice the wallpaper: English style, lack of style . . . Then I discover the cheap reproductions of Tamara de Lempicka's art in large, loathsome frames. I try to understand the soul of a place from the sum of its objects. I examine the rest of the room. Yesterday I felt too distant to notice anything, but not today, today I let myself be fascinated. I call out with delight when I clap eyes on a cupboard filled with squirrels of all shapes and sizes.

"You're awake, I hear . . ."

The Lover walks barefoot across the cigarette-stained carpet. I offer him my lips. His hair is wet, it's dripping down into my face. He smells strange. I can't make up my mind whether he smells good or bad, cheap maybe. He dries himself, dresses, then he walks over to the table and picks up the plastic bag.

"Drink this," he orders.

"Milk?"

"It's an antidote to alcohol . . . Don't you remember . . . ?"

"I'd forgotten that."

I take a big swallow, then I dip the dry croissant into the much-too-sweet marmalade. The Lover does the same. He admits that he is sad, despondent, claims it's a weakness of the body that it takes such a long time to let go of the memories, admits that I am inside him, like a fossil. He strokes my hair tenderly, lovingly, then he gives me the Bible. I put it in my bag. Wait. For him. For something. The Lover says he'll come back soon, but then he'll bring Marlene, explains that's his way of repaying what Lou once did for him, with me. Promises:

"It'll be fine."

"What?"

"That they sleep together too."

"What do you mean?"

"I think it would do Marlene good."

"And Lou?"

"Men always want to. You don't have to worry about that."

"Right."

"Marlene is jealous of our history. That's why I want her to be a part of it too."

"I see."

I put on the same clothes I arrived in. I never meet The Lover in my husband's clothes.

"How do I look?" I ask.

"Good, you always look good, Vår."

"You're lying, but I usually do look good after love-making."

I go into the chess-patterned bathroom, wash my face, and pee. I leave the door open.

"Are you ready?" The Lover asks and sticks his head in.

I stand up without drying myself. A drop runs down my thigh.

"Are we in a hurry? I haven't had a shower yet."

"The taxi's waiting outside," he says.

I pull the chain, wash my hands, pick up the mini-shampoo and shower soap, and put them in my bag with the Bible.

"Are you sure we haven't forgotten anything?" I ask.

"Certain."

We look around one last time, lock the door, leave.

"See you, Vår," The Lover says and kisses me.

"Goodbye."

Our eyes meet: briefly, uneasily, timidly. The Lover looks away. I think: Now it'll be Marlene waking up next to him, wandering around barefoot in the old garage-atelier, now she is hanging on the walls, now it's those two who are a couple, lovers.

"Listen . . ."

"Yes?"

"Say hello to Marlene."

"Thanks. Say hello to Lou."

IN ABSENTIA

As soon as the taxi with The Lover is out of sight, it begins to rain as a sign, a symbol, of something that's over. I don't care if I get wet. I like that nature is washing me clean, that my clothes become like skin on my body and my hair is glued to my face. I like the smell of wet asphalt, of exhaust and trees, of the fresh and the rotten mixed together, old piss, vomit, grass . . .

I walk around in the city for a while cold and wet, before I get tired of it and catch the bus home. If I have time, I always prefer to catch the bus instead of the train or the subway. I sit up top, at the very front, and look at the rain hitting the window-pane. I feel as if I'm hypnotized and don't notice that the bus passes my stop. I fall asleep and only come around at the terminal. There the bus driver takes a break, reads *The News of the World*, and eats lunch. I notice that my clothes have dried out a little. I lie down on the seat and try to sleep a bit more, but I'm no longer tired. I wait. After about half an hour he drives the same way back. I jump off at my stop and walk slowly, dawdle. There's no one waiting for me at home. Lou, my darling husband, where are you when I'm at my most bored? I know, and don't ask any more stupid questions.

I open the door, strip off my half-soggy clothes, and throw them on the floor with my bag. I take pleasure in making a mess, being the unbearable brat. I'm naked, apart from the uncomfortable shoes. I'm kinky. I walk over to the kitchen, open a milk carton, and drink from it. I want to call The Lover, but he won't be home for another several hours, I think, pick up an old copy of *Dazed and Confused*, and read a couple of articles about what was hip in London four months ago, and put it down again. The ultimate pastime is channel surfing, especially during the day, I think, and channel surf for nearly two hours. That makes me feel nauseous, as if I've eaten too much chocolate.

I look at my watch, look for the cordless phone, finally find it, and dial The Lover's number.

"*Allô oui . . .*"

"It's me," I say.

"Vår?"

"I just wanted to check that you'd arrived home safely."

I can hear trip-hop in the background, something from Ninja Tune. I comment that he still listens to the same music.

"Marlene also likes Ninja Tune," he says, irritated.

"Of course," I say and don't know what else to say.

The silence is embarrassing. I can hear my own breath. I have two fingers inside me.

"Vår . . ."

"Yes?"

"What are you doing?"

"I still love you!"

"You're lying."

"No!"

"I've realized now, Vår, that you can't be trusted."

"What do you mean?"

"You're confused. No, not confused, but nostalgic. And nostalgia doesn't mean anything other than something that used to be is over now and you wish it could be again. But the truth is that you don't love me anymore, that the feeling of being in love has gone, the butterflies in the stomach. You're clinging to me, because the memory of having loved me is stronger than the knowledge of not loving me anymore."

TABULA RASA

I PICK UP MY bag from the floor and go up to my room. I'm no longer bored, but I'm sad. That's the way it is. My heart is hurting.

I lie down on the bed and kick off my shoes. I have new blisters to prick holes in. I open my bag to take out matches and needle, but then I suddenly remember the Bible from the hotel and forget about the blisters. I like that each page is as thin as cigarette paper. I tear out a text about Sodom and Gomorrah, fill it with Lou's tobacco, and roll it together into something that looks more like a joint than a cigarette but that doesn't taste like either of them. I put out God's fear-inspiring words and put the Bible in the chest of drawers by the side of the bed.

I look up at the ceiling. Tick tock tick tock. . . The sounds of the room intensify. A car passes by, several, a fire engine . . . There's always a fire somewhere in a big city like London, I think. There aren't many fires in Bø, my home valley.

I like to lie like this and look at the lights from the cars, how they light up the walls in the room before they disappear. In the corner of the room is a poster for Andrei Tarkovsky's film *Nostalgia*. The Lover was right, I think. Nostalgia doesn't mean anything other than what used to be is over, and now you wish it could be again. I haven't seen Tarkovsky's film yet. I've seen all his films, except for the one I have on my wall. Ridiculous, truly ridiculous, I say to myself, and turn on the computer.

I think: I'm lucky to have my art, my scribbling, so I have somewhere to put all my feelings.

I look out the window. It's dark. I take a bite of the milk chocolate. It feels cold being naked, even in the middle of summer. I wrap myself in a blanket. I think: Am I going to meet someone else, am I going to fall in love again, is it time for a tabula rasa? Spew up everything. Like vomit.

Ragnhild lies on an old mattress in the Painter's garage-atelier. She is naked. She is his inexhaustible source of inspiration. He is working on a picture called Anatomie d'une masturbation, *with anatomic illustrations of penis and vagina, 2 x 2 meters. Ragnhild asks the Painter to treat her vulva roughly. He says that every woman with respect for herself must know her own vulva, that she shouldn't be dependent on a man. For satisfaction. She nods. She agrees.*

After a while she understands how she can make herself achieve an orgasm, how to manipulate her vulva and make her body come and go—in waves.

"Like the ocean in a storm," she says.

The Painter nods and tells her that her vulva is beautiful. He explains that he wants to see it and finds a pair of scissors. She remembers that when she was little, she didn't want to have pubic hair, she just wanted to have a dash. She watches him cutting. The Painter claims that she is beautiful when she comes, at her most beautiful, that he has never seen her so beautiful as when she's horny. Then he shows it to her as well. He touches her in front of a mirror.

I must have fallen asleep. I lie in bed with my duvet wrapped around me, and with a headache.

"Lou?"

"Hi, darling."

He kisses me. With his tongue. A French kiss.

"Did you sleep well?"

"Did you sleep for a long time?"

"Don't know. When I came home, you were lying knackered in front of the computer. I felt so proud. There's nothing I'd rather see than you working, Vår."

"Thanks, but . . ."

I don't like that Lou gives me no chance to censor what he chooses to read.

"I took your blanket off and put you to bed. I was going to bed too, but then my curiosity got the better of me. I couldn't stop. I just had to read."

"But . . ."

"No buts."

"Lou . . ."

"Yes?"

"What are you thinking?"

"I'm not thinking, Vår, I'm reading. And you?"

"I'm thinking about our game."

"Ah . . ."

"Is it really true that you want me to fall in love with another man, the way I once fell in love with The Lover?"

"Yes, but this time it'll be different, I'll be stronger. I've promised you that, Vår."

BASHFULNESS AND BACH

When I wake up for the second time, Lou has gone, to work, chasing money. I forgot to tell him about The Lover. I mentioned him, but not that I'd seen him. Strange.

I look at my watch. I still have plenty of time. I love to lie like this, half-asleep, listening to the different London sounds, how reality changes, the buses turn into dangerous fighter planes and the female neighbor's voice into Marilyn Monroe's. I look at my watch again.

"Fuck."

Suddenly I'm late and have to run. I always seem to end up running late, no matter how much time I have to start. Next time I promise myself to keep a better eye on the time, so it can't just disappear without me noticing.

I jump out of bed. Take the world's quickest wash. A spray of perfume, then I put my notebook and a couple of other things in my bag and run out.

I take the train down to the city center, walk as fast as I can through a terrible throng of people. Rush hour. I imagine that there's a machine gun in my bag that I can use at will. I smile and envisage the blood. I'm not a particularly violent person, but I'm running dangerously late.

I buy scones and caffe latte. Wolf it down. Complain to myself: This city is full of tourists. Hurry through the throngs of people and hate everyone. I have a feeling someone is following me, a large, white man, without hair, with garlic breath. I'm running now, until the smell disappears. I arrive. No. 7. Ground floor.

"Hello," I say. Silence. The teacher looks at his watch. "I'm late," I add. He looks at his watch again. "The train was late," I lie.

"Please take off your clothes, Vår, so we can get started?" is all he says.

"Yes," I say and am about to go behind the curtain to undress unobserved. I think: Isn't it absurd, this secretiveness. As if it was the fact of *undressing* which was the embarrassing, the erotic thing . . . As if the naked body in itself didn't have any stimulating value.

"The trains in London are always late, surely you know that, Vår. Lucky they weren't canceled . . ." the teacher says and looks suspiciously at me.

"Yes," I say, and stop.

I know that he hasn't finished giving me a moral lecture yet.

"London is disintegrating. The industrial revolution happened too early here. We still suffer from that," he continues, and I can feel that he expects something more than a yes.

I take a guess:

"Sorry."

He smiles, that's what he wanted. A game. I breathe out, relieved, and look out the window. It's a warm day. The heater is still on full blast. In London they're not used to summer being more than a word, I think.

"Can you close the curtains?" I ask.

"Why?"

"Because I'm shy."

Everyone laughs, but the teacher is nice and does as I ask. I walk behind the curtain and take off one garment at a time. I walk out again, *in puris naturalibus*, stark naked. No one thinks twice about it. That bores me. They are professional and cold, every one of them, I think as I take my position in the middle of the room.

The teacher puts on some music. Bach, I believe. Classical music aids concentration, isn't that what they say?

Through a gap in the curtain, I notice the repulsive man who followed me earlier. There's something stimulating in this repulsion, to be spied on. Because here in the classroom the naked body has no value, I think, while out there on the street it becomes sexy again, forbidden and inaccessible . . . I walk up and down, showing myself to the repulsive man I don't like, but who watches, something I do like despite finding it repulsive.

"A little more to the side," the teachers requests.

"Like this?"

"Great."

I look at the repulsive man again. Suddenly I'm looking straight into his eyes. Startled, I blush.

"Is everything all right, Vår?" the teacher asks.

"No."

I request a time-out, close the gap in the curtains reluctantly, and light a cigarette. I'm cold. Why am I cold when it's so hot? Am I nervous? I look at my watch. Still an hour to go. I go to the toilet, but nothing comes. I still dry myself. Then I go back to the classroom, lie down on a mattress, try to find an interesting position. I look inquiringly at the teacher. He nods. Everyone is looking at me, looking through me, seeing nothing. No one here has the talent of The Lover, I think and close my eyes. Time passes slowly. I'm cold, I'm sweating, my bum's itching. My thoughts rove and ramble, I have wild associations. Without the gaze of the repulsive man, my nudity irritates me, I think to my great surprise.

"Ten minutes left," the teacher says.

I ask for a glass of water. Am given it. The teacher observes, criticizes, advises . . . I empty the glass in one gulp. My bum's no longer itching, but now I really have to pee. I squeeze my legs together and stare into the eyes of a student. He looks down. I give up.

"Time's up," the teacher says.

The students are wandering around, packing up, chatting, laughing. Once more I wish my bag was a machine gun, that I could shoot them down, every one of them. I'm not a particularly violent person, but lack of talent infuriates me.

LA NAUSÉE

I MAKE MY WAY toward Charing Cross station. Push people to get past them. I have to pee. With me, it's pathological. I was so keen to get away from my work that I totally forgot. Typical. Now I'm running as fast as I can, because I know there's a toilet in the train. I'm surrounded again by this smell: garlic. I run faster. Find my ticket. Fight with myself. Against the part of me that is attracted to what disgusts me. I almost stumble, that's how fast I run. My heart's thumping. I wonder why I'm scared. Suddenly I feel a cold hand on my shoulder. I jump. I know why I'm scared.

"Excuse me, you dropped this," a sensual voice is saying.

I turn around and look straight into those eyes I saw earlier, the ones that made me blush. Not because I was naked, but because I was noticed. I feel embarrassed and look down. The repulsive man hands me my notebook: friendly, polite, a gentleman.

"Thank you so much . . ." I say, and look alarmed at the little red book that, instead of being full of Mao Tse-Tung, is full of me.

I feel disturbed and get the shivers when I think about all those repulsive things the repulsive man must now know about me. I put the notebook in my bag and wish I could vanish into thin air. Then I think, how strange that I become embarrassed over what I imagine he's read, even while I want the whole world to read it.

"The book fell out of your bag this morning," he said.

He wants to get us talking, I think.

69

"I thought it was important that you got it back," he continues.

"Yes."

I can't think of anything else to say. I stand still, as if frozen to the ground. I don't dare to look into the repulsive man's eyes again. He comes closer. I let him. It's like I'm hypnotized, paralyzed, by all the things he knows. He whispers a few repulsive words into my ear and laughs. I nod and squeeze my legs harder together. I imagine a lovely, lukewarm yellow squirt running down my thigh, along the platform and down onto the tracks. Neither of us mentions what we both know: the gap in the curtains. That's a secret we keep to ourselves. I tell him that I noticed him on my way to work because there was something I didn't like. Something physical. Something I felt as I sensed him behind me. Nausea.

I say:

"The way you move your mouth. Your tongue. What you said, say. How you came up to me with your hand on my shoulder, and that I already then felt it would be difficult to get rid of you. Sly. Slimy. That's what you are."

The repulsive man smiles at me as if I have given him a compliment.

"Come," he says, "come . . ."

His voice is convincing. I obey. We jump onto the train. Together. All the cars are full. We stand in the corridor. I'm waiting for the toilet to be vacant. He whispers something to me. Because he likes to be close to me, I think, so close that he is almost spitting in my ear. The toilet sign is still red. I don't know what's wrong with me. Why am I letting myself be seduced by a repulsive man. Perhaps I'm doing it for the sake of the game, to have something to tell my husband . . .

I jump off the train at the same station as him, although it's far from home. I walk as if blindfolded, I think, because I don't know where I'm going, where I'm headed, and I don't care either.

I just follow. Until we're standing in front of the fashionable Great Eastern Hotel in Liverpool Street. Then I wake up.

"Don't worry. I'm paying for everything," the repulsive man says when he sees my terrified face. "You don't have to worry about anything."

He takes my hand in his cold one, warming himself on me like a parasite.

"Are we going to . . . ?"

"What?"

"Make love . . ."

LIBIDO

As soon as we came into the suite, I locked myself into the stylish bathroom and stayed there for ages. When I had finished, I let the tap run . . . I took my time. Rummaged around, smelled all the soaps, shampoos, and creams . . . Finally I opened the door and ran as fast as I could: down the stairs and out of the hotel.

I still haven't got my breath back. It's sick to take even what you don't want, I think, open my bag full of soap and shampoo from The Great Eastern Hotel, and throw them into a large green container. I wished it was just as simple to dispose of the repulsive man. I breathe heavily. My pulse is beating fast. I turn my head several times. He is not following me. I still don't feel free of him. I keep him to myself. He is my shame. I'm about to keep walking, but then I discover a sweet little chair next to the garbage bin . . . I've no idea why I'm taking the trouble, but I lift it up and carry it home with me.

I walk fast. Hurry. I feel nauseous. Dirty. I jump on the bus. But don't even have the energy to go upstairs. I push the Stop button and jump off again. I prefer to run. To air my thoughts. When there are about sixty meters to go, I start running like mad. I give it everything. I used to be a good sprinter before I took up smoking, but now I'm out of breath. I grope frantically for the keys to the house in my always-chaotic bag, finally find them, and open the door.

"Lou!"

No answer. I call out again. Still nothing. I put the chair down in the hallway. Our house is a rain forest of incidental junk: from old doors used as tables, pulled out of garbage bins all over the city, red velvet theater curtains haggled over at the Brick Lane flea market, glasses, cups, and ashtrays stolen from various bars and cafes, books borrowed from the library and never returned, film posters torn down from walls, art works dedicated to Lou from friends, mannequins collected from closed-down shops . . . as well as a dilapidated but charming sofa in blue synthetic leather—a gift from the landlord. I'm forgetting many things, but remember the most important: that this is how we like to live, Lou and I, in a weird hodgepodge of things.

I take off my jacket, shoes . . . Then I suddenly hear . . . music! I run up the stairs and into the bathroom. That's where the music is coming from. From Lou. He's lying in the bathtub surrounded by foam, listening to Léo Ferré.

"Hi!" I call. "Were you here this morning, or did I dream it?"

"Yes, I was here," he declares, pouts his lips, and asks for a kiss.

I give him one without tongue, Hollywood style. Then I throw off my clothes.

"So when did you get home?" I ask.

"Around four in the morning, I think," Lou answers.

"That late? Why did you bother . . ." I say.

I notice that my tone is hostile. Perhaps it irritates me that my husband borrows keys to a studio in the city to take his mistress there? Perhaps it reminds me too much of myself, of The Lover?

"I wanted to see you, Vår. I missed you. Surely a husband's allowed to long for his wife?"

Lou notices everything. Down to the twitching of my skin, I think, and answer:

"Of course."

I sigh. I'm worn out.

"You look tired . . ." he says then.

"Yes."

"Is it the writing that takes it out of you, mon amour?"

"No, but lack of writing does," I answer, and find the mini shampoo and shower soap from Hotel Mateo.

Then I splash down in the bathtub. I look forward to washing off the garlic smell printed on my body like a stamp, an example. Of how crazy I am. As if a smell could be infectious . . .

"Hotel Mateo, what's that?" Lou asks and doesn't notice any smell, because the smell of garlic is in my head, not on my body.

"A shady hotel in Bayswater," I answer and lather myself with the soap.

"Yes . . ." Lou says and waits for more.

"I was there with The Lover. He left yesterday morning. He sends his love, by the way."

"Was he in town?"

"Yes, as I just said."

"Why didn't he come here, then?"

"He came to see me, so he could forget me. It was important to be alone."

"Funny . . ."

"It was Marlene's idea. He said that seeing me again was an effort to be with Marlene, and only her. Now he wants you and Marlene to sleep together too. Do you want that, Lou?"

"To sleep with Marlene?"

"Yes . . ."

"I don't know. I've never met her."

"He said men always want to."

"He said that?"

"Yes."

"I see. He may be right."

I turn on the shower and wash my hair with what The Lover smelled of. Afterwards I feel better. I study the mini bottles and look for the ingredients. No ingredients. I rinse it all out again and go out of the bathtub. I still smell bad, but still, I smell better than before. One evil has replaced another.

"Vår . . ."

"Yes?"

I dry myself thoroughly. Try to comb out the tangles in my hair.

"What is it, Lou?"

"Nothing."

"Come on, tell me!"

"No."

Lou comes out of the bathtub too.

"Do you know what I want most in the whole world this very minute?" he says finally.

"No, but I can't wait . . ."

"Nothing."

"What do you mean, nothing . . . ?"

"I don't want to do a single thing. Nothing. I want to go to bed."

INSOMNIA

I'M IN BED NEXT to my husband. Can't sleep. Finally I get up, go down to the living room, and sit in front of the television. I surf the channels. Find nothing of interest. Just news. Old news. I walk into the kitchen looking for a piece of milk chocolate. Comfort food. I open the cupboard. Empty. Time to call Mom for more supplies, I think, and walk disappointedly back to the bedroom.

I sneak into the dark room, sit down as quietly as possible, hoping that I won't wake up Lou as I turn on the computer. I hold my breath. I look at him: how his face folds itself in sleep. I put my ear against his stomach, listen. He breathes regularly. I think, he has good dreams. That it must be good to be inside Lou's head at night. I sit down at the computer again. In the artificial light, I see the garbage chair and wonder what on earth we're going to do with it. I do my best to concentrate, not to get distracted by my stupid ideas. I must try to write what seems too difficult. What I don't want to write.

Time passes, summer, autumn, and winter. Ragnhild is on the beach with her husband. It's an overcast Sunday, it's cold. They have driven to La Grande Motte in the red Renault 5 to admire the famous architecture. Ragnhild likes ghost cities. Summer places out of season. She likes the wind. The mistral. Likes it tousling her hair until it hurts. Likes her eyes getting filled with sand. Because she can see just as well even then.

They jump back in the car and keep driving to a place with sand

76

dunes they can hide behind. Sand dunes and destroyed bunkers. They write something with a knife. Something about personal wars. Between the sexes. They travel around the whole afternoon. They are alone. They are the only ones here. In December.

Ragnhild calls the Painter. Cyril has asked her to choose. She chose to travel. He hasn't given her any choice. She explains:
"We've grown together, the three of us, like Siamese triplets. So that the two of us can survive, the third one has to be cut off. That's reality. Brutal."
She hears the wind through the receiver, the waves. Her heart is beating fast.
"I love you both, no matter what happens. Never forget that," she adds.
She regrets it immediately.
"You won't leave me, will you . . . ?" the Painter asks, almost hysterically.
He wants to do something, stop Ragnhild, take her back where she belongs, in a painting or on a bed, with him or Cyril.
She puts the phone down.

The phone rings. I start.
"Hello."
"Can I speak to Vår?" says a sensual male voice I recognize.
I'm about to put the phone down.
"Your number was in the notebook . . ." he continues.
"It's the middle of the night," I say.
I feel nauseous.
"Please, Vår, let me explain. You left so suddenly. There was so much more I wanted to say. Perhaps I was a bit clumsy."
"It's the middle of the night," I repeat.
"I'm in love, Vår. I keep getting the idea that only you can satisfy me. I know this, intuitively. I've never been mistaken before, about anyone."

"Everyone's mistaken at some time. Perhaps I'm that mistake," I insist.

I try to warn him, dissuade him, give him a chance to get away. I'm fascinated because he is ugly in a revolting way. Almost attractive. This frightens me.

"I want to be dominated. Be a slave. Because I'm too weak to make up my own mind," he says.

I get cranky. Like a sulky little girl. I answer that he's a coward. Leaving it to me to think of something. I think that's unfair. I still say I'll meet him again, on an ordinary day, in the middle of the week. Then I hang up the phone.

"Who were you talking to?" Lou asks.

I turn around, alarmed. I can only just make out my beloved husband in the weak light from the computer.

"Are you awake?" I ask, foolishly.

"Who were you talking to?" he repeats.

"No one."

"No one?"

"No one important, Lou."

"In the middle of the night . . ."

"It was a mistake."

"A long mistake."

"It was a mistake to talk to him is what I meant."

"Him?"

"A total idiot."

"Whom you're going to meet again?"

"Yes."

Ragnhild tries to avoid thoughts about the Painter and Cyril. Concentrates on the landscape instead, trees, and buildings too. It helps a little. She catches sight of a dog running fast. Something she appreciates. That time passes, that landscapes move. She rests her face against the pane, dozes, and gets lost in dreams. She takes the train because she likes to feel the distance between here and there, her and them. That's the way she is: perverse, longing, volatile. She doesn't want the journey to end.

The train's soon entering a tunnel, under the water, like an umbilical cord between two countries that hate each other, Ragnhild thinks, closes her eyes, and travels through her memories. She rewinds several years back, when the goal wasn't England but France. She thinks: I've never regretted that I left, but sometimes I have regretted that I stayed. That's why I'm leaving. Now. That's why I left. Then. That's why I leave. Again.

She knew almost nothing about France, she wanted to go there because she wanted to get away. That was what counted. New sounds, new language, new vocabulary. They were the things she was hoping for, but also the heat. Because she wanted to go down south. To Montpellier. Ravn predicted that she'd stay in that country, that she'd meet a man there. But that is not what Ragnhild wanted. She wanted to be free. She wasn't interested in finding the love of her life. What she wanted to try was charming lots of men.

"You're so lovely when you're writing, Vår," Lou says suddenly. "With your mussed-up hair, a bit red in the face, dressed in whatever. That's how I like you, casual, inconspicuous. I don't like it when you're putting on airs, dressing up, being feminine. It doesn't suit you. What suits you is looking like you've just rolled out of bed."

"Are you still awake?" I ask, surprised, and look dreamingly over at my husband.

"Are you hungry?" is all he says.

All men should know that the road to a woman's sex is through her stomach. Lou knows this too well, I think, and ask: "And?"

"If we're hungry we could have something to eat, no matter what time it is."

THE WHORE AS A FANTASY

THE REPULSIVE MAN IS waiting for me in a dull little soulless cafe, exactly the way I wanted. He asks what I'd like and orders it. I get out my crumbled pack of Vogues and light a cigarette. The revolting man tries to get my attention, acts serious, says he doesn't need to be loved in order to love. Claims that from that moment on, I can treat him however I want, it won't matter. Because he doesn't care who I am, I can be whoever I want. It wouldn't matter if I were a whore, either. He insists so strongly that I have a feeling that's what he wants. The whore as a fantasy. I answer that he knows what I do, that he's seen it, that like a whore I too take off my clothes, I make money on my body, my nakedness. Then I remind him he really isn't my style, to make sure I don't forget it myself. But the revolting man isn't listening. He's looking at me, at my face, my arms.

Asks:

"Do you have moles all over your body?"

I don't answer. His sensual voice no longer has any power over me. The repulsive man doesn't stand a chance, and perhaps that's his best chance.

I tell him:

"I play a game with my husband. If I manage to find a new man to love, he'll break it off with his mistress. But surely you must understand by now that I could never love you, or make love to you."

"Why not?"

"You make me nauseous, I've already told you that."

"I thought we were just joking."

"No, with you I'm very honest. You did say I could treat you however I like."

The repulsive man looks down, sad.

"I was lying. I'm a human being too, Vår."

A tear runs down his cheek. He lets it run. I feel no sympathy.

"The truth is that I'm interested in writing about you," I say. "You inspire me, as material. That's why I came. But I don't want to see you again. I'll have to make do with what I have. Information. Impressions. The rest I'll have to make up."

I'm as repulsive as possible. So the repulsive man won't have anything to regret.

"By the way, I have moles all over my body," I say, get up from the chair, put out the cigarette, and run away.

THE HISTORY OF THE EYE, OF O

I TELL LOU ABOUT the revolting man, that I have a special knack for attracting volatile men. Unbalanced men who believe they have found their sister-soul in me. He is interested.

Asks:

"What is it about you that attracts that type of man, Vår?"

I reflect.

"Ordinary conversation bores me, perhaps that's it? I don't know. Do you think it could be that simple?"

"No."

"I'm open. I'm sure they notice that. That they can talk to me, sleep with me . . . That the potential is there, even if it isn't always fulfilled."

"I understand."

"Do you?"

"No."

"You don't?"

"Not quite . . ."

"But no one does, do they. I don't either. Do you, too, think I'm perverse, Lou?"

"No, only in the way you're perversely interested in the perverse. What about me?"

"No, only in the way you have a refined understanding of the incomprehensible."

"Apropos incomprehensible—"

"I need people like him, like the revolting man, the stranger, if that's what you were thinking?" I interrupt.

"Yes, actually, it was."

"I use them, but don't always fulfill their desires or expectations of me . . ."

". . . or yours, of yourself," Lou adds.

"Do you think I'm a coward?"

"Yes. You're like most people, scared of what's disgusting."

I nod. Lou is right.

"I ran away, ran from the repulsive man, from the stranger, from everything that's frightening. I didn't follow through with my plan to test myself. I want to be a *Madame Sans-Gêne*, but instead I'm just prudish and mean. I'm scared of what's disgusting. That's the way it is."

"No."

"Yes. I could neither have eaten shit nor drunk piss, slept with my father, nor killed my mother . . . I'm an amateur. The desire may be there, of course, but the get-up-and-go is lacking."

"Ditto."

Lou insists that we still have much to learn, both of us, when it comes to crossing boundaries, bending them. He asks if I know the author Pauline Réage?

"No."

"She wrote an erotic-pornographic novel in the 1950s," he tells me. "She could neither paint nor write poetry. So this was her way of flirting. To be heard. Loved, too. By her de Sade-loving lover."

"Did it work?"

"Yes. He stayed with her till he died."

"How beautiful," I answer. And mean it. Because I'm a romantic at heart. "What's the book called?"

I feel expectant. Like most French men, my husband is well informed when it comes to history, philosophy, and pornography. He walks over to our dilapidated bookshelf, picks out a couple of books I didn't know we had, and puts them on the table. I read: *The Story of the Eye* by Bataille, and *The Story of O.* by Pauline Réage.

"This, Vår, this is C and D in the perverse alphabet, according to de Sade and Sacher-Masoch," Lou claims.

2:

TENDER SOULS

Réage, Bataille, Apollinaire, Breton, Aragon . . . I'm reading Lou's books. I read about perversity through history. About Donatien Alphonse François de Sade. About how we gave his name to a category: sadism. But de Sade was not a violent man; from what I understand, he only used violence if someone declined to use violence against him. In frustration. Like the time he beat up a prostitute and forced her to blaspheme against God because she refused to abuse him. "Do unto others as you would have them do unto you" and "Whom the Lord loves he chastens," doesn't it say something like that in the Bible? This is a matter of interpretation, of course. But can de Sade and the Bible be two sides of the same coin? I laugh and make a rhyme for myself: *Why do the good ones go bad, and the bad ones good? How sad. Why walk on bodies dead, if you want to get ahead? De Sade was also a philosopher, remember?* He didn't just think with his willy. But unfortunately he died before Leopold von Sacher-Masoch was born. They would've had a lot to talk about, I believe—humiliating things, subservient things . . . Because it was Sacher-Masoch who gave his name to masochism.

I sit quite still. Lots of people are walking past our house, but these steps, these unhurried but at the same time light and lively steps, they stand right outside our door, waiting, I could almost swear it. I have an unpleasant feeling that we'll have visitors on Sunday. I don't like that. The day God rested, I want us to rest too.

"Lou, there's the doorbell," I call, surprised, alarmed.

"You want me to open?"

"No."

He finds a bag and begins to pack: towel, swimsuits, and books. We've got many plans for the day. We're going on a trip to Brighton to look at the ramshackle pier, buy sugar floss, ride the carousel, swim, admire the waves, read and read, and then take the train home and make love all night, until we're spent. We have many plans, so I don't know why—curiosity, maybe— but I walk over to the window, open the curtains. A lovely breeze blows into the room.

"Who is it, Vår?"

"Jane Birkin."

"Jane Birkin? What're you talking about?"

"The swinging sixties. Serge Gainsbourg. *Je t'aime. Moi non plus.*"

Lou looks at me with a strange expression.

"The sun's shining. It's a lovely day," I add.

He closes the bag, comes over, puts his arms around my waist and kisses my neck. He looks out, looks down, looks into my eyes: will, will not . . . I shrug.

"Do what you like, darling."

The doorbell chimes again. Lou goes downstairs to open it. I sit on the windowsill and watch.

"Hi, it's me!" Sidney calls, in an uncertain voice.

She blushes. She's wearing a soft summer dress and carries a backpack.

"Are you going on a trip?" Lou asks.

"Well, I . . ." She sounds as if she doesn't quite know how to say it. "You invited me, don't you remember . . . ?"

"What?"

Lou starts to laugh.

"But it's true! You said that Vår was going away and so we could be together . . ."

"That's impossible, you've got it wrong, Sid . . ."

"No!"

"But . . ."

"I've really been looking forward to it," she interrupts with pleading dog's eyes.

Lou seems bewildered.

"Vår is here," he says and rolls his eyes. "I'm sorry, but I think you'd better go home again."

He rolls a cigarette, lights it. Sid finds her asthma spray, and she, too, inhales. She doesn't say anything. Doesn't take the hint. Asks with her body what she hasn't got the courage to say.

"Sid, please . . . It won't work," Lou says then.

He interrupts the unspoken. Doesn't want the eyes to become words, the body to articulate the sentences.

"It's Sunday today, and tomorrow is a bank holiday . . ." he continues. "Vår and I . . . it's so rare that . . . we . . ."

I agree. I only wish one thing—that Sidney would take the hint and leave.

"I won't be any trouble," she promises. "I'll make myself so small, so small. I can't bear the thought of going home. Besides, it's a good opportunity for Vår and me to get to know each other better . . ."

"Well obviously, but . . ."

A car drives past. They say something I can't hear. I become quite irritated. My husband isn't comfortable, I can feel that. He turns and looks up at the window, at me. I blush. I don't know how to explain . . . my curiosity. I don't have to, I'm in luck. Because it's Lou who has something on his mind, something difficult, something he tries to air with me.

"Vår, is it all right if Sid stays over . . . ?" he calls after a long, intolerable silence—not for me, for him.

I reflect. Enjoy their torment. Not very nice of me.

"It's my fault," he says. "It seems I didn't know you were going to be here, and then I promised to be with her . . . you know how forgetful I can be . . ." he adds.

"Oh well . . ."

You have to take the bull by the horns, isn't that what they say? Or the rabbit by the ears . . . Not that I consider Sidney a dare, she's only a hare. I laugh to myself at my dumb rhymes. I think: two girls and one man, instead of two men and one girl . . . Why not? It is important to test one's limits, how far one can go.

THREE

Lᴏᴜ ᴛᴀᴋᴇs Sɪᴅɴᴇʏ's ʙᴀᴄᴋᴘᴀᴄᴋ, and the two of them go up to the first floor. To me.

"We have to sleep here, the three of us," he apologizes. "This is the only bed we have."

"That's fine," Sidney assures us, "for me, at least. But if Vår wants me to, I can easily sleep on the floor."

"Of course not," I answer facetiously. "Tonight, you're going to be our little baby and sleep in the middle. We'll look after you so well," I add ironically.

"I'd like that," she answers. "When I was little, I ran into my parents' room because I was afraid of the dark. That was before my asthma. I was a happy child, then, I miss that."

I'm thinking: I never ran into my parents' room in the middle of the night, even if I was afraid, and I often was, too. Was lying in my bed with a hammering heart and clammy hands. I wish I'd had the courage to be afraid, more often and more honestly. I look at Sidney. I'm impressed by her weird form of courage. This girl-child that she still is, as if she's gotten stuck in childhood.

She tells us:

"My room was always closest to the staircase, so I grew up with the idea that if something should happen, I'd be the first victim. Besides, our house lies in quite an isolated place, surrounded by forests, so there's not much chance of escaping to the nearest neighbor."

Lou takes Sidney in his arms.

"Little Sid," he mumbles fondly, softly, so I can hardly hear him.

I look at them, observe them as if they were a couple. I don't like it.

"I'm not little!" Sidney shouts. "I'm a big girl who's soon going to move into a studio."

She laughs because she's enjoying being in my husband's arms. I glance at her surreptitiously. She *is* attractive. Too attractive, perhaps. I'm looking for a blemish, something to become fond of, to desire. Apart from the asthma. Because as long as I can't find that, she'll remain a stranger.

"Can I bum a cigarette, Vår?" she asks suddenly.

I look at her, suspicious.

"Should you smoke, with your asthma?"

"No . . . not really. But . . . it's silly, isn't it?"

"Yes."

Lou laughs. He seems to think it's hilarious. I give Sidney a Vogue and take one myself as well. And that's when I discover the blemish. Her weakness is her anatomy. Her fingers. The skin on her fingers. The fingertips. Those holding the cigarette. They're yellow, almost orange. A nice color. Stains. She smokes, coughs, and uses the asthma spray in turns. It's a ridiculous sight. But sweet. I think that her skin must be so thin, so delicate, so sensitive that the nicotine is absorbed into it. I'm fascinated and can't help staring. I'm on the verge of being rude. Sidney realizes this and feels uncomfortable.

She explains, a little apologetically:

"It's impossible to get rid of. I've tried everything. Scrubbed with chemicals, or something sharp. It works for a while. The stains disappear. But then they come back and I have to start all over again. Now and then I take the lighter and try to burn them off."

I want to kiss Sidney's sore fingertips. I clear my throat.

"This could sound a bit strange. But I like you a lot better now that I've discovered the blemish, the weakness of your anatomy. Perhaps we could become friends. . . ?"

Friends . . . These words . . . I hope they'll be well received. That they'll grow and blossom and become a tree . . . a threesome.

"You two weren't supposed to become friends," Lou says.

PSYCHIATRY AND SIDE EFFECTS

TONIGHT YOU CAN BE our little baby and sleep in the middle, I suggested, for the fun of it, but it seemed I was the only one who got the joke.

I can hear them whispering to each other during the night. When they think I'm asleep, Lou tells her about his father, *the psychiatrist*: he who claims that the patients you treat harshly always come back. That they become your most faithful clients. While those you treat kindly disappear immediately and find another psychiatrist. Sidney says almost nothing. Because she's a listener, I think. Modest when she is with Lou. She lies very still. I almost believe she is holding her breath. Lou continues. He is used to being a voice. I lip-synch while he talks, because I know the stories by heart. Because Lou never gets tired of empathizing with his own father's stories.

He whispers:

"One of my Dad's patients thought his leg was making him depressed, that the root of all his sins was in his leg, so if only he could get rid of it, he'd feel a lot better. One day he went to the train station and put his leg on the track. It was smashed to pieces and had to be amputated. Since then he's been happy. He lost a leg, and my Dad lost a patient."

Sidney puts her hand over her mouth. She only just avoids punching me. But she doesn't notice anything, thank god. She is engrossed. Coughs softly, almost soundlessly. I think: that's what she likes best about my husband, his stories.

He continues:

"Another patient used a knife on her drunken husband after she'd talked to my Dad. He stood by her side in court. She was found not guilty."

I can hear that Sidney has problems swallowing.

Lou adds quickly:

"It's not easy growing up with a father who's a psychiatrist. He listens to people's problems all day and when he comes home, he wants to relax. My Dad never listened to me."

Then he stops. Suddenly stops talking. Sidney holds out a hand to Lou. But my husband is blind in the darkness, insensible, noticing nothing.

THE FACE OF JANUS

SIDNEY IS THE FIRST to get up, although I've been awake the longest, lying there looking at her for hours without moving. The sleeping face . . . I become obsessed by it. Sidney's face in sleep looked almost old. As if all her youth was left behind in this real life and only the old Sid went with her into her dreams. I get a kind of premonition that Sidney will grow old very fast—not gradually, but overnight.

Unaware of my gaze she walks over to her backpack, takes off her nightgown and folds it neatly. Then she wriggles her thin, delicate body into cut-off denim shorts and a checked shirt. I observe the bashful Sidney unabashedly. Watch how she makes herself at home. Fishes out Lou's tobacco from the pocket of his pants as if it were her own. Sits down on the floor, rolls a cigarette, lighting it as she picks books from our shelf, has a quick look, flicks through a few pages, and puts them back. Then she stands up and walks over to my desk. Has a look at my notes, too, but fortunately she doesn't understand Norwegian. She walks over to the window, opens the curtains. A heavy air wafts into the room. She coughs.

"It's humid," I say. "I think there's a storm coming soon. I've got a headache."

Sidney starts.

"You're awake, Vår?"

"Yes, I have been for a long time."

She blushes. Becomes bashful. In hindsight.

"It's early yet," Lou adds. He too is awake. "The wind might still come and clear the air . . . Now and then the wind's so strong, so intense, that it's like it's screaming it wants to stay with us."

"But not today," Sidney says.

"No," I say.

LA DOLCE VITA

THE THREE OF US make breakfast like a happy little family. But the only thing I can think of is the two of them, Sidney and my husband—easy movements, skin, smiles, laughter . . . I struggle to get anything down, despite my stomach rumbling.

"Aren't you hungry after all, Vår?" Sidney asks without a hint of irony in her voice.

She has become her old self again, I think. She spreads a thin layer of Marmite on her toast.

"Yes, but not for food, for life," I answer a bit too arrogantly.

Lou looks at me. Looks through me. Understands the jealousy . . . I drink my juice in one gulp, fill my glass again, and repeat.

"But you're thirsty, at least?" she says.

"Yes, that I am. Thirsty for new experiences."

"I'm not like you, Vår," Sidney says then. "When I've found something I want, I like to hold on to it."

She's referring to my husband, no doubt about that. She smiles, bashfully. Lou wants her to stop. He doesn't say anything, but his eyes speak for him. It's so unnatural, so unusual, this combination of the three of us. It doesn't work.

"Why don't we go for a walk?" Sidney suggests.

She obviously doesn't like this heavy silence forced upon us. She sees it as her responsibility to break it, I think.

"What do you think, Vår?" Lou asks nervously. "Is that a good idea?"

"No," I whisper in such a low voice that I can hardly hear it myself.

"It's not all that important to me, to go for a walk . . ." he says then.

"Why don't you go . . . I prefer to have the two of you out of here rather than in here."

JUST A FEW LITTLE SCRATCHES

*RAGNHILD WANDERS AROUND IN the gallery between the many Fridas.
"Frida Kahlo's art is a silk ribbon around a bomb," André Breton
wrote. That's what Ragnhild wants her words to be. She thinks
that if she takes all these titles and puts them together, she has a
story. About herself. Because Frida's paintings don't just refer to
experiences in her own life, but also in Ragnhild's, in everyone's,
Ragnhild thinks. She opens her notebook and writes: "My Birth,"
"Roots," "The Tree of Hope," "The Dream," "Diego and I" . . . She
crosses out the last one, changes it to: "Cyril and I."*

*Then she goes into the hallway to find Cyril. He doesn't know
she's in the gallery. He comes walking toward her but doesn't see her,
because he only has eyes for Beverley. Ragnhild hides and watches
them in secret. She doesn't see what Cyril was talking about, the
platonic side. What she sees is more concrete. She feels that they're
growing inside her like the roots of a tree. She wants to cut her
stomach open with a knife, to get a big, cold pair of tongs and tear
them out.*

*Cyril stares into Beverley's dark green eyes. In her look there's
a new expression Ragnhild didn't know Beverley was capable of. A maturity. Her eyes are steadfast and open, no longer filled with the vigilant and reserved expression she usually
wears.*

*Ragnhild surveys feelings on the brink of explosion. She listens to
their kisses inside herself. Feels their wet tongues all over her body.
Beverley's movements are languid. She probably isn't aware of it
herself, but Ragnhild notices how Beverley's whole body changes*

from being touched. She has a detestable and provocative half-smile around her mouth. She finds her asthma spray and breathes in.

    Ragnhild jots down as much as she can, until she gets too tired. It's a terrible burden. She feels dizzy and scared. Her eyes are wet. She can no longer see what she's formulating. Her hurt feelings are crying for help between each line.

PORTRAITS OF HURT EGOS

I SIT AND LISTEN for Lou's steps for a long time without hearing them. The rain is just a slow drizzle. I see a rainbow through the window. It's still humid outside, but the sun is shining. Then it stops raining, and the rainbow disappears. I close the curtains. It's really idiotic to sit here in the dark on a bright day like this, I think, light a cigarette, and close my eyes. I listen: Far away, closer. I notice Lou's slightly clumsy and confused steps, but also Sidney's slow and unhurried ones. Sidney and Lou, what a couple. Quite a husband I have . . . I want to run down the stairs to greet him, wag my tail, and get a cuddle. But instead I sit here quietly waiting.

As they open the door, I turn off my computer and put out the cigarette. Sidney shakes her short hair, wet from the rain, and reminds me of a dog.

"How silly to sit here in the dark, Vår," Sidney comments and opens the curtains.

"You're so clever that you're not real . . ." I mumble.

"What?"

"Nothing."

"I see. Anyone want a cup of tea?"

"Yes please," Lou answers.

"Vår . . . ?"

"If you're making one . . ."

I pick up a biography of Frida Kahlo and read without knowing what I'm reading. Lou seems restless. He sits down on the floor, rolls a cigarette and lights it.

"Vår, I . . ."

"Let's talk about it later, darling," I interrupt and keep turning the pages pointlessly.

"Thanks . . ." Lou says, and closes his mouth.

Sidney comes in with five o'clock tea: three cups with milk froth.

"How kind of you," I say reluctantly.

I don't like that Sidney tries to be nice to me. I become irritated. She sits down next to Lou on the floor and takes a couple of drags from his cigarette. We sit for a while without talking. It's quiet. Only the sound of swallowing, of smoking, of mouths drinking and clocks ticking. Finally I'm the one breaking the silence.

I read:

"'Trotsky sent Frida a nine-page letter after they had broken off, begging her to take him back. *Estoy muy cansada del viejo*, Frida wrote to a friend. I'm tired of the old man.'"

I look at Sidney. I look at my husband. None of us are old. I wonder who'll get old first.

I continue to read:

"'In a letter from Trotsky to his wife, he says: "I love you so much, Nata, my own, my undying, my true love and my victim!"'"

"How awful!" Sidney exclaims and stands up.

"Where are you going?" Lou asks and puts out the cigarette.

"Cleaning up."

"Cleaning up?"

"Yes. Any objections?"

"No, but . . ."

She comes over to me.

"Finished, Vår?"

"Hold on . . ."

I gulp down the rest. Lou does the same. Then we give the cups to Sidney so she can take them to the kitchen.

"Vår . . ."

"Shh . . ."

Lou shrugs.

"It's not your fault, dear,' just leave it . . ." I comfort him.

We sit there without moving, like pillars of salt. When Sidney comes back, her eyes wander. She sits down. Counts to ten. Takes out the asthma spray, breathes in, breathes out . . .

"It doesn't work," she says suddenly.

"What?" Lou asks, surprised.

"Me, here. It's a mess."

"Why do say that? I think it's going quite well," Lou claims.

"Yes," I add.

"No."

"No?"

"It was stupid, Lou. I just wanted, just had to see . . ."

"See what?"

"The two of you together. See if I could handle it. Your other life."

"Oh . . ."

"From now on, I'd prefer not to know. To have a relationship with you, Lou, as if Vår doesn't exist."

"But . . ."

She looks at him with tears in her eyes.

"I'm not like you two. I want to be, but I can't do it. I try to be calm about it all, to be open, playful, but when I look at Vår, it's as if she's sticking hundreds of needles into my heart."

TO HIDE BEHIND RHETORIC

LOU SITS AND STARES out the window. He doesn't say anything. I sit down next to him. The house is quiet. Only the ticking of the clock and the sound of anonymous steps, of cars in the street—not very many, but then it is Bank Holiday.

"You do understand it was just a lie, darling?" I ask.

"What was?"

"That you had invited her here, of course."

"I got really confused, I have to admit. But you didn't have to . . ."

". . . accept?"

"Yes."

"Still, I did. Because I love to do everything I shouldn't do." I run to the window, close it.

"What is it, Vår?"

"Thunder, didn't you hear? I've felt him in me all day: Grandpa Thor. You see, I imagine that it's him running across the sky with his hammer."

There's another thunderclap. The lightning lights up the whole room as well as the face of my husband. It is beautiful; nature's forces, rage, a god's fury, joy.

"By the way, what are your plans tomorrow after work?" I ask.

Lou looks discomfited.

"I'm going for a walk with Sidney. You?"

Sidney sticks to him like a leech, I think. Weeks have passed, and what have I done? I've wasted them. I've been a poor player.

"Me . . . ? I'm working with Holly. But that's during the day. After that, I don't know yet."

"Are you modeling nude for her? "

"Yes, I have been, but now she'd rather do a portrait of me."

"Surely that's a compliment."

"It certainly is. I'm proud of being paid to keep my clothes on. You get so tired of being naked."

Crash of thunder. Grandpa Thor is truly angry, I'm thinking. It's beginning to blow as well. I imagine that Grandma Margit is the howling wind trying to sing him to sleep. So we are both right, Lou and I, regarding the weather.

"I can't believe it," I exclaim.

"What?"

"That Sidney slept here."

I lie down on the bed. Lou looks at me, resigned, with an expression saying: I thought we'd finished discussing this, darling . . .

But instead he just says:

"Did it matter?"

"Yes. It made me see a side of you I didn't like."

MASQUERADE

I DON'T SAY ANYTHING, look around, look at various sketches and paintings hanging on the wall, look at my own and other people's naked bodies.

"Come over here!" Holly shouts enthusiastically.

"What is it?"

She shows me the canvas on which my portrait is going to be painted. 36 x 26 inches.

"Isn't it fantastic to think how you can truly create something with a canvas and a few colors . . . ?"

"Yes."

I look out of the window: the sun is shining, the Thames . . .

"Are you lonely, Vår?" she then asks, observant and sensitive.

"Why do you ask?"

"You seem so sad."

"How's Henry?" I ask instead.

In the reflection from the window, I can see her face changing.

"Vår, I . . ."

"You'd rather not talk about it?"

"I don't know how you can bear it, sharing your husband with . . . What's her name again? Sidney, isn't it?"

"I don't want to be owned by anyone," I answer, "and so I can't own anyone myself. To me, life's more interesting that way. Variety. Of course it's difficult, but the opposite demands even more."

The words, the memorized words, flow out of me. I answer without thinking, without listening. I answer what I believe in. The way I have decided it has to be.

"Perhaps you're right, Vår, but I wish that for once life could be, I don't know, easy. That I didn't have to fight for everything: men and art."

Then she stops. Looks at me in the way only she can. Intensely, probingly, with these large, round eyes of hers.

"You've changed," she claims. "I can't put my finger on it. Maybe it's too deep beneath the surface."

"I'm not in love with The Lover anymore," I inform her, drily and brutally.

"You're sure?"

"No, you can never be sure."

Holly looks at me again. She's skeptical. Believes I'm fooling around. But neither of us is laughing. She lights a cigarette. Menthol. A green packet with a lovely, almost repulsive scent.

"It feels strange to stop loving someone you've been so much in love with," I admit. "To think that a life with The Lover is over."

"It's even stranger to love someone you haven't loved before," Holly says. "That a life with Henry has begun . . ."

She opens the window. We need air. Confined feelings are set free.

"The Lover and I . . . We could never get enough. It was on the border of cannibalism . . . I really loved him, I truly did, I almost sacrificed Lou. But then it turned out to be wrong after all. Because now it's over. Now I feel something else, less painful, safer . . . Friendship."

"It's the opposite with Henry and me," Holly says.

Both of us want to talk about something else, not to talk at all maybe. Holly puts on the white jumpsuit she always wears when she's working, lays out the paints, sable brushes, and gets ready. She puts out the cigarette and puts on some music: Karlheinz

Stockhausen. Contemporary music to get inspiration, I think.

"Whiskey?" she asks spontaneously.

"Yes please."

"What I want you to wear is on that chair over there," she says, pointing.

"OK."

She opens the whiskey bottle while I walk over to the chair and put on a black skirt, a patterned sweater and a helmet from the Second World War. They're a strange mixture of epochs.

"I thought it was supposed to be a portrait," I say. "Why all these clothes?"

"Even if I paint a portrait, Vår, I need the whole you to get the right impression. Mind and body belong together. To be able to paint the small details, you'll have to know the whole big landscape . . ."

"Obviously," I say, and sit down on the chair.

"Could you look out the window, darling, at that large birch in the park?" she asks.

"OK."

I try to find a suitable expression.

"Do you think much about death, Vår?"

"Yes, it frightens me."

"Keep that thought."

"About death?"

"Yes."

We both sip our whiskey. A dog walks past and pisses on the trunk. An ailing dog shuffling along. Ownerless dog, I think.

"That's right—sad, melancholic. That looks good," Holly comments. "I'm really looking forward to painting your eyes, Vår. They're blue, but with a yellow ring around them, as if they're on fire. It'll be such fun."

I can't help grinning. Besides, her enthusiasm for painting puts me in a good mood. It's a paradox. When I arrived I felt sad, but tried to hide it behind a cheerful expression. Whereas

now that I feel more cheerful—almost happy—I have to hide
again, this time behind a melancholic mask. Life's a masquerade,
I'm thinking, a play in which you have different roles. But you're
often wrong, and use wrong expressions for the wrong occasion.

OH, SHOW ME THE WAY TO THE NEXT WHISKEY BAR . . .

TIME PASSES QUICKLY WITH Holly. I look at my watch.

"Ten. Already!"

I stand up and glance quickly at the portrait. There's not much there yet. I only have a vague idea of the form of the face and the beginning of an eye. I walk toward the door.

"Where are you going in that costume, Vår . . . ?" Holly asks, laughingly.

I look at myself and blush.

"Sit down," she commands. "There's still whiskey left in the bottle . . ."

She unscrews the top and refills our glasses. I turn around and come back.

"Do you have plans for tonight?" she asks.

"No."

I gulp down the drink and ask her for another. Holly laughs and does the same. She is afraid of being alone, I think. Only her and the canvas. That's an intimacy she fears. I do understand her. I fear the white screen of my computer.

THE DOMINO EFFECT

WHEN I GET HOME, my husband's still out. I walk into the room. My head's buzzing. Just one more glass, I'd said, and it turned into the whole bottle. I enjoy talking with Holly. She's like an angler who throws out his reel and I keep getting hooked. I feel free and uncensored. All in the name of art, of course, so Holly can get to paint my fiery eyes. We listen to each other and are in a situation where we don't really need to talk, the painter and the model, and so we become unstoppable. All tension disappears, and we chat away. Think thoughts we've never thought before. A bottle of whiskey gives you courage, and it also makes you an idiot. Sentimental.

I suddenly begin to snivel. I'm alone in my house, crying. I don't know if it's because I'm drunk or perhaps just needing someone to sing me a lullaby. I wish Lou and I could destroy all of humanity and just be the two of us. But it doesn't work. We need each other, but we also need the others. An audience. Because surely you don't really exist before you've been seen— the way a feeling also doesn't exist before it's been given a name, or a book before it's been read. We need someone to pat us on the shoulder when things go wrong and spit in our face when things go well. We need perspective, opposition, banalities, clichés, and completely new ideas. We need a stage to perform on.

The ridiculousness of tragedy hurts me, while the misery of comedy makes me happy. I start to laugh. I want to laugh myself to death so I can no longer feel any fear. Tears of grief turn into tears of laughter, lovely and warm down my cold face. I don't want to be passive, I want to be strong and independent my heartache, like a broadside ballad performed in all its seductive beauty. My wounds haven't healed, but that's because I constantly pick at them, study them, describe them . . . And why? Because the personal is global and the global impersonal. We're all unique, and that's what makes us so similar.

I straighten my back. Upright and proud I fix my eyes on the wall, like a painting. Later I throw myself against it and hurt myself. But my body is now so relaxed, so loose, that I don't feel any pain. I see the bump and observe the blue, purple, and yellow colors beginning to form, but don't feel anything. Numb. I sit down on the floor and pull up my shirt, but for whom? For a lover I no longer love? Or for a man who sleeps in other people's beds? For myself, maybe?

I run down to the kitchen and search desperately for more alcohol. Find a half-empty vodka bottle. Open it. I think about The Lover. The Lover and Marlene. The Lover before Marlene. I think about The Lover I once loved. And in my stupid, nostalgic, sentimental, and heroic mood, I find the phone and dial his number. It's the middle of the night, but I don't care. I want to talk to my lover, my savior, I want to see him, take him in my arms, and worship him. Wake him up. Hear his crabby and apathetic voice and laugh at him.

MORNING MESS

I TURN AROUND IN bed. My thoughts are whirring. I float, fly. Open my eyes wide, despite my never-ending love for the Sandman. I turn around again. Back and forth. I have a terrible headache. I'm restless. Settle down. Lou is lying in bed next to me, exhausted after yet another walk with Sidney, I think. It must be nice to need so little: two arms, two legs. I wonder what they talk about, whether they talk, or whether they just exist with each other, in the city . . . I wonder about when he came home . . .

He must have tiptoed in the door, taken off his shoes, and crept up to bed. I stroke his back, ponder what he hides behind this wall, what's making this body move, the soul, what's making Lou Lou. Can personality be defined, explained, demystified, put away in a bag? I tickle him behind his ear. Everything is unique, different from me and my genes. There's still no one who's more like me than Lou, mentally—not my mother, father, or my big brother August. I study him while he sleeps. It always used to be Lou who woke up first and studied me. He would say that he was proud and surprised to see me there next to him. That he still couldn't fathom it. That he really got me. That I said yes to us.

I try to close my eyes, but they just pop open again. I run down to the kitchen looking for milk. Find a carton that has passed its use-by date, but still drink straight from it. I spit out the milk and pour the rest into the sink. Then I go up to the bedroom and lie down again. I look at my watch: five thirty. In an hour or so Lou will wake up. Then I'll tell him everything.

WAITING FOR GODOT

LOU IS DRESSED IN his finest clothes: a worn pair of jeans, an old t-shirt with *The Ballet School* across the chest and a suit jacket he bought at the flea market in Skien. He's nervous.

"Vår . . ."

"Yes?"

"Do you really want to forget him?"

"The Lover?"

"Yes."

"It's important to forget, to allow new things to happen," I answer.

"Will you forget me too?"

"No. Never."

"Me neither."

We become silent.

"Vår . . ."

"Yes?"

"What're you thinking about?"

"I love you."

"Me too."

I give him a kiss.

"Lou . . ."

"Yes?"

"Do you love Sidney as much as you love me?"

"Of course not."

"Is that true?"

"No. I love Sidney more than everyone."

I look at him, shocked.

10

"I'm joking, Vår. It was a joke."

I push him down on the bed and begin to hit him. He hits me back. I pick up a pillow and throw it. He pulls my hair and fights like a girl. I scrape my nails down his back. He bites my nipples.

"Ouch!"

"*Aïe!*"

The doorbell rings.

"They're here," Lou declares.

"Yes, they're here," I repeat.

We walk over to the window.

"Yes. There they are."

"Yes."

SUB ROSA

I TRY TO REMEMBER the introduction. What we said. If we said anything. I only remember afterwards.

Marlene undresses. Just like that. While we're having dinner. I look at her. Her body. We all look at her. The Lover, Lou, and I. She doesn't give us a choice. This closeness, this intimacy . . . It's forced upon us. I establish that her nipples are very large, on the border of being vulgar. I'm surprised to see how stiff they can become. I study her body. Touch, it, only just. Her skin is hard, firm, not soft. That surprises me, this coarseness when I touch, this almost maleness.

I take her hand in mine. We compare hands. Hers are fat, bloated. She bites her nails. I don't know what to say. Her hands are ugly. It just slips out. She pulls it quickly away. I take her hand in mine again. She lets it happen. I'm charmed by her ugly hands in the same way Sidney's nicotine-stained hands once charmed me. Marlene's voice changes, becomes brittle. She claims that she wants to know everything I remember, no restrictions. I don't ask what, I understand, instinctively. I tell her about our clothes, that they were strewn all over the apartment, that we did it everywhere, The Lover and I. That we were like wild animals while Lou was watching, but that we held something back, that I bit my hand not to scream. I admit that this just increased the sexual excitement.

I look at Marlene surreptitiously. Her reaction. No reaction. She stands there, free from jealousy: not beautiful, but attractive.

Her breasts, her ass, the running mascara . . . Yes, there's something about Marlene. A kind of surprising form of liberation. I understand that she is an intelligent girl pretending to be stupid. It's easier that way. Then she doesn't have to prove anything. I look out the window: the cheese in the sky, the man in the moon . . .

"There aren't so many clouds in the sky anymore," Lou says.

"Tomorrow will be a nice day," The Lover says.

"Looks like it," I say.

"The rough weather's subsided," Marlene says.

I wrap myself in a blanket. It's not that I'm cold, but I like to have something around my body. Something warm. Something that can hide my sex. Because I'm not wearing anything under my skirt this time either, in honor of the old days. But I don't feel relaxed. It seems too obvious, too desperate. I cross my legs.

Marlene tells us that she is no longer shy. That she has posed naked for her lover, for other people. That she is a muse like me, a painter like her darling. She says it like that, straight out. It's quite beautiful, how she says it.

The Lover explains that he likes her German accent, that it reminds him of Romy Schneider's voice: the one that makes all Frenchmen go weak at the knees. He says it makes him melt. I glance at the man I no longer love. We're all waiting for it, for him to continue talking.

He confirms:

"It's true, Marlene paints. She spends most of her spare time standing over a mirror examining her own sex."

He throws a glance at Lou. We laugh. We begin to get drunk. We no longer talk about the weather. About this phenomenon that fills the void between people. I peer at my old lover and his young lover. Men are so obsessed with age, I think, and feel morose.

Exclaim:

"You like young girls, and when they get older, they don't interest you anymore."

The Lover admits that yes, that's true. He doesn't even apologize. Says:

"I dream about finding The Woman, the one who'll be there forever. I've imagined I've found her several times, even believed for a while it was you, Vår, but I was wrong, every time. But I don't think it's like that this time," he says and looks lovingly at Marlene and smiles.

I think: Skin. A skin that has lived, experienced, been touched. I think: That can be beautiful as well. I look at Lou. Lou is looking at Marlene. I can see that Lou likes her, too. Her youth, naivety, she has an effect on him. I see that Lou's cheeks become warm, he drinks more that usual, quicker, he laughs more than usual, louder. The atmosphere becomes intense. The Lover fills our glasses and offers his Gitanes to each of us. We light up at the same time: four cigarettes.

A minute's silence. Marlene looks out of the window and screams. A car crashes into a lamppost. People are passing, stopping, talking, staring, gaping. I ask Marlene to close the curtains. I grab the opportunity to dissect her with my eyes as with a knife. Her hair is dark red, almost like wine. I imagine that she has taken a bottle and poured it over her head. I stare at her, and suddenly she stares back. Eyes on the back of your head—so they do exist, I think. Slowly her lips begin to tremble and she moves them from side to side to reveal her two irresistible front teeth. And then a beautiful smile. Laughter. She looks at Lou, who looks at The Lover, who looks at me. I fill our glasses with more alcohol, while Lou puts on *Venus in Furs* by The Velvet Underground & Nico.

I sip my drink, light a cigarette and sing along:

". . . Kiss the boot of shiny, shiny leather. Shiny leather in the dark. Tongue of thongs, the belt that does await you. Strike, dear mistress, and cure his heart . . ."

Marlene gulps down her drink. Lou sits down next to her, while The Lover moves closer to me.

BETRAYAL

I open my eyes: Marlene sleeps. She breathes heavily. Doesn't snore. Her lips are swollen. She smells of sleep. I put my nose close to her breath. Lou's head is resting against her naked breasts. It amuses me to think that he has betrayed Sidney. It's mean of me, but I can't help smiling. Lou snores, only just, a kind of rustling sound, like a lonely wave by the ocean.

I close my eyes again. If only Sidney knew that my husband can't really be trusted, I think, that no man can. The Lover was right, men always want to. We were both right, because women usually want to as well.

"Vår . . ."

I turn in the direction of the voice.

"Yes?"

I try to move. My body's tingling. I smile without moving my mouth.

"What is it?"

"Come closer."

The voice contains everything: desire.

"I thought we were supposed to forget each other, hone away the fossils . . . We probably haven't been so good at that . . ." I say.

"You're wrong."

"Wrong?"

"In order to forget, you have to remember everything, each little detail. That's the only way to begin to wipe it out."

"Is it late?" I ask.

The Lover looks at his watch.

"Yes. Marlene is very keen to take a walk in Hyde Park before we leave tonight," he says, and sneaks his fingers in between my legs.

"Perhaps we should get out of bed soon?" I ask.

"Perhaps . . ."

His fingers are inside me now. I have to bite my lips to stop from moaning.

I stare at him with a challenging look, roll out of bed and throw on my Pollock sweater. Then I tie a towel around my waist and make myself ready for a shower. The Lover follows me. We continue to make out in the bathroom. He pulls out his fingers now and again to smell them, sniff each aroma, like a dog, or a wine expert.

Explains:

"I try to identify the various sources, to see what you're made up of: sweat, urine, a little perfume, maybe, skin, ovulation, menstruation, semen, spittle, etc."

Then he washes his hands, while he continues to talk:

"I like it when the smells of your sex mix with the smells of the soap and turn into something in between."

We enter the shower together, rinse off everything that must be gone, one last time.

Afterwards we make French breakfast: freshly squeezed orange juice, café au lait, croissants, pain au chocolat . . .

THE BETRAYED. THE BETRAYER

I HOLD MARLENE'S HAND while we walk through Hyde Park. We're desperately trying to get close, find some kind of solidarity.

She says:

"I wish I was still an unborn child, a fetus. Because when I fantasize about what it would've been like inside Mom's stomach, I long to be there. I wish I could go back into the warm darkness. I'm almost certain that I was born with a deep sense of nostalgia." She also says: "Things like that have made it difficult for me to be present in my own life."

I nod sympathetically and squeeze her bloated hand harder.

"Are you coming?" the men shout.

"Yes!" we shout back.

But we walk slowly, enjoy sharing this femininity, which men can only get a small glimpse of. It's so rare—harmony between two people of the same sex. We walk past a rock. I smile. She asks me why. I show her the rock and wonder if she thinks it's big?

"No, nothing out of the ordinary," she answers.

I tell her I know someone who had sex behind that rock. I explain they were so horny they thought no one could see them.

"Who were they?" she asks and titters.

"That's not important," I say and blush. "It doesn't concern you."

She doesn't quite understand, but is sensible enough not to dig further.

"Why don't we catch up with them?" she suggests.

"If you want to."

Lou and The Lover are waiting for us on a bench further down. A couple of squirrels are jumping through the trees behind them, playing. Marlene runs toward her boyfriend, kissing him, stroking his hair, and whispering something that makes him smile. Then she walks over to my husband and sits down on his lap.

Says:

"I'm a little girl who picks her nose in the dark of her room and rubs off the gob under the mattress."

They laugh. The men.

"You're such a naughty girl," they answer.

I want to scrape my nails down her back and scratch it open, make long, raw marks. But I don't do anything, just laugh with them. Until I'm the only one. The others suddenly turn silent, serious. It starts to rain. First a little, then more and more.

We run into a cafe. Lou orders cocoa and cheesecake for all of us, while Marlene rolls a monster of a cigarette, lights it, and gives it to him.

He takes a puff and says:

"Everyone knew who I was. That I was the betrayed husband. In such a small place by the sea. It was difficult. I mean, it was difficult to live in such a small place."

He looks at Marlene, but not at The Lover and me. "You'd have to be blind to ignore that they loved each other. That's why we moved to London: first Vår, then me."

He takes several puffs of the cigarette. Marlene, the restless one, sits stock-still. The Lover and I stiffen.

Lou's eyes seek me, he continues:

"Our relationship can only survive in a big city, in a capital, in a city with asphalt and clamor, with mess and junk and an unstoppable mass of people."

I nod. It's true. I want to add something, but Lou hasn't finished, and by the time he has, I'll have forgotten my train of thought.

He explains:

"To succumb to the conviction that love is a phenomenon as brittle as porcelain is something I want to do unobserved . . . I want to live my stories in peace. Therefore: in a city like this, and only in a city like this, can I be the betrayed, can I be the betrayer."

I LIKE LONDON . . . IN THE RAIN

IT KEEPS RAINING ALL day, pouring down. I put my head out the window to soak my face. It's lovely. I feel my hair dripping, down my back . . . It tickles. I laugh because I'm ticklish. I see lightning, immediately followed by Grandpa Thor. I wave to The Lover and Marlene, then I close the window. When I can't see the taxi any longer, I jump back into bed. Lou puts on an album we got from The Lover and Marlene where someone sings, "I like London . . . in the rain . . ." over and over again. The whole song. Just this one sentence. We sing along. Drown out the thunder.

"I like London . . . in the rain . . ."

The air is sultry and oppressive. Soon I feel a headache coming on. I ask Lou to turn off the music.

I say:

"In the Amazon there's a bird that, from the moment it starts to fly, it can't stop. If it stops to fly, it dies. I'm that bird."

Lou is silent.

"Have you written that, Vår? How beautiful."

"Isn't it. I wish they were my words."

He reflects. For a long time.

"Hey . . . Don't you know whose words, Lou?"

"No."

"Henning Mankell."

"Henning Mankell . . . ?"

"My father reads Mankell," I answer and put my fingers around his neck.

I squeeze. When his face changes color, I stop. Lou coughs. I go and get him a glass of water.

"Vår, have you lost your mind! Why did you do that?" he asks, alarmed.

"To make certain that you're alive, darling, that you're mine . . ."

A DREAM PLAY

LOU SLEEPS RESTLESSLY. THRASHES back and forth in his dreams. Clings to me and lets out little screams. I lie naked next to him, without the Pollock sweater. I've washed it, folded it neatly and put it in the shoebox with the other things from The Lover. I wake Lou up. He looks at me with wide-open eyes. He has a hard-on and there's a wet spot on the sheet.

"What were you dreaming?" I ask curiously.

He tells me about a dream sequence that keeps returning, more an atmosphere than an action.

"But what?" I insist.

"I dream that I'm masturbating in public places, on the tube, in cafes, in various streets, in dressing rooms, anywhere. And I don't care if people are watching. The only thing that matters is the rhythm: first slow, then faster and faster. Until I come. But no shame. No modesty."

I ask him to continue. The dream turns me on . . . I sit on top of him, on his already stiff member.

Ask:

"If I manage to fall in love with a new man, the way I once fell in love with The Lover, you'll dump Sidney, then it'll be over with you and her, won't it?"

"Yes."

"Do you regret saying it?"

"No."

I love this feeling: Lou inside me. He is calm. First he moves slowly, then faster and faster . . . Just like in the dream. Until I can feel him coming.

I promise:

"I'll do my best."

3:

SOMEONE

I WANT TO ASK my stomach to relax, my feelings to calm down. I'm missing someone and am no longer myself. I look out the window and want to jump. I like the thought of jumping, but hate the idea of landing. What I want is to fly. Fly away with someone. I try to be strong. Don't want Lou to know, to see that I'm suffering: him and Sidney . . . Don't want to show myself either.

So I take out my notebook and call Jäje, a Swedish boy I met at a Tricky concert. I clear my throat several times to find out if my voice works. Then I become silent. I hear his voice in a recorded message. Again and again. Every time I call. I listen. Not to what he's saying, but to him. How strange things like that are; when you hear the voice without the person, without the physical image taking your attention away from what you're hearing, the voice takes on another tone. I like the Swedishness of his voice. I find it sexy. Because it's a nice Swedish accent. But Jäje isn't at home, Jäje is never at home. I call someone else instead. Then I put down the phone. Alexander isn't at home either.

I wonder who else I can call. I have the choice between Ian, Kenneth, Romel, Jean-Patrick, Dean, Elwin, Momo or Anik. It's Anik I'd prefer to ring. But Anik is taken, as they say in English. It's always like that. The one you want doesn't want you, and the one you don't want wants you. That two people should want each other at the same time is almost an impossibility. Because one is always running after the other, and when one gets tired,

the other often begins. That two people seek each other simultaneously, catch up with each other and meet, is a miracle. It has
so far only happened twice in my life, with my husband and The
Lover. Because the problem is that when you try to fall in love,
it never happens. As if God decided not to give you what you
want most of all. The trick is therefore to pretend not to look.
Unless you manage to convince yourself, God sees through that
too. Until you've given up all hope and become yourself again,
then everything is totally possible again . . .

BLIND

LOU IS FLICKING THROUGH *The Guardian*. It's a long time since we've had an evening together, but today we decided to have some fun after work. We're sitting in a cafe in Covent Garden trying to find something to do. I ask if there's anything on at the movies. I want to be in the dark with Lou. He suggests *The Texas Chainsaw Massacre*. He's never grown out of the thrill of being scared.

AN HOUR LATER IT happens: I have to hold his hand. He's sweating, he's jumpy, and I find it irresistible. Because I like my husband petrified.

"Vår, tell me what's happening," he begs, pulls his hand away, and covers his eyes.

I think that it's almost like going to the movies with a blind person.

I whisper:

"Listen to the dialogue."

He hears a scream from the auditorium and screams:

"Is she dead now?"

"Almost," I whisper and ask him to lower his voice.

Lou looks nervously through his fingers and discovers a figure hanging from a huge hook.

"You said she was dead!"

"No I didn't, I said almost."

"Sshh!" someone calls out.

Lou closes his eyes. But it's too late, he's seen it, and for many weeks now he'll have nightmares because of this horrible scene. I know this. Because it happens every time.

When the film is over, we walk through Soho's striptease district looking for an okay bar. We find one and order a Guinness each. I light a cigarette. Through the smoke I glimpse a beautiful smile. I ignore it. I look at Lou and smile at him instead. We talk about the film, about films generally, about all the ones we'd like to see, about all the ones we have seen, about Harmony Korine, if we like him or not.

"Gummo," I say, "reminds me of my home village. That's how it touches me. As if 'white trash America' was another version of Bø in Telemark."

"I miss Bø," Lou answers, "not the yobbos, but Bø nevertheless."

I blush. I can no longer ignore the smile behind my husband's back. Our eyes meet: light blue against dark blue. I can feel my groin beginning to tickle. I pretend not to notice, but smoke more than usual, lose my concentration.

Lou asks about my parents. How they are.

"I don't know," I admit. "As usual, I'm sure."

"And August?"

"No idea. There's no sibling love between us. No interest . . . But we've talked about this before."

Lou looks down.

"I know it's worse for you, darling," I add. "You don't even have siblings not to get along with."

"I don't care about that," he answers, opens his tobacco pouch, takes out cigarette paper, and rolls a smoke.

"So what is it then, darling, you suddenly seem so gloomy."

"Dad's stopped working," he says and lights the cigarette.

"What? Why haven't you told me this before . . ."

"You haven't asked."

"Has it really gotten this bad?"

"Yes. Dad's on sick leave now. Instead of being a psychiatrist, he's being treated by one."

Lou tries to be ironic, to laugh at the situation. But he's not able to.

"And your Mom?"

"She copes. That's all she does at the moment. Waits."

We turn silent. Lou puts his curly hair into a ponytail. As he's doing it, the whole unfamiliar face appears.

"She gives him his medications," he adds. "Well, she's a pharmacist. Isn't it fucked?"

"Yes."

I stare into the unfamiliar eyes. They stare back. They give me a strange feeling of having been stared into before. They are light, light blue, almost translucent.

"Are you listening, Vår?"

"Of course."

I look at Lou, can see that he's talking. But his voice mixes with the background music and becomes indistinct, like when something is out of focus and you adjust the lens to get a clearer image. That's what I'm trying to do with Lou's voice.

"The small pleasures in life—he doesn't see them anymore," I hear him saying.

I take his hand. Stroke it.

"They'll come back, Lou."

I notice that I'm no longer part of the conversation. I nod sympathetically, but absently. I can no longer separate the music from Lou's voice so the sentences make meaning. I give up. Lou looks at his watch. He seems worried.

"What is it, darling?"

"I have to go, sorry."

"Now? This late? I though we . . . that this was . . . our evening . . ."

I almost get angry.

"Do you want me to stay, Vår?"

"I . . ."

I look into the unfamiliar eyes and change my mind.

"Don't worry about it," I say suddenly. "I'll have another Guinness . . . Read for a while. I'll be fine."

"It's embarrassing, Vår. I promised you this afternoon, only I forgot that I'd promised it to Sid as well. I enjoyed this time with you. I just wish I could stay for a bit longer . . ."

"Don't worry about it," I repeat.

I try not to appear too keen. Don't want to be suspicious. Don't want to be exposed. I feel something very, very strongly. I want to strangle this feeling before it strangles me.

Lou gets up and gives me a kiss. Outside it has started to rain.

"It's you I love," he whispers.

"I know," I whisper back.

He runs out into the rain. I wave and buy another Guinness . . . Then I return to my seat, fish the old *Dazed and Confused* magazine out of my bag, and skim through an article where Patricia Arquette talks about her collaboration with David Lynch. But I can't read, can't concentrate. I find my notebook and write something instead.

"Hi," I hear an unfamiliar male voice say.

I continue to write. My heart is pounding.

"Hi," it repeats.

I turn and look straight into his smile, his eyes.

"Hi!" I say.

We look at each other. Intensely. Directly. He asks if the seat is free.

"It is."

Could he bum a cigarette? I hold out my pack of Vogues with a smile. He takes one, lights it, doesn't seem to worry about the embarrassingly feminine about it. He radiates poise, self-confidence, which is both attractive and repellent. He speaks American. And I think that his self-confidence has to come from there, from the USA.

"I was born in Portsmouth, Virginia," he explains, "but I usually say that I'm from New York, that sounds more exciting. And you?"

"I was born in Porsgrunn, but I'm from Bø . . . I mean, Norway."

"Ah . . . Norway. I thought you were French."

"No, I'm not . . . It's not me who's . . . I'm Norwegian."

"Yes."

He says he's sorry, but he doesn't know much about Norway, the only thing he knows is Edvard Munch's *Scream*, of course, the famous scream.

I tell him I forgive him and say that I'm sure he knows other things, too, like Edvard Grieg, Henrik Ibsen, and Knut Hamsun . . .

Yes, when he thinks about it, he probably knows them too. And that it's cold. Terribly cold. In winter. He says that he has heard about a depression called SAD. If he remembers correctly, it stems from people not getting enough light, just like plants. He wonders if it's true that there's no light at all at certain times of the year, but constant darkness.

"Yes."

He repeats the words:

"Constant darkness." As if he enjoys them.

I say:

"Constant light."

I like the way he moves his mouth. His tongue. What he says. How he came over to me, direct, casual, with a simple hi, and that at that point I already knew I wouldn't get rid of him.

I light a cigarette and get a glimpse of myself in the bar window. Cars whizz past. I'm almost ugly. I think: Without that ugliness there wouldn't be anything special about me, anything to study. That's what becomes beautiful, that which is ugly. I have newly shaved armpits and my mother's shoes. I never learn . . .

"What are you thinking?" the American asks.

"Nothing," I say. "Nothing at all."

Or, no, as a matter of fact. I tell him I'm thinking of him. He answers that's what he's doing too. Thinking of me. We smile. Such a silly smile you always have in the beginning, blissful, and with a glint in the eye. We don't see it ourselves, how stupidly in love we are already, how we devour everything the other says, the words. We don't see it ourselves, because we only see each other.

The American drinks more coffee, while I drink beer. Time flies. I think: if you're truly attracted to someone, so that you don't see anyone else, so everything else seems ordinary, then you become attracted to yourself as well, then you, too, seem irresistible, as if the other's force of attraction is projected back onto yourself.

The American repeats my name. Says it over and over again, so that I have to listen, so that there is no way around it, the word. He says it as some sort of thought, as if the whole idea of me is contained in this name. The mystery. He explains that his field is music and he makes a note for each letter in my name: a "Spring Sonata" as opposed to Bergman's *Autumn Sonata*. He says that he is composing a piece which he carries around inside him, and that at this moment, I have become part of it. I think, a little too early, spontaneously: it feels as if I have met the third man in my life. But I say something totally different, something much safer.

I say:

"Every woman with any self-respect ought to have a lover."

I tell him that I'm married, that I already have a husband: Lou.

PYROMANIA

WE LEAVE THE BAR arm in arm, the way I imagine Sidney and Lou perhaps would have done it, are doing it, now. We play at an experience we don't have, don't know, because everything's so new, and we're so new to each other. The rain has stopped, the moon is shining instead. In moonlight, every girl is beautiful and the men aren't too bad either, I'm thinking.

The American and I are on our way to a place that isn't his but where he still feels at home. In Primrose Hill. It's a long walk, but by the time we come to Kentish Town, we only have to cross a bridge and walk down a street, and there we are, in front of a red door.

The American lets me go in first. I turn the lights on and tiptoe into the living room. It's a good house, clean and nice and aromatic. It has been quite some time since I was in such a house, I think, and recognize the neat smell of lemon, and self-fulfillment and independence. Perhaps I recognize it from Lou's parents' house?

"Isn't it nice here?" the American asks.

"Well, yes . . ." I answer.

He walks into the kitchen, pottering around. When he comes back, he carries a bottle of wine and a coffeepot. Then he asks me to come with him into his room, *the paunch*—which is the weird name he's given to this storage room that's changed to a guest room every time he visits. The name repels me at first, but when I see the room, I think it fits. There's only room for a mattress in there, otherwise it's bare with one oval window, like an eye on the world.

"Do you never drink?" I ask and fall down on the mattress, roll up the duvet, and put it behind my head.

"Oh yes, I drink heaps: coffee, water, juice, I drink a thousand different things . . ." the American answers and lies down next to me.

"I mean alcohol."

"Never."

"Why not?"

"Because I exaggerate everything. I moved to Amsterdam to get sober. I thought that if I could manage that in the city of temptation and sin, I could do it anywhere". He pours a glass of red wine for me and a cup of coffee for himself.

"Cheers."

"Cheers."

I kick off my shoes. Why did I wear these today too? I push them into a corner. I have blisters. Besides, the yellow color has rubbed off on my feet. It's not a pretty sight. I ask the American if he could get me a needle?

"Of course."

He comes back with a small sewing box with needles, and Band-Aids. He tells me he knows the house like his own pocket, that the woman of the house used to be his woman, but that now she's married to another, just like I am.

I'm about to ask if it's a good or a bad memory, this thing with the woman, but before I get the chance, he says:

"I love the fact that you love your husband, it makes everything so much more exciting."

He looks at me. Can see that I'm pensive. He says that at some time, at another time, he will tell me everything. Everything he remembers . . . So that nothing will separate us. No memories, good or bad.

I nod and kiss him. I barely touch his lips. Then I take another sip of my wine. I ask if we have to be quiet. The American shakes his head and whispers that it's all right, they've never said anything before. But we continue talking in low voices nevertheless, because it brings us closer together. The American takes out a needle from the sewing kit, lights a match, and disinfects it with the flame. Then he gives it to me. I prick the first blister and squeeze out the drops. I say thanks, but he doesn't hear me. Instead he lights another match and stares at it. He seems fascinated. I ask if everything's okay. Is there something wrong? His gaze seems to have become distant. He explains that a thought came to him, about something he'd forgotten, something from long ago, and then an image suddenly appeared. He tells me it started accidentally.

"I threw a match into the forest, out of sheer frustration," he tells me. "It set fire to a dry bush that burned down. I thought it was a beautiful sight, but the fire burned out almost immediately. I was disappointed and decided to come back. It took a whole week. This time I brought more matches. The sight of the raging fire fascinated me. Then it frightened me and I wanted to run away, but instead I just stood there."

I open the oval window, I feel strangely fired up and excited. I tell him about my house that burned down when I was a little girl. An old house from the beginning of the nineteenth century. I tell him that I was playing with burnt bits and pieces that I found in the garden: forks, shoes, an old stove, a broken mirror . . .

The American says sorry. Says he hadn't thought about that before, the other side of a fire.

I answer that it's a good memory. That we share a good memory.

I stroke his shoulders. They are taut, his muscles like small knots in his neck. I think: the American isn't handsome, but he's attractive. I like how the coffee has smudged his teeth and discolored them. He reads my thoughts and asks for a description.

An outsider's. He wants to know what I see. I tell him that he looks like a vagabond, someone who lives in life instead of in a house. A restless soul, I'm thinking, walking from country to country, from woman to woman . . . Then I ask what he sees, if he sees anything beneath the long bangs, if he sees me. He answers that it's impossible to put a label on me, that I'm neither masculine nor feminine, but not androgynous either, neither woman nor girl, but something in between.

"Your looks," he says, "are not from a particular country, and you don't have any physical features that distinguish you, apart from the white hair. It's the sum of everything that makes you unique, not the content." Then he adds: "I feel better in the company of women, I don't know why, men make me nervous."

I think: The men I like feel better in the company of women, while the women I like feel best in the company of men. I wonder if they are the women the men meet, and vice versa. Whether the men I like feel better with women, who feel better with men, who feel better with women . . . The American asks what I'm thinking. I answer that it's hot. That I'm thinking how hot it is. I take my clothes off and put them on top of my shoes. Old habit. I am naked. I am observed. By a man. He looks at me and takes off his clothes too. I have the feeling that I can never get enough. That there are no limits. That even with a gag in my mouth and a rope around my neck I would feel no pain.

The American says:

"Your allure is bestial."

I hold my breath until I'm dizzy. Breathe deeply, without breathing out. The smells of our sex are overwhelming. I don't mention this to the American. There's no need. He senses it too: my smell mixing with his. The whole room seems to be filled with them, with our sexual appetites. I've noticed something I can't explain. I'm attracted to men whose smell I find revolting. Even the smell of the repulsive man had an almost intoxicating effect on me, in all its garlicky disgust, because the most sexual men also have the strongest smell, I think. That's why I can no longer imagine making love with a man who doesn't smell. It would feel wrong. Like making love with a hypocrite.

THE FAMILIAR IN THE FOREIGN

THE AMERICAN'S PENIS IS hanging limply. He throws away the used condoms while I light a cigarette. He admits that the first thing he explores in a woman is her vagina. Because all women are so different. Down below. He says that mine reminds him of an orchid he once saw in Glasgow, or perhaps it's the orchid in Glasgow reminding him of my . . . He can't be certain. I feel ignorant. Because I'm unfamiliar with this diversity. Among women.

The American refills his cup with coffee while I take another sip of wine. I read the label: *Le Sang du Calvaire*, that is, The Blood from Christ's Suffering. I think: Even after death, they don't leave him in peace. What an idiot he was, he who put such blind trust in his father.

"Cheers," I say again.

"Cheers," the American repeats.

Then we kiss each other. He with his discolored teeth, I with my wine-blue ones.

I say:

"When I was seven, we went on a ferry to Denmark: my father Aslak, my mother Billa, my brother August, and me. Only Dandelion, my brother's dog, was left behind. The fire made us long for the sea, away from the mountains in Bø, away from valley life to the open sea, to the horizon. But the sea made me sick. It was so lovely to be free, free to be totally, utterly sick. Everyone left me in peace. No one worried what I was doing.

"But while I was hanging like that over the railing, a small boy came over to me. We were of an age, but didn't speak the same language. He was shy but dried my mouth every time I spewed. I had a high fever. But he wasn't afraid of my bacteria."

The American puts his fingers over my mouth. Through his bangs I can see that his eyes are shining. I remove his hand without a word and let him continue the story where I finished . . .

". . . we lived in some bungalows outside Copenhagen. Visited Legoland, Tivoli, H. C. Andersen's house, The Little Mermaid . . . Back in the bungalows, I met two Scandinavians, a girl and a boy. She was around my age, and we fell in love immediately. We spoke different languages, but understood everything. Each other. I cried when we parted, and I've looked for her ever since."

We decide that we have met each other before, the American and I, when we were both seven and were on a holiday in Denmark. He was the boy on the ferry, I the girl he played with outside Copenhagen.

I light a new cigarette and take the last sip of wine. Then it's empty. I leave the paunch, balance on an imaginary line across the living room floor, like a tightrope walker. I never became a ballerina or an acrobat, the way I'd always dreamed of. But you have to smash some dreams in order to realize others. I walk into the kitchen and get a carton of milk from the fridge. I let the milk stream out of my mouth, down my body, all the way to the floor. I'm terribly thirsty. And a bit drunk.

I peep at the American through the keyhole. He's putting the Band-Aids into the sewing kit. It makes me smile. Because tonight I'm happy. I think that I smell of girl. I don't want to wash for a week, so that all of me can smell as strongly as my vagina. I'll do that for the American, give up all hygiene, give up all shame, take the risk it is to become emotionally involved with someone outside marriage. I stand in the opening of the "paunch" and ask if he wants tea after the coffee, or if that's too much, if that means he won't be able to sleep.

He answers that he doesn't want to sleep, with me there, but enjoy every moment, together. Then he adds that he wouldn't mind cinnamon tea with sugar, but no milk. I say that sleeping is also a way of being together, but that I'll give him the tea he wants.

"You're right," he says, and is already looking forward to it.

I go back to the kitchen, open a cupboard, and take out two tea bags. I'm humming to myself. Everyday life. I think that everyday life with this man, that yes, if he asks, I wouldn't mind trying that one day.

I walk back to the paunch and lie down on the mattress. The American asks me to wait there. I put sugar in his tea, but not in mine. Then I stir it with a teaspoon, before I lift out the teabags, squeeze out the water and put them in the ashtray. I'm about to take a sip when I see the American carrying an impressively large instrument. I wonder, won't we . . . He shakes his head and claims that the sound will only push its way comfortably into the dreams of those who are sleeping.

There's not enough room for the "three of us," so the American sits on a chair in the doorway. He explains that this is his life, his great love: a cello.

"The only woman I've never left, and who has never left me," he says.

THE CELLIST'S FINGERS

A RAY OF SUN comes in through the oval window and blinds me. I don't open my eyes: they are heavy, drowsy, and full of sleepy sand. I feel terribly hot. I kick off the duvet. There's a strange smell in the room. The smell of sex organs. His and mine. I think it smells nice. I don't open my eyes. Try instead to remember the American: his face; his light colors, light eyes, teeth, how his upper lip protrudes a little because of his slight overbite. But what interests me most are his fingers. The cellist's fingers. Those caressing the cello, touching me. I try to remember all this. How I reacted. I remember that I thought of the woman. Of the woman's body between the American's legs. That the sounds coming out of her were those of an orgasm, that she screamed, moaned, and he became more and more excited, and I more and more aroused.

I turn to kiss him, but he's gone. I open the door to the room beyond, toward the living room, and discover a sweet man with rumpled hair wearing my t-shirt at the other end of it, in the archway to the kitchen.

The American has made breakfast. I stretch, roll around, kiss him, and am so happy. He lies down next to me, and we eat together in the American way. I love it, that each country has its own breakfast culture. I praise the food, say it's delicious, but very filling. I need at least two cigarettes to digest it.

He wants to know my plans for the day. He wonders if I have to go home to my husband, or if I can stay here with him. I assure him that I want to stay here with him. I stress the words with and him. He understands, but still suggests that I should give him a call, just in case. Says that if he'd been my husband, he would've been worried.

TELEPATHY

I WALK INTO THE hallway to call my husband. Curl up in the black leather chair. I feel strangely nervous. My stomach is tingling, small sparks of a bad conscience. The phone rings for a long time before he picks up.

"Yes, hello," Lou finally says in his urbane French-English accent.

I can't get a word out.

Silence.

"Vår, is that you?"

Continued silence.

"Where have you been, where are you?"

"I'm not at home. I . . ."

"Don't say anything, just listen," he interrupts.

I get more comfortable in the chair, change my position.

Lou explains:

"As soon as I had run into the rain, I realized . . . But I didn't listen to myself, just let the droning of the traffic drown out my growling stomach. Besides, I was probably a bit excited as well, about this feeling that I had wanted so much."

He stops.

"Are you still there, Vår?"

"Yes."

"I'm so exhausted. Last night . . . how can I repeat it to you so you can understand, the humanity, absurdity, of sitting at home trying to experience telepathy. That instead of continuing to walk with Sid, I broke away and waited for you, mon amour.

I have hoped for, I have wanted, both things. You're listening, aren't you?"

"Yes."

"I took off my clothes, closed my eyes, and just existed: thoughts, feelings, emotions . . . I wanted to be him."

"Who?"

"The man you're falling in love with."

I answer that it's my responsibility to deal with what's happening, to describe my feelings. But Lou isn't listening.

"You looked at him, and he looked at you. You were of an age. He had blond hair. He was your first blond. Is. I think that's how it began, in the bar, behind my back. In a banal way. That's why I didn't realize it before I was on my way to Sid. I wish I'd never left."

I answer that he's exaggerating. That I'm merely doing what he wants, falling in love. I answer that we're playing according to his rules.

Lou swallows his own spittle, his own pride, and continues:

"This is what I believe. I believe he took you home to a house in one of the better parts of town. I believe he played music for you there, that you made love several times during the night. Interrupt me if I'm wrong."

"You're right."

His voice wobbles, but he continues nonetheless, on the verge of tears.

"I can't decide which instrument he plays, I believe it's something with strings, something with feelings at least, something erotic . . ."

"Cello," I point out.

"What?"

"He plays the cello."

"Oh . . ."

Lou interrupts what I still haven't articulated and says that he has a bad feeling about this cellist, that there is something reminding him of The Lover: passion.

He says:

"I hate passion."

I answer:

"I love passion."

Then both of us fall silent.

"Is it really happening, Vår, or are you just fooling around with me?"

"It's happening . . . finally."

He stops breathing. For a few seconds. I'm almost certain of it. Then he asks when I'm coming home. He says now; that I don't have a choice.

I answer that you always have a choice.

THE SCENT OF FOREST AFTER RAIN

It's impossible to deny that the American and I are about to happen. That a whole chemical process beyond our control has been put into action. The only thing we can decide is whether we want to enjoy it or not, whether we want to participate actively or passively.

The American speculates about what we should do today. He is no longer nervous when he mentions my husband. He kisses me, as if it were our very own secret. I think about The Lover. Try to forget Lou. But in a moment like this it is impossible to stop it: the comparison. It's raining. Rain is unpleasant on a day like this, because it's summer-cold out there, almost frost. It really is idiotic to run out on the street, I think, and stop in the middle of the road. The American looks alarmed and pulls me back onto the footpath. I want us to do it: let the rain wash everything away, let the rain be the most essential aspect. It's pouring. That's how it is, brutal. We run. Then I suddenly stop again. I hold the American's arm. Walk slowly. Insist that I want the rain to drown me, here and now. I wonder if that's possible.

We lie down on the footpath. I no longer think about The Lover, I no longer think about Lou. I don't think. I feel the drops on the inside of my t-shirt that no longer smells of me, but of the American, and I already love the runny nose that I hope is on its way. That would be good, because I want the American to leave something physical with me. An illness.

He asks if he can pull a few hairs from my scalp. Says he wants to do what they did in the Victorian age, string small pearls on them and make a necklace to remind him of me. I cover my ears. Don't want to destroy the moment. The present moment. Then I take my pocket knife from my bag and give it to him, close my eyes, and tell him to cut off as many small hairs as he thinks he'll need. He winds them around his forefinger and puts them in his wallet.

I try not to think about it, that he is going to leave. He puts something in my bag too. A cassette? I don't interrupt, I let it happen. Patience. I wait. The rain. I stick my tongue out, but there are no more drops. The sun. At first I think that's it, but the sun doesn't come out. Just grayness, gloominess. As a warning of more rain. Later. Soon.

I shiver. The American says this is madness. That we have to stop. He takes off his wet summer jacket and covers me. My lips are blue, not from red wine, but from the cold. Autumn in summer. Why not? The weather, just leave it, I think, incomprehensible and schizophrenic. My teeth chatter. We try to warm each other. We walk. A little faster now. A car, several cars. Traffic. We try to get to a forest. A small forest surrounded by cars. The sun still isn't shining. I say that I don't think it will shine today. That it's already too late. That our only hope now is the moon. Moonshine. The American doesn't answer. He doesn't care.

"Whatever."

He claims that the weather, no matter what kind of weather, doesn't matter. He almost sings. At this moment in the forest we are, both of us, close to each other. The scent of forest after rain. It is everywhere. On our bodies. We stay completely still. The American whispers things that are going to happen. Things that have happened.

Says:

"I'm soon going back to what's mine."

"I know," I answer.

He lies and says he doesn't love me. I dig my nails into his hand, but he insists that it's true.

I want to know:

"Why? Why this lie?"

He answers, defends:

"You've made me believe in everything again, eroticism, passion, the unexpected, anything. But to mention it is like opening a dam and letting it flood you. Love. To say I don't love you is much safer."

I jump into a puddle.

"Yuck."

The American repeats:

"Don't."

The opposite of what he feels.

JOURNEY TO THE END OF THE NIGHT

IT'S LATE. WE'RE HUNGRY. We catch a bus in the direction of Kentish Town. I run up the stairs, while the American buys tickets. I'm lucky, find a couple of empty seats at the front. I throw myself down. Buses make me nauseous. Almost seasick. But it's fine here. I unzip the American's wet summer jacket. The material is dripping, like drops from a gutter. It is the thought that warms, I think, and get lost in my dreams.

I like that the bus is driving on the left side. That the traffic is opposite, "wrong." I still notice things like that. Like the red phone booths, the red mailboxes, the comic policemen: *bobbies*, with their funny helmets . . . No matter how long I live in London, I'll always have a touch of the tourist in me.

I close my eyes. Look. I think that it's important that I write about the atmosphere, the sounds, generally, about the smells and the stink. This mixture that is London. The dirt in the streets, in the people. All these things. The decadence. The decay. The birds that stop flying in certain areas. Where the sun isn't accessible. The rain. The wind. Places without trees. The lack of greenery, but also the abundance. The many parks. How to express all this, capture the atmosphere, lock it into words? I want to describe the smells, the smell of a polluted city: exhaust, smoke, garbage, piss, vomit. Things like that. The smells of rotten meat, overripe cherries, dog poo, grass, trees, flowers, bird shit, summer sweat, rain, water, fruit, vegetables, baby sick, the smell of love, of sex . . . Natural smells, smells accompanying the sounds. The mute sounds. More like noise, or lack of silence, lack of stillness. The everyday in suicide, murder, abuse. The screams that follow such actions, the tears . . . The sound of something pouring. But also the twitter of a few birds. Yes, that, too. The sounds of wind, of leaves falling from trees, insects, people whispering . . . Shy sounds. Like combing your hair, the eyelashes whipping your face, laughter, smiles. Things like that exist as well. A certain beauty.

I open my eyes. Can't see anything. Or . . . yes . . . the American: finally. He sits down next to me. I hold him in my arms. Hold him hard. Warm him. I want to wring him, like I would a wet cloth, squeeze out all the drops, all the tears, all the dirt, all the filth that is in all of us. So that only what is beautiful is left.

We lean into each other. We don't talk. Don't exchange a single word, only stillness. We sit in stillness and wait, in motion. I put my head against his stomach. I listen. Want to know how the piece of music is growing, developing. Sounds from the bow. Vibrations. "Good vibes," as we say. Want to listen to the rain outside and the cello playing inside him. We swap positions. I ask him to listen to my story. Feel how it's growing. Inside me. I admit that there's nothing I would rather than him inspiring me and filling me with life. Fertilizing me and making me pregnant. With music. He nods. We want the same thing together.

MASCULIN, FÉMININ

WE JUMP OFF THE bus, buy a couple of bagels with cream cheese and salmon at a Jewish newsagent's that never closes, and enjoy them. Later we walk across a bridge, down a street, and then we arrive at the red front door in Primrose Hill.

It's late. The man and the woman are asleep. We sense it as soon as we walk in the door. The stillness. I put down my bag, take off my damned shoes, and pad into the living room barefoot, with my feet covered in Band-Aids. Then I take off the American's wet jacket and the rest of my clothes and hang them on a few chairs.

It's strange to think that I'm here, in someone else's house, in the house of a woman and a man I have never met. The only thing we know about each other is the smell, and the odd sound. The only thing we have in common is the American, I think, and walk into the paunch.

The American and I wake up late and go to bed late. We have planned to do that every day until he goes back to Amsterdam. I prefer it that way: to live in the illusion that he and I are a real couple, that this life, this borrowed life, is ours.

The American takes off his wet clothes as well. Then he kisses my sore feet, cares for them. He's so clever, so good, so different. No one else has ever taken the trouble, I think, made it a routine, a ritual: lighting the matches, disinfecting the needles, the Band-Aids . . . I love this attention from a man. He is sweet, soft, feminine, and virile . . . all in one.

I am cold. The American notices everything, down to the

nubs on my skin, goose bumps, and hair standing straight up. Discreet hair on my upper arm. These hairs that Lou for some reason likes so much. This somewhat androgynous part. Fair hair on fair-haired girls, it's almost sweet, I think. Tiny floss on my face too. It's not vulgar.

The American leaves and comes back with his full suitcase. He opens it and offers me some black clothes, the only color he has. He gives me a pair of much-too-big corduroy trousers, a pair of socks, a man's underpants, and a very ordinary sweatshirt. I love this American look on me: tomboy, boy-girl, *la garçonne*. Lou, too, would have liked me like this, I'm thinking, masculin, féminin, like in the Godard film.

LULLABY

We lie down on the mattress, the American naked and I fully dressed.

"The smell of salt water and the sound of seagulls . . . It must've been the first things touching my senses," he whispers in my ear. "Smells and sounds are my favorite sense impressions, perhaps you've noticed?"

I nod. I want to hear more.

The American continues:

"I was born in Portsmouth, Virginia, 1975, in a seaport in the USA, but I've told you that already. A few months before you came into the world: Porsgrunn, 1975, and then Bø, the mountains. Sea air and mountain air, Portsmouth and Porsgrunn, a seaman and a milkmaid, a musician and a writer . . . It's difficult to know where life leads you, so far from the starting point, and yet not. I was alone at school. The others were fascinated by me, but scared of me. What I wanted was to melt our bodies and thoughts together: lie on top of each other. I dreamed of being a toilet: girls would come, lift up their dresses, and pee in my mouth. I also dreamed that I had to sit in a circle of boys, that I was forced to crawl around and smell their legs: feet, all sorts of feet, sore feet, my feet, your feet . . . This early sexuality has never left me. The raw and the beautiful things about bodies. The smell, the heat, and the sharing of all kinds of secretions, fluids . . ."

He stops, grabs my feet, takes off the sweater, the pants, knickers, and the black socks he lent me. Then he strokes my

toes. It's lovely. Even if it tickles. I think: I want to feel your
smell, your heat, your laughter . . . I turn to him. We lie facing
each other and breathe on each other.

"Good night and sweet dreams," I say.

TEARS THAT ARE NOT ALLOWED TO RUN FREELY

THE PHONE IS RINGING. The American runs to answer it.

Calls me:

"Vår!"

I look questioningly at him.

"Is it . . . ?"

He nods. I wave my hands, say I don't want to talk, not now, later. The American hands me the phone anyway.

"Vår, I know you're there," Lou says.

He who hates crying is on the verge of tears. Again. It surprises me. I sit down. Lou says he has something to tell me. Asks me to shut up until he's finished. Makes it very clear that he doesn't want to be interrupted. Insists that I can speak afterwards. That there's no rush. He admits that he is confused, perplexed, that the story about the American has made him think. That destructivity, love . . . That they're all strong words, and now he's scared.

I listen. My heart is beating very fast. I'm scared too. Nervous. Wonder if there will be consequences. If I have to pay for this. The American and me.

Lou is somber. Clears his throat several times before he starts. Samples the moment. That's how I imagine him: his veins prominent on his forehead. The way they always are when he thinks too much.

And then: Lou describes my feelings for the American. Hits the nail on the head. Says things that must have hurt him. Is utterly honest. Analyzes. Understands me. Leaves me with a feeling that he's been inside my head. Taken out the bits that interest him. Those that deal with the American. I haven't told him anything. But I like what I'm hearing. Find it beautiful. The way it's expressed. Find it hideous at the same time. Because they're about me, about the American, about things Lou doesn't need to know. He says everything, that he wants to know everything, without reservations, from my side.

I ask:

"Everything?"

"Yes."

I tell him that the American is about to compose a piece that plays by itself, inside him. I say that he is about to invade my life. I say that I want to invade his life too.

"Do you want me to tell you more . . . ?" I ask.

"No."

This lack of feeling on my part, that's something he recognizes. How I sometimes act without thinking of the consequences. Without thinking of him. He also understands that it may be a question of love this time as well.

And then he says:

"Come home now!"

"No. Not now. Soon," I say firmly.

SWEET MOVIE

THE DAYS PASS, THE nights disappear. The woman and the man remain a mystery I avoid solving. Their clothes in the hallway. An unwashed teacup. I ignore it all.

"Your husband is like the birds, like the trees, the wind, the sea," the American says. "He's part of nature. He is. That's why I accept him as part of you, Vår. The other side of the medallion, the price to pay . . . I want you, I've made up my mind about that, so I suppose I'll have to throw him in for good measure."

I smile.

"That was nicely put," I say.

We're lying in the park in Primrose Hill, five minutes from the house, five minutes from the red door, halfway up a slope. We're waiting for the woman and the man to finish their evening meal, watch TV, chat, listen to music . . . We're waiting for them to go to bed. From where we are, we can see when they turn out the light. We can see the window that sooner or later will be dark. The grass is tall. We're almost invisible. In the background, London hangs like a stage curtain, a prop for our romance . . .

We have walked from park to park all day. That's the sort of thing you can do in London. In Lancaster Gate we bought ice cream, fed the birds, and dropped in to The Serpentine Gallery to have a look at Louise Bourgeois's exhibition, *Recent Work*. Afterward the American drank coffee and I a glass of white wine at The National Film Theatre Cafe on South Bank, while waiting for the film *Sweet Movie* to start. At six p.m. we ran into the cinema and watched "The most bizarre images ever caught

on celluloid." Afterward we hurried down to the opening exhibition at The Photographers' Gallery, where Joel Peter Witkin
was showing his grotesque and beautiful black-and-white photos
. . . And the day passed like that, until evening.

Now a homemade paper kite is flying in the wind. The most
spectacular thing of all is nature, because no matter how desperately we try to imitate it, it wins. Art imitates life. Not the
other way around, I think.

We find the Big Dipper, the Milky Way, a black hole . . . We
want to disappear into it. Be weightless, disappear, together,
and never return. We look at the stars. We see many billions of
years back. Something that no longer exists. An optical illusion.
A delight. For our eyes.

Isn't it incomprehensible, this thing about light years, that
time is distance? I wish I could fly into space, I think, know
exactly where to stop, so I could play this scene, the two of
us, tonight, over and over again, for the rest of my life. Just by
walking slowly backward, like a moonwalk.

STRONG: THE NEED TO SPEAK FROM THE HEART. THE FEAR AS WELL

I WRITE IN MY notebook:

It is important to return to the softness, the softness of a man, that a man can also have skin almost like silk. And the whiteness. In very blond people. The whiteness on the border of red. The hair under the arms, on the legs, around the sex . . .

I describe our bodies, how they blend together. That we can no longer be separated. Because everything seems to flow. Like liquid. As if we fell in love with ourselves, via one another.

I watch him as he sleeps. I like people when they sleep—vulnerable, honest, themselves. I listen to his breath. Yes, he is still breathing. I think: A man's snoring, can that be music? I feel the form of love that exists in observation, in everything and nothing that has to do with the person. I watch how he moves, asleep. I want to say something about this, about people's scent, at night. This strange thing that happens during sleep, in the state of unconsciousness. This scent that clings to rooms and can only be aired out through open windows. I try to be aware of things about the American he himself is unaware of. I think if I can get to love something he himself doesn't know. Then I'll love him completely. Honestly.

When the American wakes up, he says:

"In my head you seem like a dream. I'm beginning to doubt reality. I'm still sure I remember it, the rain, the conversations, the kisses . . . It must be true."

He tells me he misses me. Already. That he missed me from the first time we met, and every day since. That's just the way it is.

I want to know:

"Do you love me?"

"No," he lies again.

I dig my nails into his hands while he kisses me. I let it happen. Passively. I feel his tongue around my lips, they become gooey, like Vaseline. The American claims that it's easier to say he loves my lips than to say he loves me.

"That carries no commitment. Do you understand?"

"Yes."

I wonder why he loves my lips so much. He explains it's because of their banality, almost to the point of being boring. He insists he worships them. I squint at him. I am filled with desire. I hope that in the future, we can spend more time together. I want to have him until I'm totally exhausted and the only thing that can recharge us is distance. I walk around with a burden of virility and desire. Like a man.

I admit:

"With you, an orgasm is like a momentous upchuck of the finest food and drink."

The American holds me tightly in his arms until I can hardly breathe. He says:

"You are violently, incredibly beautiful, and extremely tender."

I look at him. I fear our separation. That he is going to leave. It knocks me out.

I say:

"When you truly get taken over by a wave of horniness, your skin goes taut, your cheeks get like cherries, your tongue is rough, your lips are dry, and your eyes burn, your hair secretes oil, your hands begin to sweat . . ."

I throw myself over him. But he doesn't want to make love now.

"Wait. Are you happy with your husband?" he asks instead.
"Yes."

I light a cigarette. I hesitate.

"Usually," I answer, "because now and then we hurt each other. It's through suffering you grow, through happiness you rest." I'm saying this, hoping it, hoping it's true. The American stops asking. I'm the one who wants to talk about something else. I wonder if he's hungry.

"No."

I put out the cigarette, walk through the living room into the kitchen, and make myself a sandwich. Then I hurry back to the paunch. The American takes the half-smoked cigarette from the ashtray and lights it while I'm picking at my roll.

"To truly know each other, it's important to explore each other's sex," I say, "to feel where one's body has been, and to see the eyes that have seen what they're being told. I can feel your skin and see its milky white color. I can feel your feet on my sex. I know how it feels to have my legs around your head. But soon, very soon, all this won't be more than a theory."

The American stays silent, just stands up and gets the cello. Then he sits in the door opening. He experiments. Improvises. I look at him with admiration. I imagine that this cello-woman he has between his legs is a large maple tree I can climb, and that the bow is a Siberian horse that I can ride away on. A stallion with a dirty mane, which I can wash. I ride off to the sound of us. To happiness.

"Shh," the American whispers, as if he can read my thoughts.

He describes erotic impulses with his music. Tells me about an urge to moan, to talk faster than is possible and in all sorts of languages, to masturbate until he is raw and bloody.

"Only the most brutal and vulgar images are strong enough to express feelings of such desperation and desire," he admits. "The desire to create the most beautiful music from the most beautiful love is swept aside to make room for the most decadent passions."

I look at him.

"This is our last night together," I guess.

"No."

"No . . . ?"

"This is our last night here, that's all," the American says.

4:

WORDS DON'T ALWAYS BREAK THE SILENCE

I OPEN MY EYES. Lou? I see green-brown eyes. I can't see clearly. Am tired. I try to move. No, my body refuses. It feels too heavy. I smile at my husband. Inside myself. I don't know if he can see it.

"Vår?" I close my eyes. "Vår!"

Lou shakes me.

"What is it?"

"Are you getting up soon?"

His voice contains most of it—anger, fear, tenderness, happiness, restlessness, patience . . .

"Is it late?"

"Yes."

"How long have I been asleep?"

"A long time."

I feel hot. I remember that I wanted to get something physical from the American. An illness. I cough.

"Am I hot?" I ask.

Lou puts his hand on my forehead.

"Am I running a fever?"

"Maybe . . ."

I smile. The American is in me.

"How hot?"

"Don't know."

I put his hand on my forehead again.

"Feel!"

I cough. Demonstratively.

"I'm sure you've just been sleeping too much. No wonder you feel sick," Lou says and stands up.

"Where are you going, darling?"

"Nowhere."

He walks over to the cupboard, finds a towel, and throws it to me.

"You should have a shower," he says. "You still smell of him. The American . . ."

I take the towel and wind it around me. I don't want Lou to see this body that doesn't belong to him. I stand up. I want to shower off the American. Not for my sake, but for Lou's.

He looks sad, takes out tobacco and cigarette paper.

"Shouldn't you be at work . . . ?" I suddenly ask.

"Yes," he says and lights his cigarette.

Then I remember how desperate he was on the phone.

"I haven't been able to . . ." he adds.

"I didn't think you'd take it so hard," I say.

"Me neither."

I pout and am about to kiss him.

"Your lips are all sore and swollen. It's probably best that you don't kiss anyone for a while . . ."

"Oh don't be silly."

"Why not?"

"Ok, be silly then, if you want to."

We go silent. The air is stuffy. That Lou has slept with the windows closed is a really bad sign, I think.

"It's terribly clammy in here, don't you think?" I ask.

"No."

I break into a cold sweat, perhaps because I'm still tired, I think. Not physically, but mentally.

"Lou . . ."

"Yes?"

"No, never mind. Nothing."

"All right then. How exciting."

"Have you missed me?"

He doesn't answer. Blows out a big cloud of smoke. I repeat the question. Still no answer. He keeps on smoking. Breathes in deeply. I bottle up, walk over to the door and into the bathroom. I want to leave Lou on his own. Or perhaps it's I who want to be on my own. With the American.

YOU'RE SO PRETTY WHEN YOU'RE UNFAITHFUL TO ME . . .

WHEN I COME BACK, Lou is sitting on the bed reading *Thus Spake Zarathustra*. He looks at me for a long time before he puts the book away.

"There," he finally says. "Now I recognize you. Now you don't smell like a stranger anymore, just like a newly showered you. Now you can get dirty again.

He tries to pretend everything is all right, to be the old, witty Lou, and I make a new effort to give him a kiss, but he stops me.

"Have you brushed your teeth?" he asks seriously.

"Don't be stupid," I say and laugh, "it's you who . . ."

". . . who loves you."

Lou kisses me long and hard.

"I've missed you, darling. I was really scared," he says.

I look him in the eyes. I don't blink.

"What is is, Vår?"

"This is no longer a game, you do understand that, don't you?"

"No, I thought . . ."

"It's different with the American," I interrupt. "You got what you wanted."

I notice that my voice has become strangely hard. Almost angry.

"But . . . it was just playing I wanted," Lou says and looks nervously at me.

"Do you really love him?"

"Yes." I find clean clothes, put them on the bed, then I throw the dirty ones in the laundry basket. "Yes," I repeat.

"I heard it the first time, Vår. No need to repeat it."

"No."

I put my legs into a pair of washed-out blue Levis and put on a black t-shirt. Black reminds me of the black hole, of my strong attraction for the American . . . It's a positive color, a non-color, not sad, I think as I'm taking off my jeans and finding a pair of black ones.

"Lou, do you think I should put my hair up or leave it hanging down?"

"I don't give a damn, Vår."

We are silent. Uncomfortable. I know that Lou is trying to say something, but the words can't quite find their way into his mouth. He clears his throat.

"Were you disappointed when you woke up and saw that it was me lying next to you in bed?" he finally asks, throws away the empty tobacco packet and takes one of my Vogues instead.

I think, what an awful lot he's smoking.

"Just admit it, Vår," he says.

"A little, maybe."

He gets up and walks toward the door.

"Don't go."

"Why not?"

"Come and give me a hug."

He gives me a hug.

"I hate passion," he whispers in my ear. "It's just destructive. An impulse."

"No, I don't think so . . ."

"Love is positive. But passion . . ."

"I love passion," I say. But I don't have the energy to continue this discussion. Not now.

Not ever.

I think: Artists are the best lovers. They're more sensitive to the touch. A painter, a musician . . . It seems obvious. I decide: All my lovers will be artists.

"Shh . . ."

"What is it, Vår?"

"You're so pretty when you're unfaithful to me . . ." Black Francis from The Pixies is singing in the background.

The phone rings. I throw out all the clothes in the laundry basket. Lou looks at me as if I'm mad.

"Are you looking for this one?"

"Yes."

I tear the phone out of his hands.

"Hello," I say.

Silence on the other end.

"Is there someone there?"

"Yes . . . I'd like to . . . I mean . . ."

It's a light voice. Feminine. I'm disappointed and pass the phone to Lou. He gives me the rest of the cigarette.

"Do you want me to leave?" I whisper.

He nods. I close the door. You can hear through it. I sit down on the stairs and take a couple of puffs. Then I change my mind and walk into the bathroom, throw the cigarette butt in the loo, and flush it down. I don't want to listen after all.

WHITE NOISE

Lou is changing his clothes. He tries to get himself ready, combs his hair and puts it in a ponytail. Then he changes his mind and rumples it instead. He doesn't want to look like a gentleman, I think, not when he's going to betray someone: stab a knife in Sidney's heart.

"Are you going to write today?" he suddenly asks.

"Maybe . . ."

"I like you best when you're writing, Vår. It makes you more alive, sensual. Besides, you'll have a thousand things to write about now. You shouldn't waste it."

"No."

I ignore the irony in his voice. He's not allowed to be destructive.

"Remember to keep a certain distance, darling," he continues. "It's important to be critical, even when you're in love. Especially when you're in love . . ."

"I'll do my best."

I am calm. Cold. While Lou is trying to be provocative.

"Tell me about the American!"

"No."

"Yes!"

"No!"

"Please, please . . ."

Lou frightens me. His mood can swing from one extreme to the other.

"Please . . ."

175

I think that if I hurt him, it might be easier for him to hurt Sidney.

"Okay."

"Don't be afraid. You'll hurt me, wound me, I know that. But it'll be much better afterwards," he insists.

I feel almost solemn. But I'm unable to utter a word.

"Well, was he boring . . . ?"

"No!"

I don't want to talk about the American, but I don't want to keep silent either. I want to communicate without words. But with meaning. I want the American to tell it himself, about himself. I have an idea:

"Have you seen my bag?" I ask.

"Your bag . . . ? It's in the hall, I think."

I run downstairs. Open it eagerly, my heart pounding.

"What are you doing, Vår?"

"Nothing. I'm coming!"

I'm searching feverishly. My bag is cluttered. I panic. I pour everything out. Find a lot of junk: invitations to various night-club events, a broken eyebrow pencil, movie tickets, Vaseline, a Sainsbury's discount coupon, wallet, pocket knife, travel card, sun cream, a copy of the magazine *Dazed and Confused*, my Walkman, a crumbled piece of paper with the Stranger's phone number, my notebook, a stolen ashtray, but no . . . Yes, finally, the cassette!

My whole body is smiling. I run up the stairs, walk over to the stereo, remove The Pixies, and replace it with the American's cassette. It's a blasphemy to share this moment with my husband, I think. But I don't know what else to do. I want to give Lou an idea about how superfluous words can be. What I want is for him to understand a feeling, a mood. Cello: deep, melancholy, melodramatic.

He turns up the sound and makes himself comfortable. I close my eyes. It's not a good recording. The speakers crackle.

White noise, like on television when there aren't any more trans-missions, or when the radio setting is between two channels. I like the concept of white noise, that it contains all sounds the same way white light contains all the colors. The crackling finishes, and I hear the American's voice. He clears his throat solemnly and talks with his for me exotic New York accent.

He says:

"This piece by Olivier Messiaen, "Louange à l'Éternité," was performed for the first time in 1944 in a concentration camp. The cellist played an instrument with only three strings. The audience consisted of about 5,000 prisoners."

That's all he says. Lou sits totally still. It must be strange for him to hear this voice, I think. To hear the voice that means nothing to him, but is still filled with meaning. I'm calm. Because I know that the American was once on the other side of the silence. His pulse was beating, his hands sweating. I light a cigarette. Breathe the smoke in, then out again. Then we hear the cello sound. At first, very softly, then it becomes stronger and stronger until the whole room is vibrating.

I say:

"I love this sound, and the silence that follows. It's like becoming deaf. Finally you hear nothing."

"Mm . . ."

Lou concentrates so intensely that he fails to listen. That's a good sign, I think, even if it's a bad recording. The sounds of the American fill the room, fill us. I can see that Lou becomes affected as well. I feel brave, foolhardy.

"What he can do with his instrument, he can do with me," I tell him eagerly.

Too eagerly, perhaps. Lou starts to laugh. It's not a good laugh.

"It's beyond belief . . . You're beyond belief . . ."

"I don't mind that you laugh at me, rather the opposite," I say then.

"I see."

"It's like a *catharsis*," I continue sincerely.

"Okay."

"Because I have a tendency to take myself too seriously," I defend myself.

But there's really no reason to continue like this, defending myself, I think, and close my eyes again. I try to forget everything else. Everything except the tunes and the man who brings them forth. I am in his arms. I am the cello. I am the concentration camp and all the prisoners. I am everything. It has to do with him. I bring all of me to meet this music, to meet him whom I miss: yesterday, the day before yesterday, tomorrow, the day after tomorrow. I don't know when I'll see him again. I don't know what I'm going to do to make time fly, the time between now and then, between him and me, to lessen the waiting time, to make it milder . . .

"The cello," I say.

". . . is the only woman he has never left, and that has never left him," Lou interrupts.

I look at him, dumbfounded. Because these are the American's very words.

"How did you . . . ?"

"It's a cliché, Vår. I'm just playing with clichés."

"Oh?"

"I've seen through this American of yours."

"Seen through?"

"Can't you see that he's clever with feelings, that he's experienced, that he's done this before?"

"No."

"Are you really that much in love?"

"I don't want to tell you any more," I answer, defiantly. "If I tell you, you'll destroy everything. Analyzing it, tearing it apart."

"Is it that fragile, Vår, this relationship, that it can't tolerate a bit of criticism?"

"No."

I light another cigarette with the stub of the other.

"But . . ."

"The cello is his personality," I say, and breathe in the smoke.

"I see."

"It's almost as if it's become a part of him, in a physical way: a form of extension of him, his sex, his ego."

"Interesting . . ."

"Without it, he would still be exciting, but not in any sense as sexually attractive. He'd seem naked, and a little lost."

"Yes, he probably does know his art," Lou admits.

I smile happily. It's important to me that my husband also likes the American.

"I like the music, not the American. Don't misunderstand me," he adds, reading my thoughts.

"Of course . . ."

"But he's much better than I thought, I'll admit that, much better than The Lover. The Lover might well have been a first-rate lover, but his paintings never impressed me . . ."

"Perhaps he wasn't so good with faces," I say, "I'll agree with you there, but he painted fantastic bodies, and they were always original . . ."

"I don't know, Vår, if his art was all that original. He always painted the same thing. He always painted you."

THE DROP

A BUMBLEBEE FLIES INTO the room as Lou walks out. I close the curtains, turn off the light, and turn on the one in the hall instead. Then I wait for a while. It works. It flies out. It's quiet after the bumblebee. I open the curtains again. The sun is shining. I don't know what to do with the sun in a city like this, in a city without sea. I open the window fully. Then I put on the cassette with the American playing cello again: *Louange à l'Éternité.* A tear rolls down my cheek and into my mouth. I like the salty taste, as if the sea also exists within my body.

He can say whatever he likes, it doesn't matter, just to hear his voice is enough, the bow caressing the cello. I talk to him. I tell him what I'm going to do. I take out my notebook and open the document *Anatomy. Monotony.* I wonder how I can change this very personal story into literature.

I'm thirsty. I go down to the kitchen and make tea. Cinnamon tea. The American's and my favorite. But what I really need is something cold. I fill a large glass with ice cubes and water. Then I sit down in front of the computer again.

I'm sweating. I don't quite know where to begin. I braid my white hair. I stand up and open the wardrobe. I'm definitely not ill, just in love, but that's an illness in itself, I think, and decide to put on something more summery, like a dress. I take out the only black one I have.

I look at myself in the mirror. My legs are white, I like that. My face is covered with freckles, I like that, too. I walk down to the kitchen again. I'm not hungry, but I want something anyway. I'm frustrated. I'm restless. Eat a piece of cake. It's dry so I put sour cream on it. It still doesn't taste good, but I still eat it. I look out of the window. It has started to rain. The last time I looked, the sun was shining, and now it's pouring. You turn away, and everything changes. I, who love change, am now suddenly scared of change.

The tea has gone cold, the ice water warm. I try to write, but can't concentrate. I . . . I can only think of the American. In a strange way, it stops me from writing about him. I find pen and paper and write to him instead. The same thing over and over again:

I'm not scared that you don't love me, I'm scared of not loving you . . .

LES LARMES

It's so quiet that I hear myself breathing, hear my pulse, my heartbeats, I hear steps: careful, light, on tiptoe.

I walk down to the living room, jump out. But Lou isn't in the mood to be frightened. He lies on the sofa and cries. It's strange to see this very feminine side of a man. To see Lou with his mother's tears in his eyes. To see him transform grief into something beautiful. I'm proud that he finally dares.

Lou explains how Sidney was dressed. That she'd looked more beautiful than ever. Her back. He explains that he'd mostly been sitting there looking at it: her spine. How lovely her hair grows from the nape. Because he'd been unable to look her in the eyes.

He says:

"I just played with words. The effect they can have on someone else. Rhetoric. How far I can go. But I forgot myself. My own vulnerability."

They'd been sitting without saying anything for a long time. The atmosphere had been heavy. Unnatural. Beverley had understood at once that something was wrong. They had ordered meals, but had just picked at the food. Instead she had smoked many cigarettes, more than usual, rolled them, one by one, without stopping, without coughing, without using the asthma inhaler.

She'd chosen to sit so she was mainly in profile, facing away from Cyril, staring out of the window, so that he couldn't quite see her eyes, whether or not she was crying. The sky had suddenly become overcast, and a terrible wind could be heard through the walls. A wind that had been like waves, like the sea and sea gulls, he'd thought. And then it had started to rain. As if the sky had also been crying. These had been her words.

She says:

"It was quiet between us, and slow. You didn't need to do much. Early on you knew my sex almost by heart. It was soft, calm, and quiet. There was a perfectly normal harmony between you and me."

She talks in past tense, as if it were already too late. It rains outside, and inside her as well. Cyril thinks: melancholy. How it changes a person. He sees a young girl growing up, maturing.

He says:

"Every woman with respect for herself must know her own sex. You shouldn't be dependent on a man. For satisfaction."

He gives her a compliment. Claims it's a good thing: a masturbating girl. Says he likes it: the thought of it. He smiles, a strained smile. Tries to contact her. But Beverley is still looking out of the window, at the empty street, at the rain. She observes how it lashes the window, whipping it, you might say.

She asks the waiter for a glass of tap water with ice cubes, if that's possible. The food has gone cold a long time ago. They don't order dessert. Cyril thinks about the physical aspect of her, that there's nothing physical about her, at the same time as she radiates this eroticism she is unaware of herself. He thinks that it was this contradiction that had first attracted him, that this was the first thing he'd noticed. He knows already that for many weeks to come, perhaps months, she'll continue to be a part of him.

He makes a banal effort to kiss her hand, a pathetic effort not to show too much, too many feelings. But Beverley pulls her hand away. She's picking at the candle, letting the wax drip on the palm of her hand, watching it harden, fascinated, nervous, making small squares and putting them under the flame again. She asks what she did wrong, tells him she did the best she could. She doesn't understand. Asks if there's someone else, if that's the reason. Cyril answers

*that there's no one else but there's someone else for someone else . . .
He says there have been many before her, that there'll be many after
her. He's as detestable as he can be. Hurting her. Unnecessarily. For
her own good, he hopes.*

    He explains:

    *"The women I choose are too young. They have to know what
faithfulness is before they can think about being unfaithful. They
must first meet the man of their life. And then they can meet me."*

    *He claims that he needs a woman with experience so that he
doesn't need to have any experience himself.*

I look at my husband. He has a snotty nose and his eyes are red.
He's still crying. But more quietly now. More inside himself. I'm
glad his grief wasn't degraded to something more masculine, to
anger. I think: it's important to know what hurts, what does the
most damage, so that you can choose whether or not to avoid it.
It was never my intention for it to be simple. I still feel sorry for
them. Because it isn't easy to feel happy with a weeping man in
your arms, I think, and wipe the snot from under his nose and
hum him to sleep. I wait until I think he's asleep, until his body
is limp and heavy. Then I go up to our bedroom to get our duvet
and undress him and tuck him in. I think: I love Lou too . . .

THE PSYCHE

I WAKE UP ON the sofa. Bewildered to find myself in the living room. Lou has left. So he's gone to work, I think happily. Because it's important that he does something now, is active. If not, he'll just hang around at home grieving over Sidney. And I couldn't stand that now in the middle of my own happiness.

I look at my watch. I'll model for the class again in a few hours. I'm sick and tired of being naked, of displaying my body. For money. I pretend that it's for the sake of art, of course, but it's for the money. I want to save for a trip to Amsterdam. I want to buy a piggy bank so I can put all the money in it and only break it open when I think I have enough. I haven't told Lou or the American yet, but of course I'm going to travel.

Half awake, I pad into our kitchen and boil a couple of eggs, but leave the yolk a bit runny with the egg white firm. I toast bread and make coffee. The American's cassette is playing in the background. I eat quickly, gulp it down, dip the bread in the yolk, make a mess.

Afterwards I go to the bathroom, lie down in the bathtub, find Lou's shaving cream, and spread it over my legs. Lukewarm water is running from the tap. I clean the razor and repeat the process with the bikini line and armpits.

I dread catching the train to the city. I'm strangely nervous. And perhaps a bit excited. I suddenly remember the repulsive man. I find a box of matches on the floor and light a cigarette. Look at the flame. Let the match burn all the way down to my fingertips. I sit like this and ponder. I turn on the computer as if in a trance and start writing:

After the fire everything changes. Father withdraws into himself, works the fields and doesn't speak to anyone. Occasionally he stays away for the whole night.

"Autistic," mother claims. "Ørnulf is playing at being autistic. Just let him play, children. As soon as he gets bored he'll start talking."

But it's Dagny who is bored. Ragnhild can hear that her mother is crying. That she misses father. Ragnhild misses father too. She glances at her big brother. Ravn is sitting quietly in a corner, happy to have Ronja sleeping in his lap, snoring, drooling, like a baby. Ragnhild notices that his thigh is wet. It's disgusting, she thinks. Their closeness.

Only on rare occasions has Ragnhild had a glimpse of her brother's psyche. Because he has always been like a shadow to her. Someone who is there, but whom she doesn't understand, doesn't belong to. They have the same blood in their veins, the same parents, but here all forms of likeness stop.

While Ravn continues his existence seemingly unmoved, the others are nursing their wounds, letting the scabs grow thick, solid, only to pick them open again. It is a fantastic feeling, this pain, self-inflicted. To pick it open only to let it heal again. An eternal process. Natural. To disturb nature. Because the truth is that they don't want to be healed. They like the freedom the fire gives them, the freedom to be whatever they want, be themselves, their sick, psychotic selves. Everyone understands. A burned-down house. You can suffer for a long time from that.

MEMORY

I BOUGHT A PIGGY box from Chinatown after work, it's pink with Chinese drawings and it sits on my desk. I find all the small change I have in pockets and bags and put it in the slot. I think: the most sexual of all experiences is memory. The memory of someone you love, what he did and how it felt. The strength of memory lies in the ability to imagine, the freedom to invent, to be subjective. I concentrate on how I remember things, not necessarily how they were, and what is left, afterwards. How a memory is in constant evolution. Almost organic. What happened, the changes and how they related to the physical and mental stages you find yourself in. Sometimes you remember things you later ignore. Consistently. I dissect. Take care of what I like, dislike, what is the strongest. New experiences throw light on old ones, change them. That's why memory interests me. Because it's never the same. It becomes a recollection of a recollection, distances itself from the starting point and creates something new.

I look at my watch. Lou should have been home a long time ago. My stomach is growling, I'm hungry. I wonder what he's doing. Wonder if he is just lazing around. Drinking. Trying to forget her, Sidney, his ex-mistress. I can understand that, but I still think he could call.

I go down to the kitchen and pick up *The Checkered Cookbook*. My mother gave it to me one Christmas a long time ago. I believe all Norwegian mothers give it to their daughters.

It's the Norwegian Bible of culinary art, I think, and find the
chapter called *Dinner in Thirty Minutes*. It takes me an hour and
a half. I put two plates on the table and wait. When the dinner
has gone cold, I eat it.

I try to sleep. But it's difficult, as my thoughts refuse to cooper-
ate. The American and Lou . . . I don't know what to think. It's
only half past ten. It's difficult to go to sleep this early. My head
is buzzing. I'm hot. I'm thinking about the American. I want
to answer the phone that is not ringing. He has my attention,
but the phone doesn't ring. How long can he keep my attention
if the phone doesn't ring? I look at my watch again. Midnight.
What is Lou doing? I get worried. Try to think about something else, about the American. It's dark outside. My fair hair
is mussed up. I count the cars driving past below the window.
Look at my watch again and again, until it's one o'clock. Then
I find one of my favorite books: *Ask the Dust*, by John Fante.
Read without reading. See all the words, but not the meaning.
I close the book. It's impossible to sleep, but I can't think of
anything else to do.

THE OCEAN

Nevertheless, I must have fallen asleep at a certain point, because I wake up. I'm alone. I wonder if Lou came home last night, if he took off his shoes and crept into bed, if he whispered sweet words in my ear, if he has gone to work . . .

I look out the window. The sun is shining. I stay in bed and admire the patterns it makes on the wall, like a work by Bridget Riley. Finally I wriggle out of bed and turn on the American's cassette. I never get enough. I want to try to write something about him, like Lou suggested. I pick up my notebook. It takes time to write a novel. So long that if you had known it beforehand, you would never have started. It took Hemingway fifteen years to write *The Garden of Eden*, and even then it wasn't finished. I'd rather not think about things like that. The only thing I want to think about is the American and me.

A few months after the fire, the Moe family decide to go out to sea, drown their sorrows, find each other again, the family . . . They pack their goods and drive away in a blue Volvo 235. They are going to take the ferry to Denmark and then drive around the country, all the way to Copenhagen.

Ragnhild is wearing a red dress with white dots and almost looks like a Spanish señorita, if it hadn't been for her disheveled white hair. Ørnulf takes several photos of her hair blowing in the wind. But no smiles. Ragnhild is like her father, she doesn't smile in photos.

But then she suddenly smiles after all. Many hours later. After she has vomited and fallen morbidly in love. With a boy from America.

Ragnhild is crying when the boat moors. And before she knows it, she's sitting in the backseat of the station wagon again and longing for a boy whose name she doesn't even know. "Stop!" *she shouts.* "Stop!"

"What is it, dear?" *her surprised mother asks.*

She is sitting in the front with the father and thoroughly enjoying herself. This is the first holiday they have had together since the fire: Dagny, Ørnulf, Ravn, and Ragnhild Moe. Only Ronja was left behind in Norway, howling. And for Ravn it must have been just as difficult to part from her as it is for a mother to part from her child. Ragnhild understood that then, and she rejoiced.

"I just wanted to . . ." *Ragnhild says.*

"What, darling?"

"Nothing."

She knows her parents wouldn't understand. Young love.

"What is it, dear?"

"Nothing, I said!"

She watches the boy from America, until he is a black prick in the distance. And even then she doesn't take her eyes off him. She keeps staring out of the back window, from town to town, from beach to beach, the endless beaches in Denmark.

"Ragnhild, come on!" *her mother calls happily.* "You love to swim."

"I don't want to . . ."

"I hope you're not planning to sit in the car the whole holiday?" *her father asks resignedly.*

"Yes."

MY LIFE AS A DOG

Seven days have passed, and I still haven't heard from the American. I've marked the time, looked at my watch, counted the hours, minutes, seconds, day and night . . . I haven't missed anything. But has it helped? No. And Lou? We have walked past each other in the hallway, on the stairs, in the kitchen . . . We've been avoiding each other.

I put on a pair of flip-flops and walk over to the mailbox. No letter from the American. I go up to the living room again. Lou sits in a corner, watching me. I pretend that he doesn't exist. Absent. I don't care whether he leaves or stays at home, whether the door is being closed or opened. Instead, all I care about is what is not happening, the American. I'm entranced with longing.

"I'm here, have you noticed?" Lou asks.

"Of course, what do you mean . . . ?"

"I have the feeling that I can come and go unseen, that all that counts is the American . . . That what doesn't exist is more important. Do you know, for instance, what I've done the last few days?"

"You've been at work, haven't you . . . ?"

"No, I've told them I'm still sick. And I am, sick in my head."

"But . . ."

"After I ended it with Sid, I've continued to take the walks we did together. I haven't been able to stop it, this habit."

"I see."

"I air my thoughts the way you walk a dog. On a leash. Because they're not good thoughts."

"Sorry."

"A few days ago I got lost. That's why I got home so late, but I suppose you didn't notice?"

"I did."

"You were sleeping like a log."

"It just looked like it, Lou. I was actually awake with my eyes closed."

"Thinking about him?"

"I can't be bothered answering that."

DIRTY MESSY GIRL

THE DAYS PASS IN slow motion. My film is about taking my clothes off as often as possible. To be blasé about my own nakedness. To model nude. I make sure the curtains are always not quite closed. But no one ever comes. I'm disappointed. Because I believed in the repulsive man. That he was possessed by me. The American hasn't got in touch with me either. And Lou and I have nothing to say to each other anymore. The few times we try, it ends up with one of us being offended by the other.

Silence with Lou is something new. Something I can't get used to. Now and then I have the feeling that we are learning to live independently, apart from each other. I don't like it when he introduces me as his wife. *My wife, my stick, my hat* . . . Lou thinks I'm priggish. A word is a word, he believes. To me, a word is much more than a word. I never dreamed of finding the man of my life. I wanted to be independent. Free. Feminist. Lou, on the other hand, always dreamed about finding the woman of his life, even if he didn't dream that this woman would be me. He wanted to be dependent. Macho. But it didn't turn out like that.

"Dinner's ready!" he calls from downstairs.

"Coming!" I call back.

I turn off the computer and go down to the living room. It's been a long time since we had a meal together. Suddenly I notice that I've missed it, that I've missed Lou. It hits me how vulnerable he seems standing there in the old cooking apron my mother gave him for his birthday many years ago.

"It smells fantastic. It smells like Mom's pizza," I say.

"That's not so strange, perhaps, she taught me how to make it," Lou says.

I take a large bite and my nose gets red. Lou laughs. But it sounds more like stifled sobbing.

"Dirty girl," he says.

The conversation is unnatural. Strained. There's too much to digest. Too many feelings. We eat instead. I'm hungry. I take another piece and my fingers get sticky. I lick them while Lou studies me. He doesn't look like himself anymore, I think. He looks run-down. Worn out. The phone rings. We both hold our breaths.

"We don't need to answer it," I say.

"Just answer it."

"Thanks." I launch myself on it. "Hello," I say, my voice trembling.

"*Salut.*"

"Oh . . . it's you . . ."

"Who is it?" Lou asks.

"The Lover," I whisper, and go into the kitchen.

TO PLAY ALONG

I WALK TO THE mailbox. I do this every day. As a routine. I don't want to wait for a letter from the American, but still I do. I pick up several circulars, the phone bill, the electricity bill, a letter to Lou from his father the *psychiatrist*, payments for modeling, a box of milk chocolates from Mom, and a package to me from the American! I sit down on the doorstep and tear it open. A cassette? I run into the living room and start playing it.

"Dear Vår," the American says after much crackling. "Thanks for all your letters! I wish I could read what you write in your book as well, what you write about us . . . That I could read Norwegian . . ."

I nod. I agree.

"Are you still worried about not loving me?" he then asks.

I shake my head.

"I'm not especially fond of writing," he admits next. "It's only through music I feel I can express myself without clichés. But I talk nevertheless. Whisper something in you ear. In an effort to say something I usually play. Does it seem dumb?"

"No, no!" I shout. In a strange form of dialogue.

"I'm so afraid that I'm not able to rise to the occasion when it comes to words," he continues. "Your verbal equal. It'd be the same as asking you to record a song for me. It would be unfair."

I laugh.

"It'd be a catastrophe," I answer.

"But that's the way it is. I show my weak side and hope for the best, that it'll make me strong. I'll try to talk in short sentences. Full stop. That's how you write, isn't it . . . ?"

I nod.

"Yes."

"My chords are my words, my sentences. You understand that, don't you, Vår? The music I send is the beginning of a new project I'm going to call 'The Sexual Life of Plants,' a draft that started to take form in London, inside me, with you. But the first seed was sown in Glasgow, a few months earlier, in front of the orchid I told you about. Do you remember?"

"Yes."

"I was fertilized by you both. I want it to be a multimedia project with dancers, and film as well. I've already found a choreographer. In a while I'll take a trip to Amsterdam's Zoological Garden to write the Latin phylum I need for the piece."

"That sounds exciting," I say.

"Write more, my darling," he says. "I miss our pouch. I've lost all appetite for others. When I think about us, I think about two desert flowers waiting for the next raincloud. When will it come?"

The crackling starts again, and then the cello. I listen to the cassette again and again, until I almost lose my mind. Then I go up and turn on the computer.

On the seventh day the Moe family stop at a camping ground outside Copenhagen. Her mother has stopped asking her daughter if she wants to swim, her father has stopped asking if she's going to stay in the car, and her brother keeps his distance. Ragnhild is left in peace. She stares into nothingness, until a black spot appears, a black spot growing bigger and bigger, becoming a person, a little American boy, a young man, a cellist . . .

AS A CLOWN WOULD SEE IT

THE DAYS PASS LIKE a cool wind, moving imperceptibly forward. I write to the American and send him pictures. He sends me cassettes. I follow the development of "The Sexual Life of Plants" with keen interest. I love it. To be part of a creative process. Outside of myself.

Lou opens the door and takes off his jacket. I turn off the cassette. It is late. He must have been out walking again, I think, crying.

"Are you hungry, darling?" I ask absent-mindedly.

"No."

"Tea, coffee . . ."

"Tea'd be good."

I go to the kitchen and make it. Lou is watching from the door opening.

"This morning I was thinking of our marriage and what a gift it is," he suddenly says.

"Oh . . ."

"I can't talk with anyone else the way I can with you. It's like breathing in some extremely fresh air. After we've finished talking, I feel good."

"But . . ."

I put the warm teacups on the table.

"We've been avoiding each other, Lou, we haven't been talking . . . You've been grieving over your loss, and I've been rejoicing over my love . . . I don't understand . . ."

"That's exactly why I've noticed it, Vår. The first days after you came home, I was only missing Sid, only thinking about her . . . But when you were with the American, I was only thinking about you." He laughs. "It's ironic, isn't it?"

I nod, and I laugh too.

"I've always dreamed about flying," he continues. "When I was little, I built little towers and jumped off them, jumped from trees and buildings as well. Once I broke both arms and almost blinded myself. A whole summer with a bandage over my eyes. I got scars. And I became fond of these scars. Because they're a sign that a man has lived. That you've tried."

"I'm not sure exactly where this is leading, Lou . . ."

"Sid is about to become one of those scars, Vår, that's what I'm trying to say. A wound that'll heal, but never disappear. And that's good. Because I like that life leaves marks, tattoos us, in a way. You'll soon be feeling the same about the American . . ." Lou says, with a certainty that provokes me.

"I don't want the American to become a scar!" I shout, losing my temper. "I don't want it to end like The Lover. This time everything will be different. Nothing will be the same . . ."

"When I first fell in love with you, Vår, it was love of the most rare kind," Lou interrupts in a calm and composed voice. "I do wish I was able to write a letter that could express the feelings I have for you. Instead I talk about Sid to everyone. It helps a bit. My friends feel that they know me and like me. They love to listen to how we betray each other, make up, and betray each other again . . . To them I'm a clown. A buffoon. And I take my role seriously. Because I like to see how those serious faces of theirs change . . . But in reality, all I want is to be with you, Vår. I love Sid, will always love her for what we once had . . . but I sacrificed her. If you love me, couldn't you sacrifice the American too . . ."

"No!"

"Why not . . ."

"Because if you're part of a game . . . You challenged me,

Lou, you played with fire . . . But I'm not playing anymore. It's too late."

He takes out his tobacco and cigarette paper. Takes his time. Pondering on something. We don't touch our tea.

"How can you love a man who calls his piece 'The Sexual Life of Plants'?" he finally asks. "It's utterly ridiculous."

He sucks nervously on his roll-up, as if it were a pipe. My husband has been digging around in my things and found my lover's cassettes, I think. But that doesn't worry me.

"I think it's a lovely, poetic title," I answer.

"In France, it's an expression for people who don't know what to talk about . . ."

"I like a man who's not afraid of clichés," I interrupt him, irritated. "Who can call a vagina an orchid without blushing. I think it's sexy."

"The more you take an interest in others, the less interesting you become to me . . ." Lou says then, almost screaming.

"You're lying," I say, calmly.

"I'm tired of this game, my game . . . but I know that after this, after the American . . ."

"There is no *after the American*!"

"You don't understand, Vår, what we mean to each other, and that's your right. Words are merely superfluous in this connection. I'll try not to act lovingly toward you, but to be capricious instead. I want to do this so you can distance yourself from me. I want you to feel the emptiness it is not to have me. I want to do it for your sake, so that you will understand. I want the absentness, want you to miss me. That's why I want you to plumb the depths with the American, that you do everything, until it's over. I promise to do the same. To plumb the depths of my grief over Sid. Only then can we take each other back and love each other, as if nothing had ever happened . . ."

THE FIGURE

I GO BACK TO work. I'm a popular nude model. I'm often used. I concentrate on how it feels to stand naked in front of all those people who study me, try to reduce my body to a shape.

"Don't just concentrate on the figure, also try to see what's around it. The atmosphere is just as important as the curves," the teacher says.

It feels dead. With all these students who concentrate on a certain point, the body, it's almost like being invisible. They stare themselves blind.

I think: If I'm naked all day, for six hours or more, I'll soon have enough to go to Amsterdam. Another thought: I can earn money on my shapes. I wonder what kind of difference there is between modeling naked and stripping. The principle is the same: take one's clothes off and pose in different positions. I think I'd feel more alive as a stripper.

I look around. Standing naked in front of so many people suddenly seems incredibly arousing. I think about the students. That in another situation any one of them would be sexually aroused by my nakedness. And perhaps they are, too, when they get home and think about what they've done. About what they haven't done with me.

TAPE RECORDER

The American has sent me another five cassettes. He's been creative and expressive.

He tells me:

"I left Warsaw today. The train was eighty minutes late, so I don't know if I'll make my connection in Berlin. I may not be back in Amsterdam until tomorrow morning, but I enjoy that it's a gamble, and it feels good to be in a machine that speeds along in a foreign country."

I light a cigarette and make myself more comfortable in bed, on my back. In the background I hear sounds from the train and foreign languages . . . I like that the American brings his tape recorder everywhere, that he stops anywhere and talks to me, that he takes me along on the journey.

"Polish women look like you," he continues. "That makes me suffer. Eyes, bone structure—you have those in common."

I smile. I like that the American is thinking about me—in Warsaw, in Berlin, in Amsterdam . . . That I pursue him.

"The piece I'm playing is called *Concerto* and it's by Witold Lutosławski," he says. "I recorded it for you so you can be there, too, be there in the concert hall with me, at least in your thoughts."

I imagine the American in the middle of the room on a stool. I envisage how he caresses the cello, plucks the strings. There has to be an open window there too, I think, so that a cool breeze can enter the hall and blow away the long bangs from his face. I want his eyes to be visible, his eyes and the slight overbite. I imagine him wetting his lips, biting them, only just. And in my dreams, I am the cello between his legs.

THE DESERT FLOWER

Pen, paper, and tape recorder . . . they are the ingredients in our relationship. It's a terrible thought, I suddenly realize, that the relationship I don't have, in Amsterdam, is more present than the one I have, in London. Lou, my darling Lou, I haven't forgotten you, I have just put you on hold, maybe.

I put in the new cassette from the American, lie down on my back and light a cigarette. It has become a ritual. I keep lying like that, looking at the smoke rings I produce. They remind me of the soap bubbles I blew when I was a little girl.

"I want to follow your movements," he says. "I want to know everything that has to do with you, I want to hear you laugh, breathe, I want to hear your lips open and close, the air between your teeth . . . I want to bite your sex and spit out two small pieces. I miss your flower. There are pictures of you on the wall in my decadent apartment. I don't hide you away, rather the opposite, I want everyone to see you. That's why it makes me angry that we're apart from each other, that you're bound by your marriage. I thought I could tackle it, thought your husband wouldn't be a problem . . . that he was like the birds, the wind, that he was . . . But I don't know if I can stand it much longer . . ."

I rewind and listen to the ending again. I want to make sure he really said: "But I don't know if I can stand it much longer . . ."

My heart's pounding . . . I have no idea what's happening. Sweat's pouring. I run terrified around in a circle. I look for

202

the phone. Finally find it in the kitchen and is about to dial his number when it rings.

"Hello . . ." I say, surprised.

"Hi, Vår, it's me, Holly!"

"Oh . . . it's you . . ."

"Is everything all right? she asks. "I haven't heard from you for a long time . . . I want to continue the portrait . . . Paint the other eye . . ."

"Me too, but . . ."

"When can you come?"

"I don't know. I'm so busy."

"Anything exciting?"

"No." I don't know why I'm lying, why I don't want to tell Holly about the American, or take the opportunity to work with her? I believe that it's because I want to keep him to myself. "What about you?"

"Yes! You remember Henry, don't you . . . ?"

"Of course. How's his wife?" I ask nastily.

"Well . . . Henry was thinking . . . we might . . . we . . ."

Holly is enthusiastic. She ignores my questions. Doesn't care. She wants to talk. Girl talk. But my ears are somewhere else. My ears are full of cello.

"Listen . . ." I interrupt.

"Yes?"

"Can I ring back later, I'm expecting a call?"

"From someone I know?" she asks inquisitively.

"No. We'll talk in a little while . . ." I promise, hang up, and dial the American's number. I know it by heart.

"Hi, it's Vår," I tell the answer machine. "You mustn't give up your desert flower. A rain cloud will soon appear . . ."

I'm thinking about Amsterdam, about my plans, but don't say anything about that.

"I miss our paunch, too," I say instead. "I . . . I can't find the right words. Love is a difficult word to express, to take responsibility for. I can say that I love you, but not that I've stopped loving my husband. I . . ."

I blush and hang up. A reflex. I always talk about my husband to the American. In all the letters, on the phone . . . And to Lou I do the opposite, I talk about my new lover. That's how I hurt them both.

I go up to my room. Lou has arrived home. He sits in his corner again, staring at me as if he were one of our many mannequins.

"What are you doing?" I ask.

"I'm resting a bit, darling. But now I'm feeling better. He jumps up, goes down to the kitchen, and packs a sandwich. I follow."

"Are you going for a walk?" I ask.

"Yes."

"Can I come? I need to air my thoughts."

"No dear, you'll only get bored."

"Why? I'd like to hold your arm and walk along the streets of London like an old-fashioned couple."

I find a pair of comfortable shoes and a summer hat.

"Please!"

"Ok. But only if you promise not to talk about the American. I can't stand it. And I'll promise not to talk about Sid. I want to go for a long walk. I want to feel it in my legs. I want to walk till my legs won't carry me any longer."

MORNING CUDDLES AND STOMACHACHE

I HAVEN'T HEARD FROM the American for a long time. Instead I have talked to The Lover almost every day and asked his advice. While the American has neither picked up the phone nor answered any of my many letters, The Lover has picked it up every time and been the "girlfriend" I didn't know I lacked.

I have a terrible stomachache. I'm thinking about the American. Perhaps he hasn't been at home . . . alone, I think. And who can blame him, because I've been an idiot. Instead of telling him about my Amsterdam plans, I haven't stopped talking about my husband . . .

Lou comes into the room with a tray of salmon and scrambled eggs. I've taught him to make breakfast the Norwegian way. It looks lovely, but I'm not hungry.

"Here!" he says, puts down the tray and hands me a little package. My heart starts beating faster . . .

"Do you want me to put it on?" Lou asks, knowing perfectly well what's in the package.

"No!"

I have an upset stomach. Lou takes the breakfast into bed with him and makes himself comfortable. Then he starts eating while I just pick at my food. Because all I can think about is what I don't want to think about. I watch him chew and swallow. I watch him roll a cigarette, for the digestion, as he says. I take the tray down to the kitchen, I tidy away, wash up . . .

do all sorts of things I don't want to do, but which delay, prevent . . . the moment. Finally I throw myself down on the sofa, open the package, and put the cassette into the Walkman. I want to be alone with the American. I don't want Lou to hear what I'm going to tell him anyway.

The crackling starts. The American's voice sounds different. Uneasy.

"I've met a girl," he says. "Her name's Petra. I saw her for the first time when I moved here, and she made me smile. Then I didn't see her again and I thought she'd left. I looked for her in a club I used to go to."

I'm humming to myself, making as much noise as I can to drown out what I don't want to hear. Still, I prick up my ears. Because in the middle of my pain I'm curious too, of course. I want to know what I don't want to know. I wish he's lying, but I don't want to live a lie . . .

"What surprised me most when I saw her again," the American says, "was that she wasn't as beautiful as I remembered. A bit of a disappointment, actually. Her voice isn't as sweet as yours either. I'm not hoping for anything special, just to destroy a myth, or create one, perhaps, about myself. In the club there are always women who try to make contact with me, but I ignore them and keep dancing. Petra keeps her distance and just glances at me now and then. I like that. It makes me smile when other men try to contact her. I laugh and feel happy that I'm the one who has invited her home for coffee . . ."

I throw away the Walkman and run up to Lou. He gives me his hand, then he closes the red velvet curtains, as in a theater.

"Why don't we go to bed?" is all he says.

"But . . . we haven't gotten up yet . . ."

"So what? Surely we can go back to bed again if we want.

I nod.

Lou turns off the light. I snuggle into his arms. He holds me long, hard. And then we make love.

TENDERNESS

WE MUST HAVE FALLEN asleep like this, inside each other, because when I wake up, Lou is still lying on top of me. I push him carefully away. He is so sweet when he sleeps. I suddenly feel an intense tenderness for Lou. Kiss him. I see this weakness in him, this brittleness. I wish so desperately that we won't hurt each other. I think: He is stronger now, and can therefore break down. I lie down on top of him. Feel this thin body against mine. Kiss him everywhere: in the cavity behind his knees, under his arms, on his eyelids, cheekbones . . . Kiss his weak points, those I love the most. Lou is still asleep. A light snoring. Like a melody. Now and then I wonder why we do this, the others, always the others, when we could've had such a good life together, just the two of us.

I turn sleepily in bed. Lou moves so I can see him better. His face: innocent, undisturbed. He forgets everything in his sleep. But when he's awake, all he thinks about is Sidney. That is the truth. He is full of angst. Remorseful. When awake, we don't think about each other. That's life's little irony. It's Sunday almost every day in our house now. But Sunday has lost its meaning. Sunday is no longer holy.

THE INTERNAL ABOUT HAPPINESS. THE EXTERNAL ABOUT GRIEF

I WOULD LOVE TO write more about all the fine things between Lou and myself, all our discussions, kisses, fucks. Things that really make me laugh. Our dreams. I would love to write about how wild and mad I am about him. That he can make my face blush up to my ears. How he inspires me. How wise I think he is. Things like that. His sensitive nipples. His flat stomach. His curly hair. His dominating nature. His almost slanted eyes. Green-brown. Changing. According to his moods. And his ears sticking, stretching toward something: his inquisitiveness. Because Lou has a good ear; an ear for music.

I remember when we went to the Royal Festival Hall and stayed there from morning till night to listen to Russian contemporary music. How we both had become obsessed by this composer: Nikolai Korndorf. And that an old woman came over to Lou because of his enthusiasm. They said hello to each other, and she gave him a few CDs. Lou is corresponding with her now. About his fascination for her dead husband. He makes copies of the CDs she gave him, gives them to his friends, who make copies for their friends . . . That's what he had wanted, Nikolai, before he closed his eyes. That the music should continue to chime long after his death.

Those are the kind of things I want to think about. All the good things. Because they are so much stronger. But then Lou says something that hurts me, and the tears come, the bitter taste, then I hit back, then we fight, are mean to each other, play with feelings, say ugly, repulsive, painful things. And then I can't think about all the good things any longer. Then I can only remember the anger. How stupid I think he can be as well. My intense need to liberate myself. Then I remember the cigarette breath in the morning. And that his teeth have almost turned brown because of the tobacco.

"To scrape off the stained enamel with scissors is madness," I tell him straight out. "Don't even think about doing that."

But he does it anyway. I smell the sweat from his armpits. See his dirty hair. Think about all the betrayals. His love for others. Suddenly I only remember ugly things. And my anger gives me the courage to write in a way that happiness never manages to do.

Lou says:

"I want to humiliate myself completely. Go down on my knees. Take you in my arms. For a second that's all I think about, the kiss we may perhaps exchange. I hope. But then you come into the room, you don't look at me, your voice is cold, uninterested. I say something you don't hear, don't register. Mumble something to break the silence. Then I, too, look another way. I don't kiss you. Don't take you in my arms. You go out again. And I didn't get to say anything at all."

MOSAIC

LOU AND I DO our best to forget the two others, and to concentrate on ourselves. We sleep. A lot. I have a feeling that's all we do: go to bed and wake up. I think about what Noodles says in the film *Once Upon a Time in America*, when he is asked what he has been doing all these years, and he answers: *Gone to bed early*. It's a frightening repartee, I think.

I hold a cassette in my hand. I walk down to the living room. Turn on the Walkman. Calmly. I try to control myself. I listen to everything. Several times. Until I know it by heart.

"I feel a strange mixture of contradictions," the American says emotionally. "I want to be in love with Petra, but the problem is that you fill most of the space I need. I still don't have the heart to make her a sacrificial lamb. She loves me, she is free, available. I love you, but you're neither free nor available. Do you understand? To be with you, whether I want to or not, would be to betray Petra."

I light a cigarette. The American puts out his.

"You and I live outside of social rules and morality, but not Petra," he continues. "She knows about you, but not that you are still in me. I haven't been totally honest. I want you, but can't have you. Totally, I mean. What should I do? I love Petra, but I'm in love with you. I wish you could come to Amsterdam, Vår."

I put out the cigarette, turn off the cassette, and go up to the bedroom again, as if in a trance. I've made a decision. I lift up the Chinese pig and throw it on the floor. It shatters easily. It's a beautiful sight. Lou is sitting in his usual corner, looking at me. I am calm. Pick up the small mosaic pieces and throw them in the bin. Then I count the money. It's a good sum. Enough for Lou and I to really enjoy ourselves, have great dinners in the city, go to the movies, go to clubs and drink all night, several nights in a row, without worrying about money. Enough for us to take a trip to Montpellier, too, I think, and visit The Lover and Marlene.

I tell Lou this, how I want to spend the money, that I want to spend them on us. But Lou just shakes his head. He doesn't want to.

He says:

"The American's testing you, surely you can see that . . ."

"What do you mean?"

"We're all playing, playing games . . . But I see through this American of yours, I've already told you that."

"What do you mean?!"

"I mean that you should go to Amsterdam, Vår, that you should see, smell, feel, and let yourself be 'fertilized' . . ." says Lou and mocks me with the American's cliché. "That you should take a chance. And if it goes to hell, if it goes the way I want it to . . . then I'll take you back."

AFRAID OF THE DARK

I DREAM ABOUT GOING to Amsterdam. But when I land, there is no one there to meet me. I wait for a while. Then a little longer. Until I realize that I've forgotten to tell the American I'm coming. I have neither his address nor his phone number with me. I can't even remember my own. Nothing. Just me alone in Amsterdam and no one to receive me. I laugh hysterically, bash my head against the wall.

However, after a few days I manage to pull myself together. I start going to all the cello concerts I hear about. I still don't find the American. Instead I discover that there are an incredibly large amount of young men who play that exact instrument. That there are a number of cello-playing Americans in Amsterdam, just not the one I'm looking for. He has disappeared without a trace.

Lou is shaking me.

"Vår, wake up!"

I open my eyes, alarmed.

"What is it?"

"You were snoring," he says.

"Lou, it's the middle of the night, why did you wake me up?"

"You were snoring, I told you."

I snuggle down in bed again.

"Vår . . ."

"Yes?"

"Can I call you in Amsterdam?"

"I'd rather you didn't . . . Only by abandoning myself fully to the American, without a thought of you, will I know what I really feel . . ."

"I hope it rains every day," Lou says, but then he changes his mind. "No, as a matter of fact, I hope the sun shines every day, with scorching temperatures, or you'll be lying inside going at it all day."

We both laugh. A forced laughter.

I try to fall asleep again. Pull the duvet over my head. I sneak a glance at Lou through a small opening on the side. He's pretending to be asleep too. We lie like that in our dishonesty for several hours. Until one of us opens our eyes. I can't remember which of us it was.

5:

SUNK INTO OBLIVION

I LEAVE FOR AMSTERDAM. Scared. I think: there are too many feelings, there's too much at stake. I'm leaving my husband to try out someone else. Why not? When I'm in love, loved . . . Then I think, I've fooled Lou, I haven't followed the rules . . . Because I don't want the story with the American to be like the one with The Lover . . .

I make myself comfortable in my seat and take out my Walkman. It's raining . . . on the cassette. The American has recorded the sound of rain, of wetness against wetness: in the canals, in small puddles, in the coffee cup, in the mouth . . . He must've enjoyed himself immensely. He has recorded wetness against dryness too: in hair, on the asphalt, on flowers, in earth . . . he has recorded rain for his desert flower, I think, as I listen to him walking into a small forest, recording sounds there too. A city forest.

"Does this remind you of something, Vår?" he asks to the blended sounds of bird-chirps and car horns.

"Yes, about the scent of forest after rain, of us in London, of wanting to get a cold, an illness . . . of wanting the other, in the body . . ." I whisper in a low voice and look around.

No one heard me. Fortunately.

"I'm trying different atmospheres to 'The Sexual Life of Plants,'" he explains. "I'm on my way to the Zoo again to record the sounds of giant orchids and other plants I come across. I want to become fertilized by their secret language. I love the idea of a plant language, a vegetal vocabulary . . . But I hate the idea of vegetating . . ."

I nod, I agree. I wait for the American to say something, but he goes silent. I can hear him rushing around in the city, jumping on trams, jumping off again. I like that he totally forgets me now and then, but that I'm still with him.

"Can I tell you how fast my pulse is beating when I think about you coming here?" he asks, out of breath.

"Of course," I answer.

"My clothes still smell of you, Vår. My summer jacket, my pants, sweater . . . yes, even the underpants you borrowed. I haven't washed any of them."

I smile. I've only brought black clothes. They're thrown together in my backpack.

"I open the suitcase with my clothes and your smell," he continues. "Put them on. Like a ceremony. Like a stripper, or a whore. Then I play the cello as someone mad, angry and happy. The vibrations through my body are you, Vår. You're playing in me. I want my words to flow out of the cassette and hold you across your mouth so you can't breathe until you believe me. That's the kind of love I have for you, honest and brutal. Nothing will stand in the way for us as long as you are here. Not even Petra."

My heart almost stops when he mentions her name. I should probably have waited a bit longer . . . Given the American time to forget . . . But perhaps I was scared; instead of forgetting her, what if he forgets me?

COFFEE AND CIGARETTES

I'M SITTING ON THE train on my way to the city center. It takes about half an hour. I find my *Lonely Planet* guide, but I immediately put it away again. I don't want people to see that I'm a tourist. I won't look at a map or take photos. I've already decided that. I want to store the memories in my thoughts, not on a device.

I ask those in the seats in front of me if they can keep an eye on my seat. They nod. I enter the narrow and unappetizing train toilet, try to apply black mascara and eyeliner while I'm being shaken back and forth. I like all the blackness to my otherwise white self, it brings out my hair, I think, and go back to my seat again.

I look out the window at the flat landscape, a bit like Denmark. I hope I'll become fascinated by everything Dutch. By this strange language that sounds like a mixture of English, German, and Norwegian . . . I look forward to hearing it with an American accent. The American . . . I have butterflies in my stomach. America . . . That gruesome and fantastic country. It makes me dream, it makes me vomit . . . My stomach is rumbling. I'm not hungry, just nervous. I straighten my shirt. I straighten my tie as well.

The train stops. My heart is beating. I close my backpack and jump off at Centraal Station. I hold my breath, look around, look at my watch. I'm early. The concert doesn't start for another two hours. I think about the American, how nervous he must be now, I think, and go into the first convenience store I see. I stand at the counter and look and look. They have neither Vogues or Gitanes. I always choose by the design on the pack, not the taste. The woman behind the counter talks to me in Dutch. I think she's asking if she can help me, but I just shake my head and keep looking, until I find them, my Amsterdam cigarettes. The packet is pistachio green, with the head of a seductive cat woman on the cover in genuine Vargas style. I point. The woman talks to me in English now.

She asks:

"Do you mean Tigra?"

I nod, but can't get a word out, as if I've gone mute. I take out my wallet.

"I may as well have two," I say at last.

I admire the retro packet. Then I walk out of the train station and light several cigarettes in a row. Chain-smoke. They don't taste all that good, but it doesn't matter as long as the pack is nice, I think.

The sun is only just shining. The city, the canals, the atmosphere . . . Everything has a spellbinding effect on me. I listen to my body: I'm restless, I'm ready. Butterflies in my stomach. Everything is just as it should be. Thank god.

I sit down in the first cafe I find to wait. I order a caffe latte. Then another one. I order so many that my body's natural trembling can soon be misinterpreted as a side effect of the coffee. To be alone in a city where you don't know anyone and don't know the name of a single street, but at the same time refuse to appear like a tourist, to take out the *Lonely Planet* guide for assistance . . . that's pure hell. It's nice to be alone, but not just now.

THE SEXUAL LIFE OF PLANTS

I WALK INTO THE auditorium and sit down in a chair. I'm the first one there. I wish I could sink down into the uncomfortable plastic chair. Disappear. At the same time I dream about running backstage to find the American, spy on him: study his nerves, the salty drops of sweat that surely will soon be running down his forehead and into his mouth.

There are five of us in the auditorium now. I hope more will come. How embarrassing for the American if he didn't play for a full house on *his opening night*. How embarrassing it would be for him as I have come all the way from London to be present at *his opening night*. This piece that's dedicated to me and the orchid in Glasgow. I feel tense. Seven of us. I breathe out. Eight, nine, ten, eleven . . . There's room for two hundred, I've discovered. Counted. I've been sitting here counting two hundred plastic chairs in all sorts of colors and shapes. Twelve, thirteen, fourteen . . . It's filling up. I take out my Walkman again.

"For years, there were no toilets in this place," the American has told me. "So when they finally got one, they set it in the middle of the stage, like a golden calf. I'm going to play my piece from this toilet-podium," he said.

I look at the red stage curtain and squeeze my legs together. I always make sure I pee before a film, a play or a concert, even if I don't have to go. I'm about to ask for the toilet, but then it suddenly occurs to me what the American said, that the only one they have is on the stage itself. I squeeze my legs tighter together.

The auditorium is almost full now. I clear my throat, although I won't use my voice for a while, and cough.

"Shh," someone whispers.

The curtain goes up. I hold my breath. The American is sitting all alone on the toilet podium. He is wearing the clothes I borrowed from him. They smell of me, I think. Then he begins to play.

There's a large screen in the background. It shows the solutions of various mathematical equations, Latin phylum, and genetic images. Everything is chaos. The dancers enter the stage, first as human beings, then as plant-like genitalia. They take root, as it were. Then we hear the sounds of rain, bees, together with strange, indefinable things, and then a kind of yellow pollen-like powder is scattered from above, seemingly to fertilize us, the audience. The American plays like crazy. Very theatrical, I'm thinking, as I watch and watch, in vain. Because I can't see the woman between the American's legs. I hear sounds and identify them for what they are—string music, not orgasm. I panic.

I close my eyes . . . I try to imagine that the American plays only for me. I concentrate until I recognize the atmosphere. Until I'm there. With him. In Primrose Hill. Until all the others disappear. And then the woman enters my thoughts again. The woman between the American's legs.

DEATH BY DROWNING

I can feel the American stroking me, first slowly, only a thin sound, stroking again. It escalates, he strokes faster, begins plucking the strings, insists, strokes, plucks, strokes . . .

Suddenly the auditorium goes totally silent. I hold my breath. Open my eyes again. Then the curtain falls. The audience clap, leap to their feet and shout: "Bravo, bravissimo . . ." While some bow. But no one throws rotten tomatoes or eggs. Everyone is civilized. The American bows with the choreographer, the film crew, the dancers, the costume designers, sound and lighting designers, and everyone else who has been part of "The Sexual Life of Plants" production.

Then the audience flock up on stage with flowers and compliments. Especially the women swarm around the American, I think, as I sit there, motionless. I notice one in particular. I feel paralyzed.

I observe this piece of theater. This is when it begins, I think. Because this is a play, a performance, that's all. But I don't want to take part in this scene, can't find my role in it, my lines. To open my mouth now would just sound false, I think. The falseness of all the others seems so natural, while my naturalness would have just seemed false. I watch as the auditorium begins to empty. The woman I noticed is also leaving.

Why can't I just stand up, run over to the American, and throw myself around his neck? I dream about being the extroverted, talkative Vår again. There are two kinds of shyness, I think. The eternally shy and the pseudo-shy—me, that is.

Shyness exists to be conquered. We perform drama or music, talk in front of big crowds, pose naked for artists . . . Yes, people do the strangest things. It's shyness that creates this get-up-and-go vitality, I think. As for the eternally shy, however, I have nothing to say. I have never known anyone who falls into the category.

The American is looking nervously out into the auditorium. Can't find me. Perhaps he thinks I didn't come after all. He looks at his watch. Looks out into the auditorium again. Back and forth until our eyes meet.

I stand up. Run toward the American, who lets go of all the flowers he's holding, and throw myself into his arms. I feel the ocean—a wave rushing through my body, and the sound of people talking becomes the cry of a seagull. We kiss until we're dizzy.

I smile. I want the American's love. I want to do everything to keep it. The feeling of drowning, of being encircled by water, slowly but surely. The legs first, then up to the waist, into the mouth, the ears, the eyes . . . People say that drowning is supposed to be beautiful if you survive the first feeling of terror, relax, let yourself sink, fill up your lungs, until your heart stops working, then you sink with a smile.

The American says:

"I'm so glad you finally came! Petra just left. I don't know if you noticed her. She . . ."

"Shh." I put my fingers over his mouth and let him suck them. "Why don't you talk about it later, the eyes of women, the ones I can feel?"

"Of course."

I do my best to hide my jealousy. A stab in my stomach. A knife being twisted. My own hara-kiri. I try to find my lines. The ones I have learned by heart. But they have disappeared. I improvise.

"I'm not to be trusted either," I say and laugh.

"That's true. I'd forgotten that," the American says. He isn't laughing. He looks at me. Intense voice: "How are you?" he asks.

"First we have to get to know each other again, then you can ask me how I am," I answer.

"You're right, Vår. It was clumsy of me." He turns silent. He seems to have doubts, but then he throws himself into it anyway, and asks: "Shall we fuck?"

I nod.

"But first you have to show me the city, then we can make love."

TWO

IT'S LIKE BEING ON a summer vacation. I mean *summer vacation,* like when I was a little girl. The whole town is on bicycles. The American is pedaling me. I'm sitting behind him with the backpack on my back, holding on to him with one hand and holding the opening-night bouquets in the other. It's windy. My white hair is fluttering in the air like a peace flag, I think, and try to avoid thinking about The Lover, about a black bicycle, about going from one man to the next . . .

The American asks:

"Do you believe in relationships, that they can last?"

"Don't you . . . ?"

"No."

It's so good to be two on a bicycle. I sneak my cold hands under his sweater, feel the music in his stomach, kiss his ears, bite them. The American laughs. He's ticklish.

"You didn't tell me what you thought," he suddenly says.

"You didn't ask," I answer.

"No."

He continues to cycle. I don't say anything. I can feel he's expecting a comment, praise . . . But just because he wants this so badly, it repels me.

"I liked it, of course I liked it . . ." I finally say.

"Thank you," he says shyly. "I wrote it for you, you know."

"I liked it just as much as I hated it," I say then.

"What do you mean?"

"I don't want to share you with anyone," I admit.

"I don't understand . . ."

"I closed my eyes." That's the truth. Very quickly. "What I saw inside me was . . . beautiful."

"But . . ."

"Tomorrow I'll open them again," I promise. "Every day a little more. Until I've seen, heard, and felt the whole piece. Then I'll tell you what I really think. Now I'm glad to see you . . . I can only come to a just and objective opinion after some time has gone by."

SUR LE PORT D'AMSTERDAM

WE STOP TALKING ABOUT "The Sexual Life of Plants." The American promises to wait until my opinion has ripened. Instead he shows me the town, better than the *Lonely Planet* guide, I think, and wonder how I can get rid of it. I have to throw it away, obviously. The American must not find out that I, in a fatal moment at Borders in London, behaved like any enthusiastic tourist and bought this book.

He stops.

"This is the 'Red Light District,'" he explains proudly, "this is Amsterdam's pride: legalized whores in windows, paying tax. Isn't it wonderful?"

"I don't know . . . Does it work?"

"Nothing really works, probably, but I think it's better this way. Now they can at least sit inside and be warm."

The curtains are opened, one by one. I put the opening night bouquets outside their windows. I don't know why. Then we keep cycling through "the sex paradise," which is almost as full of tourists as Piccadilly Circus. It seems as if the whole place is blushing, I think, as the American turns into a gloomy side street stinking of old piss and vomit. He points to a bar called Sur le Port d'Amsterdam, after Jacques Brel's classic. Isn't it typical that a bar with a name like that isn't even down by the harbor? I think. The American tells me that he likes it there. He suggests that this should be our favorite haunt. I nod. I agree. I've never been there, but I know it's right.

We keep cycling, past whores, more and more whores. The American asks which one I like best, who is going to have the last bouquet. I point to a girl with her back to us, and put the bouquet down behind her. Then my hands are empty. I like the way her hair is rolled into a bun, the old-fashioned quality she has, and her back covered with moles. Then I ask him to keep cycling. Because I don't want to get disillusioned, don't want her to turn around.

We talk and talk, cycle and cycle. Get to know each other anew. The American shows me Amsterdam, what I need to manage on my own. He wants me to get a feeling for this town, to feel it. So I say yes! yes! Because I love to sit behind him, my arms around his body, under his sweater, to feel his heart beating . . .

He stops again, at a fairly tucked-away canal this time. Then he walks me to the water, kisses me, sneaks his fingers under my skirt and into my knickers. His fingers slide in easily, I'm wet. He pushes himself against me and opens his fly.

"Sometimes I'm so horny that I'll do anything to experience this ecstasy, the physical, sex," I say. "My body revels in it. I start to shiver and am a slave of my own desires. But other times I totally forget the sex part. I forget that it's important, that I like it. I believe that if I never have sex again, I'll still survive."

"Shh."

"What is it?"

"First I want to get to know your body, Vår, then you can tell me how it works in your head."

I laugh. He is brazen.

"Okay."

He pulls up my skirt. Pulls down my knickers. I point to the houseboats and shake my head.

"It doesn't matter, that's just a plus," is his answer to my apprehension and laughs.

The American is like the Stranger, I think, he likes the taw-driness of the whole thing, the honesty. He is even more liber-ated here than in London. And I can understand that. Because this is his territory, his scene . . . I remove my backpack and lie down on the ground. I open myself fully. I feel as if I'm going to swallow him, that his head is going to disappear inside me.

WE GET ON LIKE A HOUSE ON FIRE

I TAKE OUT MY pack of Tigras and light a cigarette. Then I give one to the American as well. He says he's fallen in love with Norway, the idea of driving a car through the country without stopping, with thoughts like these—of the silence, the emptiness, the nature—and that there are so few of us.

"Between four and five million," I answer.

He likes that. The fewer Norwegians the better, as far as he's concerned.

I get up from the ground, brush off my clothes, and fix my hair. Then I put on my backpack and jump on the back of the bicycle again. I hold on tight, not because I'm scared, but because I like the warmth of his body.

The American cycles us to Schinkelhavenstraat 31 hs 1075 VP, to his ramshackle flat. The building lies in a lovely position, by a canal, but it looks dilapidated from outside as well, I think, looking at the green peeling paint. At the door there's a flower bouquet from Petra. It shouldn't be there. I'm beside myself. The American notices, pretends not to, takes the bouquet, and throws it in the canal. Then he holds me. I turn away.

"Leave me alone," I tell him.

He strokes my hair, dries my tears, kisses me where they've run, where they continue to flow . . .

"Why don't we go inside?" is all he asks.

"You go, I'll follow," I answer him in a low voice.

"I'll wait for you inside," he says, and picks up my backpack.

I nod, sit down on a bench, and fill the pages of my notebook with illegible handwriting even I have trouble deciphering. Then it starts to rain, one drop, two . . . I laugh. I stand up, take my notebook, and run inside. I stand in the doorway and laugh.

"Why are you laughing?"

"It's raining!"

The American looks at me, surprised.

"Do you miss London already . . . ?"

"No, but I miss you."

I run in and out, wet, dry, wet, dry . . . I smile, invitingly. I want to forget all the other things, all that's wrong, let the rain wash away all ugliness. I run until I collapse.

I loosen my tie and use it as a hairband instead, take off my shoes, until I stand naked in front of the American. He holds me around my waist and kisses me. Then he bites my ears carefully and closes the curtains in front of all the windows in the flat. Not out of modesty, of course, but to divert attention from everything that's going on outside. We kiss again. The American studies my feet: no blisters, no lesions . . . He almost looks a bit disappointed. It has started to blow outside. I think that if we're lucky we might get thunder too. I want a dramatic stage curtain to our film.

"Do you like it?" he asks.

He's referring to the flat. I look around. There are large piles of books on the floor. I like that. I wander naked from room to room. It's a large and airy flat. Completely different from the paunch. It isn't up to the same standard either. Worn. Pictures of me are taped to the walls, but of other girls as well. I look away. I try to wipe out, not remember. I prefer an abstract Petra. As an idea. Even if I hate the idea of her.

A box of pearls and the strands of my white hair are on the desk. He has only just started to make the chain. My eyes keep wandering: I notice a pile of letters in a half-open drawer. They can't all be from me, I think and feel that I'm entering the American's double life, triple life, I don't know how many . . .

The room I prefer is the music room. There is a cello, and on the wall hang musical "maps" drawn by John Cage, among others. They are beautiful. The American is obsessed by charts, it seems. All kinds of charts, everything from music to mathematics to world maps. And some of them seem very old, almost antique. He has forgotten to tell me that, I think. If I had known, I would have brought a lovely map of Norway with me, from Bø.

"It's much more masculine here than I'd imagined, more shabby. Perhaps that's what I like best . . ." I finally say.

I look through his record collection. We compare our taste in music. We like much of the same. The American puts on something I don't like. I walk over to my backpack, open it, pull out a dressing gown for me and a present for him.

"Here!" I say. "This is for you."

"For me . . . ?"

"Yes for you, who else . . . ?"

"No . . ."

The American blushes, holds the present, but doesn't quite know what to do with it.

"Aren't you going to open it?" I ask.

"Of course." He unwraps it, holds up the gift and studies it. "Is it . . . ?"

"Yes," I interrupt. "It is . . ."

". . . incredible."

He uses tape to hang up the photograph in the room that looks most like a living room. Then he moves closer and studies what I've written. It says: *We get on like a house on fire.*

"I wonder what'll be left of us after the fire," the American says, jokingly.

"There won't be anything *after the fire*," I answer. There will be an eternal fire, like in hell . . .

He has no answer. But I know there's something dark and destructive about him, something damaging. I think that the fire's gotten stuck in his eyes. I walk over to the backpack again and take out a photo album.

"The edges of the photos are a bit worn," I explain, "because I take them out and study them so often."

The American leafs through them enthusiastically. Then he suddenly stops. Scrutinizes them.

"What are you looking at?" I ask.

"You."

"Me?"

"Yes . . ."

We look at me. Together. Because I never get tired of looking at the expression on my face when I was little. The one that disappeared as I grew up. I enjoy seeing this expression disappear. It disappeared in the fire, in the frustration. And after the new house was built, the memories of the old one faded. We keep leafing through them. Once more the American stops.

"What are you looking at?" I repeat.

"You look like your brother."

"Do I?"

"Yes. You have the same mouth. His is just more masculine."

"I thought I was more like my mother."

"No."

I take the album from him and put it back in my backpack.

"Tell me more!" the American pleads.

"About what?"

"August."

"He's a country boy, even in the city, and I'm a city girl, even in the country," I answer, the way I have taught myself to answer.

"And . . . ?"

"Are you really interested?"

"Yes."

I rewind my thoughts.

"Apart from the large shadow, vanity is, strangely enough, his most noticeable feature," I say.

"Vanity?"

"Yes, it's true. When we were younger, he would push me away from the mirror, wanting the space to himself. This happened every morning before we walked to school, and I just had to wait for him to finish. He didn't like the wave of his strawberry blond hair."

We become silent. I walk over to my backpack and take out another parcel.

"Another one?" the American asks surprised.

"Looks like it," I answer.

He opens it eagerly.

"A dictionary!"

"Yes. I got so tired of you not understanding Norwegian," I tell him, "that you're unable to read what I write."

"Me too," he says.

"You're lucky to have chosen the cello," I add. "Because the language of music is international, just like dance. It's something everyone can understand."

He nods. He agrees.

"Teach me something right now," he pleads, enthusiastically, "anything, but not some nonsense."

"Okay." I consider. Finally I say in Norwegian: "The cello is the only woman I have never left and who has never left me . . ."

The American tries to repeat it. Then he stops.

"What does it mean, Vår?"

I explain. He's embarrassed and laughs. I take his hand and pull him with me to the music room. I want him to play for me. The American sits down on a chair and puts the cello between his legs, this *femme fatale*. He explains that he has two cellos: this one, which lives at home, and another one, which travels with him. He has two women as well, I think sadly. As if it were worse to have two women than two men . . . I look into his eyes, intensely, questioningly. He understands and admits that

he seduced Petra through his music, not the coffee. I'm sure he's
seduced all his women that way. I include myself.

I say:

"It's a simple trick. Easy."

He pretends not to understand.

"How come?"

"Because by stroking her, you show what kind of potential
you have. That's how come."

WEATHER CONDITIONS

It thunders, it rains, we stay inside and kiss all day, for several days, time doesn't count. In the evenings, the American plays the cello for full or half-full houses, to good or half-good reviews, while I open my eyes more and more. Afterward we cycle around, stop, and make love again. It's an idyllic life. We need so little, because everything's still far too much . . . But every evening when we come home and find a new bouquet from Petra on the doorstep, I close my eyes.

"Vår . . ."

"Yes . . . ?"

The American gets out of bed naked to open the curtains and the many windows in the flat.

"Are you asleep?"

"No . . ."

I laugh.

"Why are you laughing?"

"Because if I was asleep, you'd have woken me up with: *are you asleep?*"

I get up, put on some clothes I happen to find on the floor and walk toward the door.

"Where are you going?" he asks, surprised.

"To the baker. What do you want me to get?"

"Something sweet, something like you, something filling."

"Right you are."

"Vår . . ."

"Yes?"

"I wish that every time you left, it also meant that you'd be coming back."

EVERYDAY LIFE

WHEN I GET BACK, the American has made cinnamon tea for us both. He has tidied away old breakfasts, dinner remains, and other scraps from the table. He has even emptied the ashtrays and washed up with *Withnail and I* potential. We really haven't bothered, I think, we've been living like pigs, happy with each other's company. Because I actually like this mess of ours, this life, as if we were teenagers. But now the sun is shining and the kitchen is tidy. It's probably nothing, I tell myself, but I don't like all these changes for the better. It makes me feel uncomfortable.

I find plates and cups and put them on the kitchen table. Then I open the bag from the baker's. It is full of Dutch specialties I don't remember the names of.

"The sun's shining," the American says.

"I know," I say.

"So . . ."

"What?"

"Why don't we go outside and eat instead?"

"Let's."

We carry everything outside and sit on an old sheet down by the canal.

"I want it to be a new place every time we meet," he says. "I don't want anything to be routine with you, Vår. The next time I go to Barcelona. If I earn enough money from 'The Sexual Life of Plants,' it's my treat."

I think this is a perfect idea. At the same time, there's

something hurtful in this suggestion too. Because I want much more from the American than I had from The Lover. I want a life with him, an everyday life. Then the American says I had better go back to London soon, if not, he'll be keeping me there.

THE OEDIPUS COMPLEX

I push my fingers down into the American's trousers. But his sex is limp. He doesn't want to. He tidies away the breakfast, walks back into the kitchen, and washes up for the second time. I help him dry the dishes. Then he sits down at the kitchen table and lights a cigarette. I can feel something is wrong.

"I have a few things to do today," he suddenly says, absentmindedly.

"What?" I ask, inquisitively. "Can I come?"

"No. I want to be alone for a few hours, Vår. I think it'd do us both good."

Of course the American is right, but it hurts because he's the one suggesting it.

"Are you tired of me?" I ask stupidly.

"Of course not."

"Do you want me to go back to London now, immediately?"

"Certainly not. I only need time to think."

"What does she look like?" I ask, suddenly and out of context.

"Who?"

"Petra, of course," I say, immediately regretting it.

"She looks like a film star from the twenties. Very beautiful, but occasionally also very ordinary. She reminds me of my mother. She frightens me in that sense. The Oedipus complex . . . I suppose all men carry that around with them."

"Is that what you're going to think about?"

"The Oedipus complex?"

"Yes."

"No."

DIZZINESS, INTOXICATION AND PAIN

I HAVE FIVE HOURS to myself before the evening's performance of "The Sexual Life of Plants." I close all the windows and the curtains and shut out the fine weather. I study the photos on the wall. I look at the woman who looks mostly like an old-fashioned film star, but who still doesn't look very much like one. I don't like her. That is, I do like her, that's what I don't like about her. If I'd been the American, I would also have had an affair with Petra, I think, while I imagine the whole thing, scene by scene. I undress the girl in the photo. The feeling I'm left with is a kind of dizziness, a mixture of intoxication and pain.

I jump into the shower. I want to wash away the smell of the American, so he can fill me up again afresh. Afterwards I rub creams on my body and put on clothes I know he'll like. I even paint my nails black. Then I put my white hair up into a tight bun. I want to look like an old-fashioned whore.

I'm on my way out when the phone rings. I run back to get it. But when I finally find the phone, it's too late. I sit down. Suddenly I want to call Lou. But then I remember what I told him before I left . . . I put down the phone again. I miss my husband, unexpectedly. He is to me what Nietzsche was to Lou Salomé. I think: these days have passed like a hangover, but now I'm wide awake. I pick up the phone again and call Lou after all.

THE CHINESE

Cyril sits holding the phone for a long time before he puts it down. He dresses in his finest clothes and puts two clips in his long, curly hair. He wants Beverley to remember him as a charming man and not regret that she called him.

He travels on the bus, the tube, and the train. He's on his way to the outskirts of London, near a forest. He sits in a carriage full of scribbles and tags and looks out the train window without seeing anything, just his own thoughts. He's relieved when he finally gets there. Relieved and strangely nervous. He coughs several times. He feels that he has something stuck in his throat, something that tickles. His conscience, maybe? He walks past a fountain, drinks water, gurgles it in his throat. He feels better afterward. Cleaner.

It's a gray day, dismal, Beverley's house is gray, too, with a big, flashy cross above the entrance. Cyril looks in the garage. It's empty. He is glad they are alone. He looks up to the window he believes is hers. She opens the curtains and runs down.

"Hi!"

"Hi!"

There's a strange atmosphere surrounding Beverley. A confined smell you find in houses that are never aired, like summer houses in winter. Cyril thinks that Beverley is now in such a house. His observation is rude. Beverley smiles. She doesn't notice. Her sharp eyes.

"You've put on makeup," is all he says.

Cyril doesn't like girls with makeup.

"Yes."

She blushes.

"For me?"

She doesn't answer.

"Come in," she says instead. "Tell me something, anything, about the time we spent together," she adds.

But Cyril can't do it. Beverley asks him to make something up, to lie. Sometimes that's almost preferable. He tries, but she isn't listening. His voice is too low. She pretends not to notice, takes his worn suit jacket and hangs it on a hook next to a framed picture of Jesus Christ. Then she points to her room. She says she'll join him as soon as the tea is ready.

She walks up the stairs. The clattering is deafening. She carries a tea tray with brittle porcelain cups and expensive silver spoons. Cyril covers his ears with his hands.

"I've met someone," she says. But in the beginning she doesn't insist. That's why he doesn't notice. He takes her hand and strokes it. She continues:

"I've met a Chinese man."

Cyril suddenly stands up and walks over to the window, opens it and pulls the curtains aside to let the air in. It's unhealthy to live in the darkness of depression, he thinks. He knows what he is talking about. The sun is strong. The light blinds her. "Do you want me to close them again?" he asks, "and close the window?"

"No."

She squints.

"So who's this Chinese man?" he asks and pours milk in his tea.

"We've run out of cocoa powder, or I'd have offered you a cup of cocoa, Cyril, cocoa and cheesecake. But I don't have any. I'm a terrible hostess," she says instead.

"You're perfect."

They're silent, both of them, awkwardly silent.

"Would you rather not talk about the Chinese?" he asks again, hesitantly.

She sips her tea.

"Well yes. Where should I start?"

"With him, that'll be the easiest."

"Yes." She explains: "What I liked was that it was exotic, foreign: the Chinese man's long, smooth hair, beard, so different from Western men, the totally hairless body . . . That was what I fell for—his Asianness." She insists: "A very flat, broad face, tall cheekbones, large eyebrows, and the occasional smile."

"Are you going to meet the Chinese man again, Beverley?" Cyril asks.

She doesn't answer.

"Are you going to meet the Chinese man again, Beverley?" Cyril repeats.

He notices that it hurts his stomach to listen to her talking about the Chinese man, but he still asks her to continue.

"Don't call me Beverley, Cyril. It seems to strange. Can't you call me Bev as you've always done, like those close to me do," she finally says.

"Yes, Bev. Sorry."

"I'm trying to meet the man in my life, so that I can meet you," she admits then, and almost starts to cry.

He doesn't understand. He's forgotten. She helps him remember.

"You said something once about those you meet being too naive. The women, I mean. That they have to meet the man in their lives first, and then they can meet you . . ."

These words, which didn't mean all that much to him, have been essential to her. He feels ashamed.

She continues:

"I've thought about you a lot since I met the Chinese man."

"Now you're being silly, Bev, I don't understand you now," Cyril answers, defending himself.

"You're the one who's silly for not understanding," she insists.

"I see."

Neither of them knows what to say anymore.

"Sorry. I didn't mean that," she says, and moves closer. "It was a joke."

She lies down on his lap.

"Where in China is the Chinese man from?" Cyril asks then, even if he doesn't really want to know.

"He's from a small place surrounded by mountains, a village," she answers, even if she doesn't really want to talk about it. "He says it's an ugly place, but that doesn't worry me. On the contrary. You know how I am . . ."

"Yes, Bev, and I miss it."

That remark softens her.

"The Chinese man said I must never go there, and then I really wanted to, of course," she says, repressing a smile. "In a moment of madness I wanted to travel to all the places the Chinese man has been."

"So you're in love?"

"No, Cyril, no, not that."

"What then?"

"I was lonely, and he was so nice to talk to."

"What did you talk about?"

"The Chinese man isn't very good at languages, at a foreign language like English. So we talked mostly in very short sentences, and not about anything important. But now and then silence says more than words, that's what I mean by talking together."

They are silent.

"You mustn't change anything, Bev . . ."

But she isn't making it up, she isn't capable of things like lying, he knows that.

"Of course not."

"I want to know everything, down to facial expressions," Cyril says.

"Do you really?"

"Yes, you've become so good at talking about things."

That makes her happy. She makes herself comfortable.

"Where should I start?" she asks again, but this time he refuses to help her.

"That's up to you, Bev, this is your story."

"Okay."

She tells him how the Chinese man had slowly undressed her. She forgets nothing.

"I'm glad you're taking your time," Cyril says.

She looks him in the eyes. For a long time.

"I let my body relax in the arms of the Chinese man," she says.

"That's good."

She refills her cup, rolls a cigarette from Cyril's tobacco, takes a drag, and breathes out. Coughs. Gets her asthma spray and breathes that into her mouth instead.

"In a way I liked what he did to me. How he came inside me without telling me. But there was something inside me that remained aloof. When I came home, I went to the bathroom and vomited, all night, vomited up the story about the Chinese. I did it for you, to try to be like your wife, things you have told me. I tried to be a girl who is being taken in all kinds of ways, who masturbates, a young girl who behaves like a whore. But the silence afterwards, the emptiness, that was unbearable."

Cyril looks into her eyes, but avoids eye contact. They have an intense red color. Hurting.

"It's you I want," she says.

"You have to forget me," he says. He's lying. He says: "I've already begun to forget you."

ABOUT NEED AND LOSS

I PUT AWAY MY notebook and make another effort to go outside. I want to see a bit of Amsterdam before the American's concert. I check that the coffee machine and record player are turned off and that all the windows are closed. I look forward to autumn, to sitting inside freezing in a turtleneck sweater.

I take the American's bicycle with me and lock the door. The sky is cloudless. I get up on the much-too-high seat and cycle as steadily as I'm able, first through a park, then down a street, past a few canals, all the way down to the Red Light District. Here I cycle back and forth studying the whores. Most of them are vulgar, but some are cute. I look for my whore, but she isn't there. I keep cycling in a circle until I arrive at the gloomy bar the American talked so enthusiastically about, Sur le Port d'Amsterdam.

I chain the cycle to a street lamp and walk into our favorite haunt for the first time. Alone. I feel at home immediately. The interior is tasteless, it stinks, the music is a potpourri of hits from the eighties, but I like it here. The American was right. I order an Amstel and a small glass of genever. I write:

Ragnhild is an idiotic person. When she is with her husband, she misses her lover, and when she is with her lover, she misses her husband.

DANCER IN THE DARK

AFTER THE CONCERT WE'RE not sure about what to do or where to go. I cycle away in my comic style, while the American holds on to me tightly. I cycle around aimlessly. I feel that I know this city. A little better than yesterday. But not as well as tomorrow. The only way to get a feeling for a place is to experience it alone, I think, find one's own way, one's own tempo, one's own good and bad habits.

"What have you done today?" I ask the American out of the blue.

"Nothing special. I've done all the things I haven't done for a while," he answers.

"And they are . . . ?"

"Being alone."

I don't know how to respond to that. There's silence between us. Finally the American suggests going to *the club*. This club I'd suppressed. This club where he met Petra. He thinks it could be fun. To sweat a little, before I return to London.

I don't like the way he's talking. He seems so dejected. The fact he's so sure I'll leave him makes it certain that I *will* leave him. Because I can't be with a man who doesn't believe he can hold on to me.

There's a long line outside the club, but the American and I walk straight in. He nods left and right, is praised for "The Sexual Life of Plants," and gets free drinks—because everyone forgets that he's a coffee-drinking American.

But it doesn't matter, because he passes the drinks on to me. The music is loud. We have to shout to hear each other. This is the first time we dance together. Our rhythms are totally different. The American's is very Amsterdamian, while mine is more that of London. Every country and every city has its own way of doing this very simple thing: moving rhythmically. We dance. Without touching each other. Other men try to get my attention, but I ignore them. The American doesn't like all the attention I get.

"How does your husband put up with it?" he asks out of the blue.

"What?"

"The competition."

"He needs it as a proof that he's made the right choice," I answer.

"I wish I could meet someone like you," the American says.

"What do you mean?"

"I mean exactly what I'm saying."

I THINK, THEREFORE I AM

THE AMERICAN NEEDS MORE and more time to himself, to think. Every day he needs several hours for this *thinkery*, as he calls it. I'm almost missing his cassettes: a voice in a tape recorder, sent in a small parcel and received by me on the other side of the Channel; that was almost more intimate.

I walk over to his desk. Sit down. Open the top drawer, where I know I'll find the pile of letters. I take them out and count how many are from me. I'm shocked at how often I have written compared to the others. I read my letters again. It hurts. What I felt then. What I feel now. What I won't feel much longer.

I shut the drawer again, close my eyes, and sharpen my sense of smell. There is a wonderful odor in this boy-flat that is no longer very boyish, but clean, handsome, and androgynous. I didn't have the heart any longer to let the American throw Petra's flowers in the canal, so I've taken them in myself and placed them around the flat, in everything from liter jugs to chipped coffee cups and empty soft-drink bottles . . .

I dance around, from one room to the next. This flat is too big, I think then, we're drowning, the American and I. What would suit us is something small and cute, like the paunch.

I convince myself that the American needs to be alone to create music. That love-making and being in love is the cello's worst enemy, while the lack of it makes him more creative. Because he would never have composed "The Sexual Life of Plants" for me if I had been here with him. It was missing me that made him do it. I know this, understand it, but don't accept it.

In a last effort to become close to the American again, I glance at his books. I see where he has put dog-ears and amuse myself with his comments. Still, I understand the American less and less. I try to listen to his music instead, devouring John Cage, Brian Ferneyhough, and Pierre Boulez. Contemporary music Holly would like, I think. But the American just continues to slip between my fingers.

BATHING PICTURE

IT RAINS AND RAINS. *The streets of London are like small rivers, flooded. Cyril feels his feet getting wet, feels the water seeping into his shoes, socks, and trousers. He is walking in water up to his knees. He stumbles in this tide and his whole body gets wet, his skin, all the way down to his soul. A fox passes him. He wonders about that, but doesn't worry. His wet hair is plastered to his face, but he's humming to himself and is almost happy. He sees another fox, only just registering it. He's on his way to the deserted graveyard in Stoke Newington. This is how he feels, alone: the birds, nature, still alone, humming, on his way to Abney Park.*

He stays there for a long time. Because he has nothing to come home to. No one. He thinks about the deserted graveyards, trees, flowers, grass, weeds . . . How we human beings change, decompose and become compost. He thinks about nature's ways, about the parasites . . . Yes, at first that's all he thinks about: putrefaction . . . But with time, he begins to think this is fantastic, this, that we can be so useful, even after death, that there is still someone to whom we can be of use.

He lights a cigarette, thinks that there's something beautiful in this gloom, something that makes him feel at home. An old woman walks past with three Dalmatians. She says hello, so he says hello back. There are other people who like deserted graveyards, he thinks. He is loafing around, walks his round, around and around, as in a labyrinth. Walks to his favorites, the graves with the most interesting names. There are many stories to tell in a place like this. He hopes that when he dies, he can end up being a story too.

When he comes home, he finds her like this:

Her eyes are hard, staring, but at the same time it feels as if she doesn't see anything, just looks through him. She is somewhere else, nowhere. Cyril doesn't know how long she's been lying there like that, in the water, but he thinks it must be a long time. From what he can understand, what he can see: the wizened body, the wrinkles, the blue-colored skin . . . could it have been hours? He tries to orient himself, to understand. He says:

"It's over, it's really over. I thought I'd told you that very clearly."

He can see himself in her transparent face.

"You're not the one I could've loved after all," he explains, and looks at her, sadly.

Asks:

"Why didn't you take your own life?"

His comment makes her start. But she's unable to scream. Cyril is ashamed over what has happened. Holds her head in his hands. Mechanically. As if it weren't quite natural for him to have a reaction.

"We drifted apart, more and more," he continues.

He lies and lies. Soon he believes it himself. Her eyes are full of tears. She looks at him. Sees that he, too, has shriveled. And in a strange way it gives her courage. So she has meant something to him after all.

"I stole the keys from your jacket when you were visiting me," she admits, "that's how I got in. They're on that chair. You can take them back if you like."

"Thank you."

He no longer gives voice to anything. Buries himself in himself. She knows it is finished. She accepts. Because it hurts him as much as it hurts her, she can see that now, even if he doesn't know it himself yet.

"I never thought I'd do something like this, sink so low," she says,

totally exhausted, powerless. "Do you want me to leave?"
He puts his hand in the bathtub and pulls out the plug.
"Yes."
"I'll go then," she says in a weak voice.
She lies still while the bathtub slowly but surely empties out.
Cyril waits until she's left, until he can't see her anymore, then he
breaks down.

THE WATER SPRITE

THE SUN IS SHINING. As usual. I can no longer distinguish one day from the next. I take out the bicycle and cycle around for hours: through the Vondelpark, past the Rijksmuseum, the Stedelijk Museum and the Van Gogh Museum, down Rembrandtplein, Leidseplein, The Jordaan, Prinsengracht, Keizersgracht, Dam Square . . . I didn't throw away the *Lonely Planet* guide after all, and now it helps me to find my way, remember names, be a tourist.

I stand in front of a hotel and look up, imagine how Chet Baker came flying, falling . . . down, for a small second that must have been an eternity for him. I wonder what was so special about this very hotel, this street, this city, this country . . . Why his life should end right here?

There's nothing about it in the guide. I turn the pages. Look for somewhere else to visit. I have always had problems remembering names. The center of the village of Bø consists of two streets, and we call both of them Bø Street. Usually I find my way with the help of visual memory. But here in Amsterdam I have so much spare time that I've begun to learn names by heart. And the truth is I like it. I feel I get a better grasp on the town that way: soon I'll know it as well as I know London.

Amsterdam, this city of sin, I think. How beautiful it is here. No one had told me that. Just the drugs and the whores, but not the beauty. I feel a lump growing in my throat. Perhaps Lou was right after all? Perhaps there is an *after the American* . . . ? I sit down on a bench and think about the water sprite. About this

fatal creature who rules over lakes and waterfalls. Who lures
people into them with his music so they drown. The water sprite
usually plays the violin by rivers and grinding mills, but he may
just as well have played the cello . . .

LAST ACT

I ENTER THE AUDITORIUM to attend "The Last Performance," "The End," "The Finale," "Glasgow-Orchid's Death." I'm early. I have brought a small bottle of champagne for myself and a thermos of coffee for the American. He doesn't know that I'm coming early. I sneak backstage, say hi to the choreographer, the light and sound people, the dancers, the designers, the film crew . . . Yes, almost everyone who takes part in "The Sexual Life of Plants" production.

I've become like a piece of the furniture now, I think, part of the inventory. But as I'm about to run in and throw myself in the arms of the American, I stop. My stomach is like a compass asking me to walk away. The American is not alone, I can feel it. I put my ear to the door, my eye to the keyhole. I see what I expect. Except more beautiful. And I feel nothing: neither jealousy nor passion, neither hate nor love.

I sneak out of the corridor, out of the whole place, sit down by a canal, drink the content of the champagne bottle, and pour out the coffee. Afterward I sneak into the auditorium again. I make myself comfortable on the plastic chair. The curtain goes up. I watch the piece as if for the first time: without blinking. I watch it with nostalgia as well, like a memory. I remember Primrose Hill, I remember London as our honeymoon, I remember the smell of sweat, of sex, I remember all his cassettes, my letters . . . I remember my first impression of Amsterdam, of the American . . . I remember what I want to remember.

*

When the curtain comes down, I'm left with a smell.

I tell the American:

"To make a smell out of sounds is more impressive than making sounds out of sounds."

AU REVOIR TRISTESSE

WE CYCLE HOME IN silence: me at the front, the American behind me. Neither of us wants to go out and party. The end of "The Sexual Life of Plants" means the end of us, too, we both feel that.

When we get to Schinkelhavenstraat 31 hs 1075 VP, we hear the phone ringing. The American runs in to answer it, but it's not for him, it's for me.

"It's your husband," he says and hands me the phone.

I take the cordless phone and sit down by the canal. I want to talk to Lou. Alone. As the American closes the door, I see him picking up Petra's flowers, taking them in with him for the first time. I stay where I am for a long while.

When I walk back inside, the new bouquet on the table is the first thing I notice.

"This is our last night together," I say.

"This is our last night together," the American repeats.

We look at each other. We don't cry. It makes me sad, this lack of *tristesse*. Because we're both . . . hurt, we're both . . . too proud. The American turns off the ceiling light and lights the candles instead.

"What are you thinking about?" I ask.

"Me?"

"Yes, you. Who else?"

I notice that I'm not relaxed, that the sarcasm is heavy, unnecessary. The American tries to see how long he can hold his hand over the flame of the candle.

"How did it happen?" he finally asks with a lump in his throat. "Was it an accident?"

"What?"

"The fire, Vår, the fire."

He wants to talk about the fire. I can't believe it. I want to talk about us, but he slyly starts talking about the fire.

"An accident," I answer without thinking. "An accident," I repeat.

I have to admit that I've never thought about it before, the origin of the fire. I walk around the room, collecting all my clothes, and start packing.

"Now and then it's good to burn everything," the American continues. "Then you can start again from the beginning."

He smells of backstage, of her, I think. Of course, I don't know how she smells, but I can imagine she has a sweet smell, feminine, like a flower.

"You're not in love with me, you're lying, it's Petra you're in love with," I say suddenly.

I stop folding my clothes, I throw them in the backpack.

"You're the woman I've always dreamed of, but you love your husband. For some reason I accept my fate, as if it could never be otherwise."

"How strange that you should mention it," I answer. "Lou never dreamed about me. Perhaps that's why we're still together?"

The American's fingers glide through my hair. He pulls it.

"Ouch!" He pulls it again. "Stop it!"

We're no longer relaxed in each other's company. Everything is wrong. I walk toward the door.

"Where are you going?"

"To finish packing."

"I don't want you to leave, don't you understand that? I'm only pressuring you to make a decision. But all the time I'm hoping for something else."

He is breathing heavily, nervously, while I stop breathing, get goose bumps, feel cold . . .

"You don't know what you mean to me," he says. "If I'd had a woman like you, I wouldn't have shared her with anyone."

"Not even with you . . . ?" I ask ironically.

"Especially not with me!"

We are silent again. The American blows out the candles and everything goes dark. I like that we can hardly see each other, that we don't have night vision like cats, but just make out the contours of each other.

"I can pack tomorrow morning . . ." I suggest as I feel his arms move down my stomach.

His hands are covered in wax. It's lovely. I turn toward him, wet my lips . . .

"Do you sometimes think of Beverley and me?" the American asks as I'm about to kiss him.

"Her name's Sidney. Beverley is my creation," I answer.

"Sidney, Beverley . . . Simon Beverley . . . it sounds familiar," he says.

"It's Sid Vicious' real name," I inform him.

"And what do you call me?"

"I don't call you anything."

"All that counts is Lou and you, isn't it? The rest of us are just test rabbits, something you can write about . . ."

"Of course not," I interrupt and light a cigarette, inhale, and exhale through my nose. I like how the American's face appears between each puff. "I'm sorry if I've hurt you, that was never my intention. But you knew it from the beginning. It was your choice as well," I say.

"My choice?" The American begins to laugh. "It was not my choice. I was in love. And if you're in love, you overestimate yourself. At first I thought it was sweet that you were married, but now I understand that I was suffering. That's why I cheated on you, Vår, that's why . . . the others . . . Petra . . . In order not to become hurt yourself, you have to hurt others . . . I've given up."

AN EXAMPLE OF A BREAKDOWN

CYRIL BITES HIS NAILS *so badly that when he puts his fingers down his throat to vomit, he scratches himself. He likes this pain, something compatible with his disturbances. Usually he likes it. Because sometimes it's the opposite. Then he gets obsessed by whatever makes him feel refined, and wants his nails to be round and neat, delicate. He likes this pain, he insists, because even when it's different, it's still the same pain.*

He thinks: I'm happy when I touch myself and feel that my collarbones stick out, my hips. I like to get proof of how slim I am. He also thinks: alone. I'm so alone. That feeling is everywhere. He is as if surrounded by this vacuum. He walks to the deserted graveyard in Stoke Newington, because that's where he sees beauty. He thinks: it's a long time since I've been the person I like to be.

6:

TIME FLIES . . .

"Welcome on board this flight from Amsterdam to London Stansted. This is your captain speaking . . ."

I look out the window: a bird sits on the wing, a mini-plane, I think and look inside the cabin again, look at the hostesses going through the safety routines. I make myself comfortable, I have a window seat, I'm lucky. Next to me is a fat man, and next to him a small girl.

I think about the American. I miss him already. Not the person he was when I left him, but the person he was when I arrived. I look at my watch: one p.m. I wonder what he's going to do today. He's sure to take Petra to our bar that we never visited together, I think, and conjure up a picture of it in my mind. Then I try to forget: him and her, what has been and what is going to happen . . . I do my best. Soon I'll probably just remember the essential: a cello. Because I don't want to think about the female body between the American's legs anymore, instead I want to think about a musician's discipline, all the repetitions, stroking, stroking, again and again, until his fingertips are sore, until they bleed. Yes, sometimes a musician has to go that far.

"We wish you a pleasant journey . . ."

The American is best at a distance or deep inside me, I think then, and I push the red button in the ceiling. A young blond woman in a dark blue suit and conservative makeup comes up to me.

"Could I have a pillow and a blanket?" I ask.

"Of course."

She smiles—a stiff, unnatural, professional smile. As friends, he and I are ordinary, I think, socially speaking there's nothing special between the American and me, as human beings we only partly understand each other . . . That's why I don't want him to become a friend like The Lover, but that it be truly over. I'm sorry we had to leave each other obviously, but I'm happy that I'm going to be reunited with my husband. I feel that I've finally found a kind of balance.

I sit and stare into nothingness, until the fat man suddenly pokes my shoulder.

"What is it?" I say, bewildered. He points to the air hostess standing in the aisle with a pillow and a blanket. "Thanks," I say.

"You're welcome," she answers.

"You . . ."

"We're ready for takeoff," she interrupts. "Have a nice flight."

". . . have lipstick on your teeth," I whisper.

"Thank you," she says, and blushes.

The fat man tries to sleep, while the little girl is reading a Pippi Longstocking book in Dutch. I smile, because Pippi was my childhood idol, the very symbol of Scandinavian feminism, I think.

"We are now leaving the Netherlands, and in a little while we will see Belgium with its capital, Brussels . . ."

I look through the tax-free magazine but don't find my Vogue cigarettes, nor Gitanes or Tigra; instead I find YSL and Drum for Lou, and a bottle of genever for us both. I look out the window again. The bird has flown. I think about my husband. I miss him. I think that every time he takes a drag on a cigarette and blows out the smoke, this is what happens: clouds in the sky.

SWEET DREAMS

I'M WALKING DOWN AN old dirt road in Bø, a private road you're not supposed to use. All around me there's the forest, behind me the mountains. She stands at the other end of the road, Petra. She's playing hopscotch. I look at her thin, anorexic body, hidden behind a glamorous dress from the twenties. I study how she moves her delicate bone structure. I can see her vomiting in the ditch. I try to pretend that she's invisible, look through her as she picks up the pebble and throws it in front of her. Each pretends to be unaware of the other. I'm picking flowers for my mother, a large bouquet of wood anemone and blue anemone. Petra is hopping and skipping. We don't look at each other. Perhaps she doesn't know that it's me, I suddenly think. Perhaps she simply doesn't know who I am . . .

A plane flies across the sky and leaves a thin stripe, as if it has wet itself, I think and walk closer and closer, as if nothing has happened. Petra stops. The plane leaves behind a silence. I'm listening for birdsong, while I go on walking forward until we pass each other: Our eyes meet for a second, they itch afterward like mosquito bites, they swell revengefully, mine blue, hers gray. She knows who I am, I'm thinking.

"Are you coming . . . ?" calls the sweet voice of a child.

I turn and discover a boy hiding behind a tree, a boy who reminds me of the boy from America . . .

"Come on," he insists and holds out his hand so Petra can take it. "Ba ba black sheep . . ." he sings.

But she doesn't listen. Launches her fist in my face, so I fall to the ground, almost unconscious, blood oozing from my nose.

"I'm bleeding, I'm bleeding," I scream, but Petra has disappeared.

I try to move, but can't. I have a dreadful headache. The boy from America comes over to me and whispers something in my ear. I lie still, but all I hear is a ringing sound getting louder and louder until it's unbearable.

"Ba ba black sheep . . ." he sings again, picks up my flowers, and is about to leave.

"Stop!" I scream. "I didn't hear what you said."

"Who set fire to your house, Vår?" he repeats in a loud clear voice. Then he finds a match, lights it, and nonchalantly throws it away.

"You devil!" I scream and stare into the flames that quickly spread through the bone-dry forest.

"As hot as hell itself . . ." he whispers, and he disappears.

"Are you coming . . . ?" asks a hoarse male voice that sounds both familiar and foreign.

I turn and look straight into Lou's green-brown eyes. He is unrecognizable: old, with mussed-up gray hair. He really looks fantastic.

"Darling, is it really you?" I ask happily.

He nods. He's holding a bottle of water in one hand. He opens it, throws the water into the forest, and extinguishes the fire. It's unbelievable. I stand up, brush off gravel and grit, run toward my husband, and give him a long, lovely Hollywood kiss.

"I love you," I say and close my eyes.

"Ugh, yuck," he answers.

I open my eyes, bewildered.

"Ugh, yuck," I repeat, and blush.

"What are you doing?" asks the fat man and dries his cheek while I dry my mouth.

"Sorry, I didn't mean to," I say.

"How disgusting," we say simultaneously, with a little laugh.

"This is your captain speaking. We are preparing for landing . . ."

"Have I been asleep for that long?" I ask, surprised.

"Yes," the little girl says and leans over the fat man's stomach, "and you even snored."

"It's not nice to lie," I say, and I look out the window; I see London, far away from Amsterdam.

PORTRAIT WITH HACKED-OFF HAIR

I STUDY MY HUSBAND: he looks different, thin, I mean thinner, sad, I mean even sadder that I had expected. We sit down on the sofa. I hardly recognize him. I give him the carton of Drum and take out a stolen ashtray with a Sur le Port d'Amsterdam logo.

"You want to kill me?" he says jokingly.

"What's happened that you look so different?" I ask instead.

"I've gotten a haircut, surely you can see that? I wanted to know if you could love me without my curls."

"Of course I can, but . . ."

"I wanted to change something, so I changed my hairstyle. Don't you like it, Vår?"

"No, but that doesn't matter, because I love you," I say and lean into him. "I wanted to live through the story with the American without your interference . . ."

". . . and . . ."

". . . come back as if nothing had happened," I say and fish out a bottle of genever from my backpack, along with two glasses that also have the Sur le Port d'Amsterdam logo. I tell Lou that this corn liquor with juniper berry is a Dutch gin that we have to drink in one swallow. I give him a glass. "Cheers," I say and gulp mine.

"To what?" Lou asks and gulps his too.

"To us. To you and me, Lou."

"And what about the American?"

"He's nothing to worry about anymore."

"Really?"

"No, are you disappointed?"

"Oh, please. Was he a disappointment?"

"No."

"You mustn't play with me, Vår . . ."

"It wasn't the American who disappointed me, Lou, it was us, he and I together. Because I love the American just as much as you love Sidney . . . But I think you're right, this game . . . well . . . Let's try not to play it any longer."

"Or . . ."

"What?"

"Do you want to take part in a game?"

"No, now . . ."

"Shh. He picks up his bible, *Thus Spake Zarathustra*, and reads: "'In every real man a child is hidden that wants to *play*.'"

I'm about to say something, but Lou puts his finger to my mouth.

"What I want is for us to play at *not* playing," he says.

"What?"

"We've always done the unexpected, but now that's also become expected. It simply doesn't stimulate me anymore."

"So what stimulates you now, Lou?"

"I want to try something else, something new, something perhaps a bit old-fashioned; something different."

"What's that?"

"Faithfulness, Vår, couldn't that be something exciting? What I want is to try and redefine what it means to be a couple. To make *not* playing itself the game."

"What you're saying is poetic and beautiful, but . . ."

"I'm saying it too quickly. That's a mistake. You've only just arrived home. You haven't even unpacked your backpack. Of course I'll give you some time. Time to get over the American and to discover me again . . . Tell me about Amsterdam," he then demands.

"Do you really want to . . . ?"

"No."

"You bastard! You tell *me* something . . ."

"It's rained constantly, strangely enough it stopped today, quite suddenly, just before you came home . . ." Lou says.

"It rained in Amsterdam too."

"All the time?"

"No. There was thunder, rain, for several days without time seeming to pass at all, without us even knowing where we were. Until the American one day opened the curtains. The weather was nice, the sun was shining . . . Do you understand what I mean, Lou?"

He looks at me and smiles.

"Yes."

A MAN'S SNORING CAN BE MUSIC

LOU SNORES, ONLY JUST, but enough to keep me awake: this soughing sound that isn't a proper sound but something absent, the reminder of the other person's sleep, the longing. I get up. It feels strange to wake up next to my husband again. His familiar body suddenly feels strange. His smell is not as I expected either. I want to call the American and ask how he is, but I tell myself no: I don't want to destroy anything for anyone. I take a long cold shower. Then I go down to the kitchen to make breakfast, something simple: beans on toast, something arch-English. Outside the weather is autumn gray, I think happily, because now I really can't bear this summer anymore. I go up to the bedroom again to wake Lou.

I whisper lovely things to him and put my fingers down his boxer shorts. He twists around in bed like a happy worm, until the phone rings.

"It'll be the American," he says.

"Just let it ring," I answer.

"Don't you miss him?"

"Of course, but I was happy when I opened my eyes this morning and saw that it was you lying next to me in bed . . ."

"I can believe that. I'm irresistible," Lou says and laughs. He is happy again, and I am too. "You always come back," he adds.

"Yes," I say, and I pick up the phone with a beating heart. "Hello."

"Hi."

The male voice doesn't introduce himself. He asks instead if I can describe myself, describe my husband. If I do it well, he'll pay to draw us. I wonder how he got my number, but forget to ask. Perhaps from Holly, or the teacher, or someone in the class. It doesn't really matter. The most important thing is that he called, and that he offers to pay.

"How much?" I ask.

"Twenty pounds an hour. Begin with your husband?"

"French," I say.

"Go on."

"He looks like a French poet."

"Good."

"Intellectual, thin . . . extremely thin, too many cigarettes, too little food . . . Naturally thin," I add. "It doesn't help to eat."

"Interesting."

"I think he must be ideal to draw," I continue. "His bones are beautifully visible beneath his skin, and he has very high cheekbones."

"Mm . . ."

"Serge Gainsbourg," I explain. "He used to look like Buster Keaton, but now he looks more like Serge Gainsbourg, with short hair and sweet ears, a bit protruding. And his sex: despite his slender structure, it's big and dominating."

"And you, what about you?"

"I'm Norwegian, but I haven't lived there for many years and have no plans to return there. Nomadic, perhaps, someone who keeps moving," I answer.

"Interesting, but what about your looks?"

"Nordic."

"Go on."

"Isn't that enough?"

"I want to draw you and your husband in an erotic pose, for instance, when you're making love. That's why I would like to know what you look like, down below."

I end the conversation.

"Who was that?" Lou asks.

"Some quasi-artist who wanted to draw us while we're having sex."

"Is that so bad?"

"Yes."

"You're right. Always think the worst, darling, then you might be surprised for the better."

TORTURE

WE ENJOY THE LONELINESS solidarity brings, the monotony that can sometimes take on a positive form. Lou and I alone. So that for a few days there's only us, as if there'd never been a Sidney, as if there'd never been an American, as if there'd never been anyone else. Because we have to forget the others to be able to remember each other.

The phone rings but we don't pick up. Even if everyone does their best: the American strokes his cello, Sidney cries, The Lover wants to have a "girls' talk," Holly talks devotedly about Henry, and the teacher threatens that unless I come back soon, he'll swap me out for a man! But we just let it ring. Lou and I have almost no money left, but we let it ring.

Lou rarely goes to work. Most of the time, we lie inside reading, he his books and I mine. But always including the other. I read something that gives me goosebumps. It claims that they made use of the bodies of the Jews—that nothing went to waste: their bodies became soap and their hair woven blankets. I show Lou a picture of a field filled with hair: a swarm of red, brown, blond, and black. We talk about psychological torture as well as physical, and how the communists killed just as many as the Nazis. Lou is reading Aleksandr Solzhenitsyn's book about the Russian concentration camps. He believes that he'll have to stay with this particular book for at least a year, there's so much information in it, so much to learn, generally, especially for me, who knows so little, I think.

But in the evening he puts it away and opens one of the many newspapers scattered around the flat instead. He selects an article and reads it as if it were a poem, and its atrocity becomes beautiful. He reads it over and over again, like a lamentation:

"'The Israelis made a fence around the settlement, then they put in a gate so we could get to our olive trees. They gave us the key and let us come and go. Then they changed the lock and stationed a guard. But he doesn't come on the Sabbath, holidays, or when he is sick. Then he doesn't come at all and you can't get to the land. Then they declare you're not working your land and seize it.'" Then he reads the name as well, several times: "Abdul Karim Ahmad, villager. Abdul Karim Ahmad, villager. Abdul Karim Ahmad, villager . . ."

In the end we're crying. I don't know what day it was.

ASH

I wake up with a start. I'm alone in bed. The phone is ringing. I don't pick up. When the answering machine comes on, I hear cello music. I feel down and run out of the room. I can't bear listening to it.

Where is Lou? I notice a burnt smell, a disgusting smell, like rotten food, but at the same time a nice smell. I think that it must be this smell that woke me up. I try to find where it comes from. I'm sweating, my heart is beating. I run down to the kitchen, into the living room, up again . . . Lou is in the bathtub, surrounded by soap bubbles, listening to Léo Ferré. He often locks himself in the bathroom and stays there for hours, that's where he gets his best ideas, he says, but this doesn't seem like a good idea, this, though I don't know what it is yet, gives me a stomach pain. I ask Lou what he's done, what he's burned. He doesn't answer, just keeps smiling, so I hit him. For a couple of seconds I lose my mind and hit him.

"What is it, Vår, have you gone crazy?" he asks, alarmed.

On the floor is a garbage bin, and behind it a matchbox. I run into the bedroom, into the mess, stumble over my own clothes, swear, until I find my "secret" shoebox, innermost in the wardrobe. I open it and see that it's full—that The Lover's letters are still there, the Pollock sweater, and the American's cassettes. The phone is ringing again: more cello music. I cover my ears, not because it's ugly, but because it's beautiful. I run back into the bathroom.

"I'm such an idiot!" I say and kiss my husband.

Then I turn my other cheek so he can hit it. But Lou just turns down the volume of Léo Ferré and looks inquiringly at me.

"What are you doing, darling? Sometimes I really don't understand you."

"I thought you'd burned The Lover's letters and the American's cassettes," I admit and blush.

"Have you gone nuts? It's Sid's letters I've been burning . . . Why should I burn your things?"

"Did you write letters to each other?"

"Yes, but we didn't send them. We gave them to each other at the gallery."

"Oh . . ."

I think: if we're going to change, change our lives, we have to move somewhere else, the way it's always been. We ran away to London, now it's time to run away from London . . .

"I was thinking . . ." Lou begins.

". . . that we could go home to Bø," I continue without thinking. "Because we have to go where there are no temptations."

"That sounds like a good idea, darling."

"No," I say. "It's a terrible idea. Surely you understand that . . ."

"But . . ."

"You must try to talk me out of it, mon amour. You can't let me do this to us . . . Are you angry?" I ask.

Lou dries his hands and asks me to get his tobacco. I watch while he rolls a cigarette. It's a nice sight, I think: my husband in the bathtub with his roll-ups.

"I don't regret anything," he finally says. "We sacrificed The Lover, we sacrificed Sid, we sacrificed the American, we almost sacrificed each other . . . But you were worth it, Vår, you're worth suffering for."

TO CARRY A GREAT DESPAIR

I turn on the answering machine. The first thing I hear from the little machine is melancholic cello music. I don't listen to the rest but delete everything. I don't know why. I have a bad conscience. Perhaps that's why. I long for him, but instead of ringing the person I'm longing for, I pick up the phone and call Sidney. I dial her number several times only to hang up. Lou may have finished his Sidney-longing, I think, but I haven't.

I stand with the phone in my hand without saying anything.

"Hi," Sidney says.

I feel my heart beating. I remain silent.

"I know it's you, Lou, I recognize the number," she continues. I still don't answer.

"Perhaps you were wrong, that everything can be okay, unsaid. I'd agree with that . . ."

I open my mouth, but change my mind.

"Let's see how things develop, I need to be alone too. Perhaps it's best like this after all . . ." she says.

I have to say something. I can hear the fear in her voice.

"Who is this?" she finally asks, worried.

"It's me . . ." I say.

"Vår . . . ?"

"Yes."

That's all I can say. The words get mixed up.

"I can meet you in an hour," she suggests.

We walk through Hyde Park. Sidney holds my arm the way she used to with Lou, it makes me feel ill at ease. Because she doesn't feel like herself anymore, she looks old, as I'd feared.

"We came here, without discussing it beforehand, instinctively, isn't that strange?" she asks.

"Did we?"

"Yes."

A dog runs past, goes behind a bush for a poo. Then the owner arrives, takes out a plastic bag, and puts the poo in his pocket. This has always puzzled me, the bashfulness of dogs when it comes to excrement. They can shag each other from behind in full view. Do it "doggy-style," as it's called. I look at Sidney. Don't know what to say.

"It's lovely here, on this side of town," I say.

I try to avoid the words that concern us.

"Yes," she answers.

It's a foul and depressing day, we watch kids playing, parents arguing, someone riding a skateboard, others on roller skates . . . The air is sultry. I want Sidney to tell me about her and my husband, but I don't believe she's up to it.

"Don't become different," I say, "just stay as you are."

I mean as she *was*. She doesn't understand.

"You know I miss Lou, don't you?" she asks instead.

"Of course."

We're searching for an equal playing field, somewhere she and I can communicate without falling apart. But just the sight of her makes me feel wistful.

"I've changed my hairstyle," she explains. "That's why I look different. I could see you staring. I've always had a soft spot for people whose hair grows in a natural little triangle down their forehead, a *widow's peak*," she continues eagerly. "That, and men who start losing their hair and then there's suddenly a white stripe of skin on each side of their head. I think that's what inspired me to create the hairstyle I have now." She repeats: "*A widow's peak.*" How she feels abandoned.

We sit down on a bench. Sidney takes out her asthma spray.

We look around. She sees something that makes her laugh. I feel relieved. The seriousness of our conversation stuns me.

"Why are you laughing?" I ask.

She points to a rock.

I pretend not to recognize it.

"Lou and I made love once behind that rock, in the middle of the day. We were so much in love we believed no one could see us."

We both laugh. Loudly. It's almost unnatural to laugh so loudly.

I calm down, order her:

"Sit down on that rock!"

"Why?"

"Because I want to take a picture of you on top of it. Besides, the weather is so dismal today, I think it's a good motif."

"Okay," she says bewildered and sits down on the rock. "How do I look?"

"Nice. Stare into the camera so I can see your dark green eyes. Look at me as if I were Lou. That's right!"

Sidney looks at me with surprised eyes.

"Thanks," I say. "That was very special."

She smiles.

"Will you send me a copy?"

"Of course."

I put the cheap disposable camera back in my bag, then we continue to talk. By forming a picture of Sidney, concretizing her, in a way she becomes more understandable. We're both silent. It's unnatural for us to be together. We observe everything around us without following what's happening, we listen to other people's conversations without really paying attention.

"Why don't we go there?" I suggest and point to the cafe where Lou and I went with Marlene and The Lover.

"Let's."

She smiles.

"Why are you smiling?"

"Because it was *our* cafe."

"So we'll go there?"

"Yes."

"What did you used to order?'

"Cocoa and cheesecake. It was the same almost every time."

"Oh . . ." I say, pretending not to know.

"Lou's the kind of person who enjoys his little habits," Sidney explains, as if she forgot she was talking about my husband.

"Really . . ."

We both order cocoa and cheesecake. It tastes exactly the same as last time. I offer her a cigarette, then another . . . until we've finished the whole pack of YSLs. I say it doesn't matter, I have more at home, a whole carton I bought on the plane from Amsterdam. I get a lump in my throat when I mention Amsterdam. I cough. Then I pluck up my courage and ask Sidney if she can show me the ugly parts of London, what she likes best, because that's what Lou is always talking about. She says a very definite no, the ugly parts are something she wants to keep for herself, they belong to Lou and her, only the two of them. She says no, and shows me only London's lovely side.

FUNNY VERSES

I MUST THINK OF something to do. Something better than passing the time by lazing around. I start crying. Suddenly. This isn't something I try to hide—that I'm sometimes caught unaware by my feelings, that I'm an emotionalist. But I'd never have thought that I'd cry like this over Sidney; that her intrusion into my life, that her affair with my husband . . . I'd never have thought that, in this strange way, it was going to break something inside me. What idiots we have been, I think, dry my tears, stub out the cigarette, and call for Lou. He's in the living room, reading Nietzsche. I go down there too, because I want to be near him.

"I can't write," I complain. "I'm empty. All that comes is rhymes, funny verses inspired by André Bjerke, like kooky drawings, squiggles, except for in words."

"Focus on Ragnhild's fear of the village," Lou tells me, "how trapped she feels. Which is something that's in her from the beginning, but that's growing inside her little by little. Finally it feels like the turtleneck sweater she had to wear as a child, the one that almost suffocated her."

"Do you really remember that, Lou?"

"Yes, Vår, I remember everything. Perhaps you believe I don't listen, but I never forget anything."

"Oh, Lou, there are certain things I wish you could forget."

"Such as?"

"The things I've forgotten myself, you should delete them from your memory, too. For instance, do you remember what it was like the first time we made love?"

"Yes, Vår, I remember it well, it was terrible."

"Now you're being nasty."

"No, not nasty, just honest. I was just as bad as you were."

TIME HEALS NO WOUNDS, IT JUST MAKES THEM LESS VISIBLE

TIME PASSES, THE MONEY disappears, friends become memories, wounds heal, the scabs . . . But Sidney is like me: she picks them open again. Because she doesn't want to get well, I think. It's like the ruins after a fire, something hot and frightening that came into her and destroyed everything inside.

I try to visit her. I want to give her a copy of the photo on the rock, as I promised. But Sidney's parents tell me she wants to be left alone, the last thing she said before she locked herself in her room was: solitude. They respect her choice. I tell them I'm sorry and walk away. Away from this strange house with the heavy, oppressive atmosphere, as in a Bergman film, I think, just less aesthetic, with bad actors and lame lines.

I don't tell Lou about Sidney's condition, that she's just getting worse and worse, that it's tragic, this little game of ours, the consequences of it. Instead I stare out the window, stare intensely at a tree that doesn't exist: despairing, disappointed that I still haven't found anyone who could replace The Lover, that the American wasn't the third man in my life after all, irreplaceable, that he didn't become *The* American, the way The Lover became *The* Lover. I look at Lou. He understands. Puts his arms around me, kisses me again and again, until I stop looking at the tree, until I discover what does exist.

I ask:

"Why do you love me?"

"Because you're the only one I can talk to, I mean completely openly and honestly, without being considerate."

I put my head on his shoulder and close my eyes.

Lou declares in an undertone to himself:

"I've no regrets. All the hurting has been good for me."

We become silent, each with our own thoughts. I'm thinking: It's time I accept that contrary to what I believe, I'm not free. Dependence. To love Lou. Exclusively. To love someone more than you love yourself . . . For a second I feel that I could sacrifice everything for him, my life, my career, and just be his wife. But that's a stupid idea. I put it out of my mind. I could never give up everything for someone else, the way so many women have done throughout history. Because I'm angry with these women, for what they've lost of themselves.

I ask Lou:

"Could you give up everything for me, for my book?"

"No, Vår, no."

"Why not?"

"Because you would never give up your book for me."

THE WORLD DOESN'T STOP
BECAUSE WE DO

THE AMERICAN HAS STOPPED calling, stopped leaving beautiful cello music on the answering machine. I decide to unpack my backpack. It smells of mold, sweat, foot odor, and something more masculine that doesn't belong to me. I'm unsentimental and throw the whole Velvet Underground look in the washing machine. I don't want to be nostalgic anymore. I want to wash away the memories.

Afterward I dress up in something colorful, something that goes with my yellow shoes. I'm restless and take the train to town. I walk past the building where I used to model naked, no. 7. Ground floor. The teacher must have replaced me by now, I think. It's cold outside, and windy. The curtains are only partly closed. I sit down on the ground and peep in through the gap. I glimpse a naked body, hairy legs, and a pair of butt cheeks . . . I don't believe my own eyes: the repulsive man!

I button my jacket and take the train home, weak and depressed. I masturbate. I think that to masturbate is a form of incest with oneself. I think about the repulsive man. That I get horny by thinking about him makes me hate myself. I wish my body was unfeeling. I light a match. I have given myself blisters deliberately. I'm angry with myself. I can't blame myself for declining the offer from the perverse artist who wanted to draw us, but not to work with Holly's class, that's unforgivable idiocy, I think, walk down to the living room, throw myself on the sofa and dial her number.

"Hello," she says.

"Hi," I answer.

"Oh, it's you, Vår? It's been a long time . . ."

"Much too long," I say. "I should've called . . . But you know how it is . . ."

"No, I don't."

"I have a thousand things to tell you," I say eagerly. "I didn't want to talk about the American before, because I've been very busy, but now I have time. Do you want me to drop in? I can bring a bottle of genever . . ."

"No, Vår, I don't want that."

"You don't?'

"No, you weren't there when I needed you. I've finished the painting now. I worked from memory. I had to. However, I sold it to a lord. He gave me a good price. I'm happy."

"Couldn't we at least have a cup of tea?" I ask, almost begging.

"I'll give you a call if I have some spare time."

"How's Henry?" I ask instead, as if to ignore that Holly is ignoring me.

"Good," she says.

In the background I hear a doorbell. Holly goes silent, finally she says:

"There's someone at the door."

"Yes, I can hear that," I answer.

"It's probably my model," she admits. "I'm sorry, Vår, but life goes on, with or without you . . ."

She hangs up. I sit there holding the phone. I need to talk to someone quickly, before I begin to cry. The only person I can think of is The Lover.

"Have you finished with the American?" he asks, pleased.

"Yes," I answer, sadly.

LA PHILOSOPHIE DANS LE BOUDOIR

RAGNHILD IS CLAUSTROPHOBIC. CANNOT bear the thought of someone owning her. She wants to be in love, yes, loved, yes, but married, no. And even if Cyril isn't a faithful man, and Ragnhild isn't "The Woman" for him, he wants them to marry immediately.

His voice tries to convince:

"No matter what happens, I'll always feel proud of having been married to you."

That's a nice thought, Ragnhild thinks, and understands that they'll always explore together. The meaning. It's like saying yes to wonder. A guarantee of progress, art, love, and understanding.

"Yes, I want to marry you."

She knows: egotist. That she wants to be an egotist. Prioritizing herself. Cyril. But no children. No excuses. Because she believes only cowards live for others. In the shadow. Of themselves. So she says yes to being self-centered. Together. Yes to being a couple. Inseparable. To love. Life. Good and bad. Until death . . .

L'amour, it was impossible not to see it, I think, and say:

"I want to look at photos."

Lou goes down to the living room and comes back with the rose-painted, rustic-romantic album. We look at my black cape, our white roses and Lou in a suit and top hat. We look at our serious *fuck you fuck off* expressions.

"Us against everyone else, that's what we wanted to be," Lou says dreamingly.

"Yes," I answer.

"But it didn't turn out like that."

"No."

"I wish I'd never watched the *Emmanuelle* films," he says. "That I hadn't grown up with that pouting mouth, her pear-like tits, and brown curls . . . That my father hadn't bought an exact copy of her famous chair and placed it in the bedroom . . . Because that's where 'she' belonged, he thought, in a fantasy, in the subconscious . . . with Freud . . ."

"And . . . ?"

"I fell in love with Emmanuelle, with the idea of an open relationship, you know that."

I nod.

"And I convinced you that that was right."

"Yes . . ."

"And that it wasn't difficult."

"No . . ."

"But it was wrong."

Cyril believes that Ragnhild doesn't suffer, that she doesn't know, the enormous sex drive: the unfaithfulness, the lies . . . He's in denial. Her questions become more and more intense, but he always stops just before the truth, just after the lie, when he believes he has fooled her.

LES CHOSES DE LA VIE

IT'S A COOL DAY, I'm cold. But I don't mind, rather the opposite, I like it. I sit on a bench and eat fish and chips with Lou. I see it as my duty to do this now and then, as long as I live in this country. I wash it down with ginger beer. Then I become more interested in reading the newspaper the fish is wrapped in than in the meal.

"Brighton Pier is now just a shadow of itself," I read and look at pictures of the ghostlike pier in ruins.

Lou also wants to look at what's now merely a scene from a horror movie. Still, it must have been a beautiful sight. Ocean and flames. A rare sight, I think, and throw the newspaper in a garbage bin filled to the brim, with the remains of the fish and chips. My fingers are stained with newspaper ink and fat, and perhaps my face too. Lou laughs and hands me a clean napkin.

We look at the Thames: it's dirty but still beautiful, just like London. We get up and start walking, away from St. Paul's Cathedral, across the Millennium Bridge, and over to the Tate Modern. Lou knows quite a few people who work there, but neither one of us is in the mood to go to an exhibition just now. We prefer just to walk. Walk along the Thames, perhaps down to London Bridge, or over to the Embankment. We can't decide. We just walk.

"I really wish I felt a craving for London," Lou says. "Of course I know that London is an exciting city, that lots of things are happening here, that it's a thousand times better than Bø in Telemark, but it doesn't interest me anymore."

"I'm tired of London too," I admit, to my own surprise. "I've been thinking about it for a long time, Lou, but now I'm certain, now I'm ready. I needed time to accept my own suggestion. Isn't that funny?"

"Yes."

I think: it's important to forget, so that new things can happen. To see Bø with new eyes. Not like the seventeen-year-old girl who went away, but the girl who came back.

7:

HAPHAZARDLY

We've never regretted leaving, but sometimes we've regretted staying, that's why we leave, we get on a boat taking us away from Great Britain, from the island and the island mentality: ocean, ocean as far as the eye can see. What we're trying to do is rid ourselves of the past by leaving it behind. It's a lovely feeling to see the mainland disappearing, to see all that has been our lives for such a long time becoming a tiny dot, disappearing . . .

I lean my head against the window and take pleasure in the distance getting greater and greater. I think: life is short, the world is big. I want the journey to take its time. I want to feel it, the move, mentally and physically. Know which country separates me from my old life, from the restlessness and the unfaithfulness. I wonder: why are we moving? Is it a confrontation, a rebellion or a change? Was it Lou who presented faithfulness as something attractive, something new, almost arousing it's so revolutionary?

Before we left, we sold all our furniture, along with the mannequins and most of the artworks that Lou had received, so we could have some money to live on for a while. And I don't regret it: it feels liberating to let go of material things, I'm thinking, and admire Michael Landry, who disposed of all his possessions and made the destruction process itself into a conceptual quasi-art.

I look at my husband with loving eyes. He is smoking and reading the newspaper.

"I wish you were more politically engaged," he suddenly says, looking up. "You, who are Billa Bergland the politician's daughter. I don't understand why you don't make use of the opportunity to write about America when you're writing about the American. Don't you feel that America is invading us, Vår, destroying us, that Europe has to fight to protect its culture?"

"Of course, but the American has nothing to do with America, in his case it's a nationality, not a political standpoint," I say. "Ever since I was a little girl, Mom has tried to recruit me to politics. Surely you can understand that's made me totally fed up with it," I add.

"No."

"The result is that I've almost become an illiterate, politically. In a sort of silly protest. I'm not proud of it, but I write first and foremost for myself. The Lover paints, the American plays, I write . . . but what about your therapy, Lou, is that me? Eternal married happiness . . . ?"

He doesn't answer.

"I'd rather live an interesting life than a happy life," I continue. "Actually, I can't think of anything worse that eternal happiness. Because what can I write about then?"

I notice that I've said something silly. Lou looks at me, dreamingly.

"You really don't know that, Vår? Now you disappoint me."

"All right then . . ." I pull on his loathsome roll-up and wait for the cruel answer I know is coming. "Out with it then, Lou, your sentence!"

"Do you really want to hear it?"

"No, but say it anyway. So we'll get it over with."

Lou becomes serious, solemn.

"You can write about other people's unhappiness, Vår, there's enough of that in the world."

WHITE RUSSIAN

I'M SWEATING. IT'S HOT. The waves are big, the ship is rocking, we're being thrust in all directions. Lou's face is taking on a green tinge.

"Are you feeling seasick, darling?" I ask.

He nods and sprints over to the rail. I dry his mouth after he's vomited. Lou is feverish, but I'm not worried about his germs. I begin to wish that the little boy I met when I was seven . . . well, I wish it could've been Lou at that time. And as I can choose, I decide that a meeting like that never took place, that we didn't go to Denmark, that there was no boat trip, or nausea, or American boy . . . That there was no childish love, and later, that there was no Lover either, no stranger . . . Because I want my husband to be the first, the only. For all the others to be merely literature.

I squint over at my sick husband and go to fetch him a glass of water. Lou is sitting on the floor now, exhausted. He's cold, curls up in a fetal position. But it doesn't help. He stands up, runs over to the rail, and pukes again. Lou's throwing up slowly turns into a weak sound in the background. My thoughts come to a halt. A few moments later we hang over the rail and spew as a duo.

I lie glued to the window in our cabin. I can see land in the distance. The ocean rolls calmly beneath us. After a stormy night, this is like a cuddly pussycat, I think, and look around, look at the Edvard Munch poster in its cheap plastic frame and the poor landscape watercolor of the Norwegian Trollfjord in Lofoten. Then I sneak a *Princess Ragnhild* ashtray down in my bag as a souvenir, as well as soap and shampoo, before I open the dresser drawer and nick the Bible too.

Lou is asleep on the floor in a corner. I help him up into the bed again without waking him up. The spewing finally finished him. I felt better, so I wandered around a bit, bought what we needed of smokes: Petterøe's tobacco and Vogue cigarettes, then I put some money into a slot machine, lost a few coins, and won them back again: played Las Vegas on the ocean.

"Can I buy you a drink?" a man asked eagerly and looked into my eyes—brown-blue, his were.

"Please."

He said he was a Berber, but didn't look like an Arab. He also said: "I'm an intellectual without a culture."

I liked that. Then he asked me if, instead of going to Norway, I'd like to come with him to Russia. It was tempting. I was surprised that I managed to say no, when I would rather have said yes.

LEAD US NOT INTO TEMPTATION . . .

I squeeze out the water in the blister on my heel and put on a Band-Aid. Then I wake up Lou.

"We'll be arriving soon, darling," I say and kiss my husband on the forehead. "You've got to get up, my dear."

"Where were you last night?" he asks instead.

"Weren't you asleep?"

"I woke up after a while, got up, and looked for you. I wanted to check . . ."

"Check what? I had a couple of drinks with a guy I met, if that's what you were wondering? And no, we didn't go to bed together."

The Berber looks at me with sad eyes as I disappear with my husband and all our goods and possessions into a taxi.

"Was he the one you met last night?" Lou asks.

"Yes."

"Is it difficult?"

"What?"

"To resist the temptation . . ."

"To resist the temptation is always difficult. But it's even worse not to have a temptation to resist," I say, but regret it immediately, because that's exactly why we're moving to Bø.

We fight to enter the train from Oslo to Kristiansand, jam our luggage into the baggage racks, and take the rest on our laps.

Lou sits and looks out the window. My husband loves this country, this nature, its endless forests, lakes, tarns, fields . . . like a dream. And I can really understand that, because the colors are irresistible now: yellow, red, orange . . . Autumn colors.

I do as he does—look at the landscape rushing past. I want to write about the people, the loneliness, and the language here. I feel at home but I'm a stranger, don't belong, can't express what I truly feel. The first thing I notice is an old concrete factory decorated with obscene graffiti. Trees and plants are growing through the broken windows and up the walls. I find what most people think is ugly, I think is nice, and recognize Sidney in myself. I study how everything comes closer. The stations fly past, Sandvika, Drammen, Kongsberg, Nordagutu . . . I'm thinking about how infinitely close Bø feels.

FALLING TREES

Everyone is there on the big day, the whole Bergland family. They wave to us from Bø station. Mom is running toward us with such a speed that she almost scares me while my big brother August observes us in the background. I notice that he gets more and more uncouth every time I see him. He is still handsome in his own somewhat irritating way. I look around and suddenly discover his bitch. It hits me how old and gray Dandelion has become. How can she be bothered to cling to this doggy life, I wonder, while Mom tries to gather us together for a group photo.

"Smile, smile!" she says.

Dad spends an eternity getting the self-timer to function before he too runs into the photo.

What have I done? Suddenly it seems like a mystery to me. I cry and cry. Everyone thinks it's because I'm so moved, but I'm scared. Panicky. I notice all color has drained from my face, my head is buzzing, and suddenly I'm lying on the ground with everyone bent over me. My parents are talking and talking, but I can't hear anything, as if some mechanism in my head has turned down the volume. My father is shaking me so hard it hurts, trying to bring me back to life. I want to tell him that he must handle me carefully, but I can't get out a single sound. Besides, I want to go on lying here. I notice how exhausted I am: sleep, sleep . . . only sleep, and for days. That's what tempts me more than anything now. To close my eyes.

"Vår!"

I see a clutter of colors, different nuances of blue, gray, brown, and green. I stand up. Because I can't stay lying on the ground. I'm about to sit down in the big family car. But all I see is August's metal-blue Opel Ascona with its worn zebra cover, the sooty windows, the Wunder-Baum air-freshener, and the dice . . . I look confusedly at Mom.

She says:

"You know your father, Vår. The Volvo refused to start this morning. Only to be expected. It's old and should be traded in soon, just like Dandelion. But oh no . . . Aslak won't be beaten by a technical glitch. The result is that our garden has become a repair shop."

Dad is looking shyly at me, his face turning red. I smile reassuringly and get into August's car. I use the horn several times, impatiently. Then I remember all the luggage and jump out again to help. I notice that Mom notices that Lou has cut his hair, and that she doesn't say anything, no one says anything, everyone misses his curls.

"There isn't room for everyone," Dad says, "so I'll jog home."

"No, no . . ." I say. "That's out of the question."

But we don't have a choice, the car's full, Lou and I are definitely too tired to walk, Dandelion's too frail, and Mom . . . well, Mom doesn't want to walk either . . . So off we drive.

August puts on loud music and steps on the gas. The first song is "Jolene" by Dolly Parton, a song I like as well. I'm surprised that we have anything in common. He turns up the sounds, but when I sing along, he gets embarrassed and turns it off.

We drive through the center of Bø—the famous downtown of Bø, which in the evening changes into a veritable rally paradise. But now it's quiet. It isn't late enough for the girls to go to the trouble of waiting on the benches along the road, or for the boys to pick them up. For the moment, Bø is a nice sleepy little village in Norway.

August still hasn't said a word. He is driving, that's his language, I think: speed. Everyone knows everyone here, when a car drives past they stare. It's not bad manners, it's the countryside. From the time I was a little girl, I quickly began to talk the other dialect, the one you don't speak in the village. I think I did it to defy my parents, to be independent. But now I almost regret it. Because I talk like any Oslo girl, while they speak in a unique way, like genuine Bø people.

August turns right up the Gymnasbakken, Dandelion puts half her body in my lap, drools, and dirties my skirt. In the background there are two churches, the one Lou and I got married in, and the other one. They stand there, nice and grand, as if they stood in heaven. We continue to drive over Langkåshaugen, down the hill, across the river, and past the village museum. August still doesn't say anything, while Mom just keeps talking. Because Billa loves Lou, and he does his best to answer in his charming Norwegian. My husband can roll his r's, but still has a strong French accent, which I find delightful.

Then we turn left, to Ryevegen 9, Otterholt farm. When we enter the yard, the first thing I notice is the old car we once took to Denmark. Taken apart, it seems more like a toy than a vehicle, I think, and almost find it sweet. Then the sight of the new house whips me like a lash in the darkness. I search for the old one, the remains of it. But there's nothing there anymore. All that's left of the past is a ramshackle red barn. Besides, the leaves have begun falling from the trees, lying over the grave, dead and rotten.

Ravn and Ronja walk into the forest with their father to fell the trees they're going to use to build the new house, next to the old one, which burned down. It's a romantic idea to use their own resources, Ragnhild thinks. And they smell wonderfully of sweet pine when they come home in the evening.

Ragnhild believes this was when they got closer to each other.

Could have gotten. That the opportunity was there, if they'd only taken it. This is what she believes: that they get nervous in each other's company. This likeness. Physical. That they look like each other. A little too much, but never enough. She observes the uncertainty that creeps into them both and becomes part of their personality. This lack of communication that's so typical between father and son. This deficiency.

HEIL

NOTHING IS BETTER THAN simple country food when you haven't tasted it in a while, I think, just as Lou exclaims:

"Whole milk is *Heilmjølk*, just as in *Heil Hitler*," and laughs.

Then he continues to discuss politics with Mom while August is silent, Dandelion lies in her corner, and Dad and I chat about everything and nothing.

After we've finished supper and my husband says: "Thanks for the lovely food, in an hour or two, it'll fall in the loo . . ." in his charming Norwegian, and we go into the living room to watch the news.

Mom is addicted to keeping informed, at least three times a day, preferably more. Dad says it's an illness, that no one needs to be that informed. So Mom makes an effort to wean herself off the evening news, she's on a diet, as Dad says. But she falls off the wagon all the time, like someone who can't stop smoking.

While the others are watching the news, I walk over to the bookshelf by the fireplace. I take down a couple of books and leaf through them, without being aware of what I'm reading. Mom buys the best books, but doesn't read them. Dad's books aren't so good, but at least he reads them. August neither buys nor reads books, I think, and put them back. I glance at him surreptitiously. If our parents hadn't been there like a link between us, I think we would simply have forgotten each other . . .

"Shh," Lou says.

Mom reluctantly turns down the sound while we prick up our ears.

The fox farm: it's always given my husband bad dreams. Because he's never gotten used to the sound of the heart-wrenching scream of the fox. We're very silent.

"Shh," Lou says again.

Mom turns off the sound.

The screams of the fox sound like babies crying.

When Ragnhild was a little girl, she used to sneak down to the fox farm and watch the animals, fascinated. She had heard that the carcasses were sent to a factory abroad and that parts of the animal cadavers were used to produce glue. She watched the foxes being laid out on a table, getting one peg put on their rectum and one on their snout. The pegs were fastened to an electric lead. Death was almost instantaneous, and reminiscent of an execution by electric chair. Afterward the cadavers were flayed. Now and then Ragnhild got blood on her face, fox blood. It was almost a little pleasurable.

STRANGER THAN PARADISE

I WAKE UP WITH Lou's congealed semen on my stomach. I try to remember what I was dreaming and in which language, but I can't remember anything, total blackout. When I lived in France, I used to dream with Norwegian subtitles, while in England, my dreams were dubbed.

I look around, look up into the ceiling, hear steps above my head: Mom, Dad, August, and Dandelion, how they wander about. The day started for them some time ago. I wonder what time it is. But then I decide not to check after all. Because time doesn't exist here in the countryside, not for us anyway, the vagabonds.

Someone's going to the toilet. The water is being flushed right above our heads. All the pipes in the house end up here in the basement. There was a flooding in Bø in 1987 that rotted all woodwork, so now there's a moldy greenish look to things down here.

I get up, sneak around in this universe that will be our future home, at least for a while. Last night I hung the *Nostalgia* poster above our bed, like an icon, and put up the photo of Sidney on the Rock in the staircase.

I go into the bathroom to wash off the semen with *Princess Ragnhild* soap. Lou likes to take me dry, to push into me without warning. But the dryness doesn't last for long, I think, and wet a washcloth.

Afterward I go up to the ground floor. Through the window, I get a glimpse of the ramshackle red barn and the orange

threshing machine with Dad on it. It's sad to see the corn disappearing, I think, and make rosehip tea, take out Dad's homemade bread and Mom's unforgettable plum jam, along with
some *heilmjølk*. Then I wake up my husband.

"My whole life I give you nothing, and you still ask for
more . . ." I whisper in his ear.

"What?"

"Gilbert and George," I answer. "1–0 to me."

After we've finished breakfast, we go for a walk in the fairytale
forest, which is my forest. At the end of April, it's full of anem-
ones, and then nothing is lovelier, I think, as we climb the tree
with a hole in its branch. When I was a little girl, I used to climb
all the way up to that hole and whisper my secrets into it. It was
a kind of confession, I think, and jump down again. I stay sitting
under the tree, watching the leaves falling. I'm impressed by the
way they float down, graciously.

"Once while I was sleeping I peed on my sister because I
dreamed she was a tree," Lou says, and jumps down too.

I start to laugh. I get confused.

"You don't have a sister," I say and burst out laughing.

"Klaus Kinski, you idiot," Lou says. "1–1."

LUST

I keep working on *Anatomy. Monotony.* until early morning. A comma . . . That's what keeps me awake. I love to stay up wondering where to put it. Because it can change everything: rhythm, pauses, meaning. I'm awake, tired, because of a pathetic comma. I hear steps. I close my eyes immediately, lie down with my head on the pillow, and imitate heavy, calm breathing.

Lou creeps into my room, reads secretly from my computer, before he saves what I've written and closes it down. Then he lifts my body and carries me down to the basement bed, tucks me in, and turns out the light.

"I'm glad we were able to change before it was too late. That we stopped playing," he says and kisses my lips. Almost sucks them. Then he too takes off his clothes and lies down under the duvet with me.

"You're my wife," he continues solemnly. "For better and for worse. Until death do us part."

I feel his naked body next to mine. My heart, my pulse . . . it's as if a hammer has been let loose inside me. It's almost repugnant to be this horny. I turn over on my side. Lou lies close to me, pushes himself inside me, carefully. I pretend that I'm dreaming. Wriggle back and forth and utter small moans as if I'm having a nightmare. I notice that it titillates him. He grows inside me. Soon I can't stand it any longer. I scream. Like a fox. Lou comes. I can feel him shuddering for a long time afterward. I open my eyes. Frustrated. I would love to come, too, but Lou has already lit one of my cigarettes.

"Sorry I woke you up," he says with a smile. Exhausted. "Are you hungry?" he asks.

≈ CAIN AND ABEL

TIME PASSES IN A leisurely manner like nature does when it changes seasons, almost invisibly, and then suddenly you notice. We jump in the hay in the barn, go for walks in the mountains, drive to Helvetesholet, walk to Kvennøya to admire the Bø waterfall, watch Ivo Caprino films . . . do everything I remember from my childhood. There's only one thing that ruins it for me, and that's August. Every time he's in the vicinity, it's like he's carrying around a cloud, a warning of stormy weather. He doesn't have to say or do anything, his presence is enough to annihilate mine. Because I feel uncomfortable in my big brother's presence, my voice starts to tremble. Mom tells us that August has decided not to open his mouth unless he has something interesting to say, that he's just like Dad right after the fire. I ask Mom how long it's been since he's had something interesting to say. She doesn't answer.

When I think about my big brother and me, I think about two trees in each other's garden that stop the evening sun from shining in. I think that my big brother is dreaming about taking an ax and cutting me down. An ax like the one he cut his own head with. There's no visible mark from it now. The scar is hidden beneath his strawberry blond hair. It was an accident, Mom has decided.

One day Ravn goes into the forest alone, without his dog and his father. He stays away for several hours. When he returns, he has an ax in his head. He doesn't scream, doesn't cry either, he doesn't say a word. He just stands in the garden, smiling, with an ax in his head. He is wearing his best clothes: the much-too-short, light blue confirmation suit and the pink synthetic leather tie. He seems blessed. Ragnhild is almost proud of her big brother. For the first time she feels a kinship with Ravn, feels that the same blood is coursing through their veins.

No one says a word. Ragnhild is holding her breath. He stands there like a statue, proud and honorable. Ragnhild looks at her watch. It has stopped. She looks at her mother. She has fainted. Ravn still doesn't move. Ragnhild tries to call her father, but can't get a word out. She doesn't know what to do, so she just stands there, letting things happen. She watches her brother's face go white, then he falls down, lies lifeless on the floor, smiling.

Ragnhild later thinks that the fire was to blame, that the damage had always been there, the shock, but that the wound that had been too obvious inside them, well, the same wound had grown inside Ravn like a sort of tumor, first around the heart, and then slowly, but surely, it had moved to the brain.

KITCHEN STORIES

WRITING IS LIKE CREATING a child: it has your blood, your genes, but in the end, it is something else, with its own personality, its own life, different starting points, but still related, I think, as Mom calls out that dinner's ready. I save what I've written and run downstairs. I say hi to Mom and sit down at the kitchen bench the way I used to do when I was a girl, look out the window, and wait for the others. The field looks like a black ocean where Dad's used the plow. I can hear him in the laundry. He's taking off his rubber boots, overalls and washing his hands. To work with the earth, to burrow your fingers into it, that's something I know he likes. When the snow comes and covers everything, it's like a duvet covering Dad as well, I think, and let him scratch my back with his broken farm hands.

"How's the writing?" he asks lovingly.

"Good. I'd wanted *Anatomy. Monotony* to be a book about me, but it didn't turn out like that. Because the more I imagine, the closer I get to reality, isn't that strange?"

"Yes."

"Even as I try to write it the way it really was, is, I no longer recognize it."

"Mm . . ." Dad says as Lou comes into the kitchen with August and Dandelion.

They've gone for a walk in the forest again. Dandelion lies on the floor like a slaughtered animal while August and Lou seem as secretive as a pair of teenagers. I watch them and feel a sting of jealousy. Because Lou does with August what he did with Sidney, he is leaving . . . me.

He comes over to me and gives me a kiss. We sit down, the whole Bergland family and Lou, and eat a lovely dinner while Dandelion looks at us with hungry eyes. Mom's pizza is famous: mince, the mushroom, onion, dry mustard . . . Lou's version is good too, but nothing beats the original, I think, and cut off a large piece before I pass it on. Someone's smacking their lips. I'm not certain who. We don't talk, which says everything about the food. The phone rings. Mom gets up and goes into the hall.

"Billa Bergland," she says. B. B. as in Brigitte Bardot, I think and laugh while Mom says *oui, oui* and *très bien* and other French words while she looks helplessly over at Lou.

"It's your father," she whispers.

He gets up and walks into the hall. Closes the door. Lou hates anyone to watch him doing something he's bad at: talking on the phone. Mom tiptoes back. I take a sip from the beer and cut myself another piece of pizza. I make a mess. Soon my face is covered in sauce.

"What plans does Lou have while you're staying in Bø?" Dad asks suddenly, and helps himself to a large piece of pizza too.

"He likes to go for walks," I say and try not to look angrily at August.

"He can just walk and walk. That's why it's good to be here. What I hope is that he's going to discover something on one of his walks, a passion."

"Yes, let's hope that," Mom says.

"Yes," Dad says. "Are you happy to be back in Bø?" he asks.

"It's strange. Lovely and nauseating at the same time," I answer. "It's such a contrast to London. But now and then, nature can communicate as much as people can, more perhaps . . ."

"Yes," Dad says, chews and swallows. Then he takes a sip of beer as well. "If you listen to nature, you always learn something," he says. A magnificent bull elk walks across the lawn. "I feel that I'm in harmony with nature. I'm sure that I was an elk or a tree in another life."

I smile, Aslak Bergland as the king of the forest, I'd like to believe that, I think, and continue eating.

Lou comes back. But something is wrong, he sits down silently, like August usually does, and continues where he left off eating. I notice that August is looking at him, studying all of him, as if he liked him.

"How's your father?" Dad finally asks.

"Not so good," Lou answers. "Dad's started working again. But he isn't helping the patients, he just sympathizes with them. He hardly has any patients left. He knew it himself, that the ones you treat badly are faithful for the rest of their lives, while the ones you treat well go off immediately and find a new psychiatrist . . ."

We clear the table, go into the living room and turn on the evening news.

"Is it really like that?" Mom finally asks.

"Yes, that's what it's like. When patients talk about how depressed they are, Dad answers that he can really understand that, as terrible as this world of ours is . . . His patients don't make any progress, they just become as ill as ill can be."

MELANCHOLY AND THE SEAGULL

I SEE THEM DISAPPEARING: Lou, August, and Dandelion. I see them sit down in the Opel Ascona and drive off. I see that my husband tries not to be like Lou. I force myself to think that it's good that "the boys" can do something together, without me, something masculine. That's something I'm missing: femininity. A girlfriend, not just an old lover I can call. I look at myself in the mirror, feel sorry for the mirror image and take a bite of milk chocolate, not because I'm hungry, but out of old habit. Perhaps I ought to start eating baked beans instead, something nostalgic from England? I muse.

I am totally silent. Listening to . . . myself. To how I am, inside. The uncertainty is always lurking, waiting to take root in me. In Bø, it doesn't take much before I begin to feel small and insignificant. I sit still and listen to the silence. It's incredible how silent it can be in the countryside. So silent you can hear the bird wings like a lonely ballad, yes, so silent you can hear yourself think.

I look at the computer: nothing happens, no miracles. The desk: the same one I've had all my life, four drawers on each side, all full. I close them again and try to concentrate. On the shelf next to the desk is a book by Jon Fosse. I would rather read that than writing myself. I tell myself that for each sentence I write, I can read a sentence in his *Melancholy*. But there is this one sentence. I can't find it, instead I walk over to the window as if in a trance, light a match, and take it over to the flowered seventies curtains that I used to love.

"Vår!" someone is calling. "Vår, are you there?"

"Yes . . ." My heart is beating. I blow out the match, sit down on the small bed, agitated, breathless . . . "Come in!" I call back.

Mom is looking at me from the doorway.

"Am I disturbing you?"

"Yes, but come in anyway."

She sits down on the small bed, holding a pile of political documents. By giving me life, she also gave me death, I think, find a pack of Vogues, and light a cigarette. Then I hand one to her as well, *my murderer*. We are silent. We listen together to the sounds of cigarettes. Seagulls. I ask Mom about the seagulls, how long they have been here and how they came here. She explains that a few years ago, Norwegian seagulls began to emigrate inland.

"Do you think you can finish writing your book here?" she asks, anxiously.

"I really hope so," I answer.

My head is whirling in every direction. To be back in the village of my childhood has had an effect on me, like the slide of snow from a roof. Now I'm lying on the ground covered in all the dirt.

LA CORRIDA

RAVN, RONJA, AND CYRIL kill time in Ravn's hot rod. Cyril is studying this phenomenon from the inside. He's playing with the dice hanging from the rearview mirror, playing the dice-man, watching cars parked in rows at the petrol station. Ravn opens a bottle of beer and gives it to Cyril, then he opens one for himself too.

"Cheers."

Ronja is lying on the backseat enjoying herself. She loves to be one of the boys. She is patient, old, and refuses to die . . . Ravn is waiting for darkness to fall, for the streets to empty; the two streets making up the town center. So they can start the game. There's a strong wind. The police radios are on at full volume. The atmosphere is on pause. The streets empty. Slowly. No one is in a hurry on an evening like this. Saturday. The clocks are ticking. It's getting late. One beer, two . . .

Cyril can't remember anything anymore. Alcohol. In his blood. He wants to go home to bed. To go home to Ragnhild. Feel her warm body against his cold one. Sleep. But Ravn tells him he has to stay, that this night will be different from the usual ones. Cyril is counting cars. He moves from twenty and down. He counts the cars disappearing. The streets emptying.

Two hours later there's oil on the street and the cars are racing each other, gliding down, making stripes, back and forth the same stretch. Even the odd tractor is taking part in the game . . . The wind is blowing in the street signs and makes strange sounds. There's kissing and fucking. Texas . . . in Bø, Cyril thinks, and looks around. He notices that something is happening, something that shouldn't have happened. Everyone is holding their breath. Over there on the footpath is a student with long black hair and black clothes. Everyone obviously is thinking about it, but only one loses control, and that's Ravn. He opens the car door, runs down the footpath . . . Ronja tries to run after him, but isn't able to catch him. She stops, breathless, and watches, she too is a spectator now. Ravn is furious. Ravn hits out. Cyril thinks that it's like a corrida the way it is in the arena in Nîmes, in his hometown. Because to be a student surrounded by joyriders is just like being a bull in the arena, it's suicide.

EMPEROR NERO'S JOY . . .

I'M LOOKING AT MY watch. It's late. The sky is full of stars. I can see that Saturday is about to become Sunday. I miss Sunday being meaningful. I establish that my husband is still out with my big brother and his old bitch instead of being home with me. I take out the Bible from *Princess Ragnhild* and begin to look through it. I never used to read the Bible voluntarily, eagerly, as I read it now. The Bible is an artful book, I think, I don't know whether it makes me foolish, or wise, or if I may as well be reading a cookbook . . . I put it aside, make myself comfortable in the chair, and close my eyes. Things don't stop existing just because they no longer are, I think.

Outside the sky is raging. The wind sounds like a wolf singing in the treetops. I like a bit of rough weather, to feel it on my body, get red cheeks, become really cold or wet, I think. How lovely.

I lie down on the small bed and feel something sharp under the mattress, something that must have been there all the time, but that I've overlooked. I put my hand in, find a book, open it at random, and read:

"Knut Hamsun had developed an erotic passion for light— sunlight, lamplight, even ordinary daylight; Drude Janson thought he had gone mad. She was shocked when she entered his room one day and saw that he stood looking at the curtain he himself had set alight. The sight of the flames gave him a strong satisfaction, and he told her that he could really understand Emperor Nero's joy at watching Rome burning."

I believe in the meaning of the accidental.

I, A WOMAN

IT'S SO LATE THAT it's early. The sun is winking at me from above the mountain. I'm thinking about women in literature and wondering whom I like best. I love Lila in *Lila Said*, Catherine in *The Garden of Eden*, Hermine in *Steppenwolf*, and Velma in *Velma Variations*. That is the kind of woman I want Ragnhild to be: playful, different, amoral . . . A woman Hamsun would like to dislike, I think, or Thomas Bernhard . . . one of history's many ingenious male chauvinists. I want Ragnhild to be a woman who ridicules all men who are hostile to women. They fear her just because they haven't met her . . . I think.

There's a knock on the door.

"Don't come in!" I scream. Lou puts his head carefully through the door anyway. "Lou, mon chou . . . Are you back already?" I ask.

"Am I disturbing you?"

"No. Everyone else disturbs me, but you—never," I answer.

"I hope you'll take the time to describe these strange feelings of alienation in your own home. The sudden light, the accommodating forest . . ." Lou says then.

I look at him, surprised.

"Did you have a good time with August?" I ask instead.

"Yes."

"Really?"

"Yes," Lou repeats, takes off all his clothes, and jumps on top of me.

"What are you talking about . . . ?" I ask from the floor.

"Nothing."

"Nothing?"

"There are a thousand other ways of communicating . . ." he says mysteriously.

"That's true, but . . . August has never left home, he must seem so boorish to you . . ."

"There are many ways of traveling too," Lou continues in his mysterious way, and takes off my sweater, pants, and thick socks . . .

I feel the cold floor against my naked body. Lou smiles slyly. As if he knows something I don't . . . I kiss the small hollow in his neck, just at the hairline. Then I turn over on my stomach. I like that it's hard, uncomfortable. Lou enters so far into me that it almost hurts.

"I've noticed something terrible," I suddenly say.

"What, darling?"

"The egotism, Lou, egotism . . ."

"What do you mean, Vår?"

"The orgasm, Lou, orgasm."

"I don't understand . . ."

"Me neither, but now I see it so clearly."

"What?"

We change position. Lou prefers that I'm on top.

"I've become more and more masculine. Have you noticed?" I ask.

"Masculine?"

"Yes, I'm no longer satisfied unless I come. Like a man who hasn't had an orgasm, I'm first and foremost seeking my own pleasure. Now and then I forget my partner, just like you."

We change position again. I prefer Lou to be on top.

"That's fine, Vår, just forget me. But it's easier to have an orgasm if you forget yourself."

LE VOYEUR

I LIGHT A CIGARETTE. Lou takes a couple of drags too. Then we go down to the basement and lie on the bed. I like it to be soft, warm, not sexual. On the shelf in front of us is a green papier-mâché sculpture I gave Lou one Christmas many years ago. It's a kind of portrait of him as a thin sexy singer with a silver cock and a snake microphone. Lou the Martian, I think, because he really lives on another planet. He has seemed so distant lately . . .

Cyril is walking around in the many hallways. It's a large wooden house. He tiptoes into the toilet. But as he turns on the light, the radio comes on automatically. He thinks that this must be his father-in-law's idea. It's a good idea, but at night it's a nuisance. You tiptoe into the toilet and end up waking the whole house because of the damn radio. Cyril almost has to smile. He creeps out again. As he closes the door and turns off the light, the radio goes silent too.

He walks past Ørnulf and Dagny's room. He wonders where they are, if they're inside or outside. He bends down and looks discreetly through the keyhole.

The first thing he notices is the morning sun coming in through the open window, making a stripe on the floor. On this stripe stands his mother-in-law, naked, smoking a Vogue her daughter has given her—like an Edward Hopper picture, The Woman in the Sun, *1961, Cyril thinks. Because he remembers details like that, he who has worked in a gallery. The loneliness, the longing, the melancholia . . . All this is to be found in Dagny's naked figure,*

321

in her posture. The cigarette is burning and burning, soon there is only ash left. Cyril is wondering what she is seeing, what is happening behind the open window. Or is she just standing there lost in her own thoughts, looking at the foliage, the leaves falling from the trees . . .

TAXIDERMY EPIDEMIC

Two months later:

Lou and August are inseparable. I work and work while they laze around: it irritates me. Because I want a husband I can be proud of, one who creates, like The Lover and the American.

I take a break from writing out in the yard. I kick the ground and watch the small pebbles rolling across the gravel. I pick up a handful and throw them straight up.

"I had that many, I gave away that many, I got that many back . . ."

If I sharpen my senses, I can almost feel August's presence in his absence, I think, and go back into the house. I sneak up the stairs and into my big brother's room . . . August and Vår . . . Why were we given names like that? I ask myself and whirl around until I feel queasy. I don't really like merry-go-rounds, rollercoasters, things like that. I feel dizzy and lean on a shelf. I grab something raw and yucky that looks like a dead mouse and drop it immediately. I'm about to scream, but then I remember that I'm not in my own room. I look around. In a corner on the floor, the mouse's pelt is squeezed flat. Then I see a kind of mini sculpture in glass fibers imitating it. What the hell does this mean? I ask myself, and to my great surprise I find a book on the bedside table with the explanation.

"Taxidermy comes from Greek, means the arrangement of skin, and is the art of making dead animals look alive," I read.

Further down I learn that you often start by freezing the dead animal before you fleece it, flatten the pelt, and treat it for later use. Then you make a sculpture that the pelt can be fastened to, as well as glass eyes, false teeth, a false tongue . . .

This is sick, I think, and put the book away. I can't believe it, that August believes it, that he can give Dandelion eternal life by stuffing her like a toy . . . His whole room is full of pictures of this bitch. He has even hung up the one of the family in front of the fire where she appears like a stroke of felt pen above us.

I feel queasy and lie down on the bed, on a hairbrush with strawberry blond strands of hair in it. I pull them out, twist them together, and put them around my neck like necklace, a bit like the one the American once wanted to make from my hair, I think, and tighten it. Strangling is supposed to be erotically stimulating, but it doesn't work for me. All I can think of is Dandelion. I tighten it even more. When I was a little girl, I often tried to strangle myself to test God, to see if He would do anything to keep me alive . . . My face turns red. I let go. I'm too curious to choose death. Too old to believe in God . . .

ELK IN DECLINE

Mom calls "Dinner's ready!" I run out of August's room, but then I stop. Because I suddenly remember that I'm already sick and tired of the Norwegian country food . . . tired of it all. The honeymoon is over. I'm no longer nostalgic for everything Norwegian. I'm longing for something that isn't, something I don't know anything about.

I hear a shot, then another, and another . . . I run down the stairs and halfway I meet Mom, Dad, August, Dandelion, and Lou . . . in the apple garden lies the king of the forest. His blood is running out of his body and down onto the yellowing grass. A new specimen for August, I think callously, while the hunters carry the elk away. Lou collapses. He begins to cry. He's more vulnerable when it comes to animals, I think. Because even if he knows about bullfighting in the arenas of Nîmes, he's used to meat being something you find nicely wrapped on supermarket shelves, not a beautiful animal running free in nature.

HAPPY TOGETHER

SHOCKED, I WALK BACK to my room and sit down in front of the computer again. I dream about this book. About opening it, reading it, smelling it, closing it. Soon. I feel that the end is breathing on me. I make myself comfortable. Am I relaxed? Do I have everything I need? Are my feet cold? Am I hungry? No. My fingers are sweaty and yucky. Everything is as it should be. I look out the window. Winter will be here soon, I think, and it will cover everything, and soon I'll disappear as well . . . I don't say a word. Concentrate. But words become everything.

Cyril feels like a bird. A bird of passage. Where Ragnhild goes, he follows. He has no Plan B. Didn't put any cushions under the window. He just jumped.

He sits down on the bench in the street. Then he takes the tobacco out of the inside pocket of his jacket and starts to roll a cigarette. This is something he is good at, this "handiwork." No one rolls a cigarette as elegantly as he does. Smoking always legitimizes waiting, he thinks, and takes a deep drag. Because even if no one comes, you can sit and do nothing with a cigarette in your hand.

He looks at the joyriders. They're driving up and down the street at least sixty-four times, some more than that, but he can't be bothered to continue counting them. Finally there's Ravn in his hot-rod car with Ronja. Cyril puts out the cigarette under his shoe and goes to sit in the car with them. It's great to just drive back and forth like this, he thinks, it's like being rocked to sleep.

"Do you have a light?" Ravn asks while Ronja licks his face.

"Of course."

Cyril takes his lighter from his inside pocket. He likes how the flame throws light on the ruined face of Ragnhild's big brother. Because Ravn always has a black eye or some other injury from a fight. The only thing missing to make him really handsome is a broken nose or tooth, Cyril thinks, and almost falls asleep. Without Cyril noticing, Ravn drives him back to the farm. Here he stops and opens the door, so that Cyril can go home to his little sister and sleep. But Cyril remains in the car. He thinks it's important to test himself, see how far he can go . . . He closes the door, opens his eyes.

Ravn steps on the gas pedal and doesn't stop until they've reached Lifjell. Then he runs out of the car and into the lovely mountain air that makes his head whirl more than alcohol, Cyril thinks, and hurries after him.

"Wait!" he calls.

Cyril can hardly see anything, just the starry sky, hardly hear anything, just the silence and Ronja rambling around in her old and worn-out way. Then they're suddenly standing right next to each other. Cyril looks into Ravn's gray-blue eyes, and sees that they have a yellow ring around the iris, just like Ragnhild's, as if they're on fire.

JE SERAIS L'OMBRE DE TON CHIEN

ALL I CAN THINK of is my husband, and my big brother. "What's interesting about your brother, Vår, is that he has this naivety combined with a kind of wisdom," Lou once told me. "Because August is definitely a country boy, slow: his steps, his thinking . . . but also a savage: a true joyrider driving rallies through the streets, fighting, and wearing cowboy boots. I like him because I don't understand him. The lines of his mouth just barely turn up at the edges and give him a kind of charm. When he smiles, I see you, Vår."

I continue writing. But I don't know why I bother. I'll never finish anyway, never get it finished as long as we can't finish with others, I think, and feel a sting inside me, feel it hurting.

I leave the computer on and run out in desperation. I need air. I hear the sound of dead leaves against my feet, a hissing, whispering, living sound. I run down to the waterfall. The water's cold. Soon it will turn into ice. The sun is still shining, a sun that seeps through your clothes, a persistent sun you mustn't allow to tempt you. It's so easy to take your clothes off for the sun, I think, and button my jacket.

I look for Lou, but don't find him by the waterfall. I run into the forest: the rustling of trees trying to shake off their dry leaves drives me crazy. I want to ask nature to be quiet. But then I think, it's important to approach nature without prejudice, to judge it on its own terms. Because nature shouldn't have to adjust itself to us. We should adjust ourselves to it, I think and look everywhere.

Ragnhild is bored. She walks into the forest, deeper and deeper. She hears a sound and walks in its direction. Her heart is pounding. There's something about this sound, something piercing. Like long nails against a blackboard. Ragnhild feels almost intoxicated. This screaming. It hurts to listen to it. But she doesn't cover her ears, rather the opposite, she sharpens them. Then she screams.

    Ronja is lying way down a hole, caught in an animal trap. Why isn't she with Ravn and Cyril? Ragnhild pats her head lovingly. Coolly. She's never been especially fond of animals. Ronja licks her face gratefully. That irritates Ragnhild. That Ronja doesn't notice. The coldness.

    She still doesn't expect this, what she does then. It's as if she isn't herself anymore, but as if something else acts via her, something instinctive . . . A hatred. A moment of intense and unfounded jealousy. Ragnhild cries. Ronja licks her tears. But instead of freeing the poor, innocent, lost . . . Ragnhild squeezes, as hard as she can. She is sweating, sweating, biting her teeth together . . . And Ronja's half-blind eyes, she can't bear thinking about them, begging her . . . Ragnhild runs away. She had held life and death in her hands, and she chose death.

FADE OUT

LOU ENTERS MY ROOM at a run, without knocking. He insists that he was looking for me earlier. He asks where I was. I answer that I was looking for him. I look at myself in the mirror. Like a Dorian Gray character, I expect the worst, a scar on my soul, a sign. But nothing is visible.

"Have you seen Dandelion?" Lou asks in a worried voice.

"No, isn't she with you?" I answer in an unnaturally loud voice.

"We went for a walk in the forest, we were talking, we forgot her. When we remembered her, she was gone."

I stay silent. Don't say a word. Don't know whether I'm happy or jealous, angry or proud. My brother's probation is over, I think. Then we both go silent. In this silence there's an expectation of the other. I turn away from the mirror. Our whole lives we see ourselves inverted, and we believe it's right, then know it's not right, but believe it is anyway, as we can never see our true selves. Lou looks into my eyes. In his eyes I see myself. It has started to blow outside. I wish that the loneliness would spread itself around me like a Russian shawl embroidered with roses.

"We have to get away from Bø," I say finally. "We've been here for two months, can you believe it?"

"Yes, Vår, I can, and it's been lovely. You and I, and nature. I haven't missed her one bit."

"Who?"

"Sid, of course."

I grab his short hair, pull and tug . . . But Lou doesn't fall. Instead he hits back, even harder. My cheek is burning.

"To betray me in Bø is to betray me doubly," I tell him. "Everyone knows who I am. That I'm the deceived wife. It's difficult. I mean, it's difficult to live in such a small place. That's why we have to move away from Bø," I repeat. "I was right, because even if it was my suggestion, I knew deep down it was a kind of utopia to believe we could live in the country."

Lou sits down on my small bed, finds his tobacco, and rolls a cigarette. In the background we hear August's desperate shouts for Dandelion.

"You weren't right, Vår, you're scared, that's something else," he says.

I give him *Princess Ragnhild*'s ashtray and a lighter.

"Scared . . . ?" I ask, startled.

"Of finishing your novel, of binding yourself, staying in Bø, being with me . . . That's why you're making up a totally improbable story. Feeding your fantasy the way you feed a stuffed animal . . ."

"Have you read what I'm writing?" I ask worriedly.

"Yes. When I was looking for you earlier, your computer was on. I thought it was an invitation."

My face changes color.

"That you fantasize about your brother and me is one thing, but that you actually believe in it, that's incredible . . . Perhaps you do it because you want something to happen. Something you can't put into words."

I breathe a sigh of relief. I had been thinking something else. I give away nothing. Instead I say:

"Now you're making matters worse than ever, darling. You're making me feel like an idiot. Either I have to leave you or forgive you. I haven't decided yet."

"That's the stupidest thing I've ever heard," Lou says, and adds: "I've been thinking for a long time what mark I'm going to leave behind. I was seeking some kind of passion, something you could be proud of. You know how interested I am in art?"

I nod.

"But even if I wanted to be like The Lover, I'm no painter. That's why I wanted you to forget him. What I hadn't considered was that you could forget me too. That hurt, of course. But I couldn't hate the other one either, the American, because his bow made such magical sounds."

I nod again.

"'What's your therapy?'" you asked me arrogantly on the ship. Oh yes, I noticed that you were looking down on me. As I said, I was looking for some kind of passion. Nietzsche is a passion, but again a passion for someone. I knew it wasn't good enough. That unless I could think of something soon, you'd leave me, that I couldn't keep you with me just by playing, or *not* playing. I had to think of something more ambitious. I was already beginning to write in London. I began with a letter to you, a letter that was supposed to express all my feelings. I composed it when I was out walking. After I finished with Sid, I had such a lot of spare time. But I never wrote that letter. Only when we arrived in Bø, did I finally find my story."

"What?"

My heart stops. For a fraction of a second I'm actually clinically dead. Lou pulls on his cigarette, which has almost burned down. He blows out a big cloud of smoke and puts it out. I get smoke in my eyes. It stings. He strokes my cheek. It gives me an unpleasant feeling, as if his hand were a slithering little animal. Then he jumps out of my little bed and finds a plastic bag . . . I'm watching. Paralyzed. See him taking out a pile of papers written by hand and letting them fall on the floor. Hundreds of them. I'm almost angry. Angry because he's secretly been writing and not saying a damn thing to me. I'm burning inside and out. From jealousy. It's unfair. I don't like myself in a moment like this. It isn't a pleasant feeling. I strangle it before it can strangle me.

I pull myself together, swallow and ask:

"What's your book about?"

"August."

"August?"

"That's why we've been together so much. Like a parasite, I've trotted along to joyrider parties, car rallies, and walks in the forest . . . I've even learned a few things about stuffing animals."

I choke. I don't want to talk about anything that has to do with my big brother.

"August was flattered by the fact that someone was interested in him," Lou continues. "Flattered to be the center of attention, a story, words. Because unlike you, I'm interested in your brother. But I didn't want to say anything, it was supposed to be a surprise . . . I've been carrying this secret around like a pregnancy. Of course I've noticed that I've irritated you. Lou the lay-about is what you've been thinking, right? The good-for-nothing . . . and I've let you think it, because it's given me strength and courage. Because deep down I did hope that one day you'd be proud of this. I've been going for walks in the forest and writing. August has been good enough to keep his mouth shut. You couldn't get even a whiff of it," Lou says.

I'm ashamed. I run over to the window, open it wide. I can't believe my own ears. I laugh at the moon that isn't a moon, at the sun that isn't a sun, at the glowing sky. The wind is still blowing. The room is filled with a strange mist. The few leaves left are being shaken off the trees, looking like snowflakes in the sky.

"Fire!" I scream in alarm. "There's a fire!"

The red and ramshackle barn is like cat's eyes in the night, lighting up the sky from our farm and many farms uphill. Dandelion isn't barking. Never again. I'm crying. All the awful feelings are pouring out: arrogance, jealousy, anger, laziness, greed, avarice, gluttony, fornication . . . Lou licks my tears the way a dog would. Devotedly. It's unbearable. The conscience tormenting me. His thin arms hold me. He wants to run outside, help, find Dandelion . . . I hold him back. Fire sirens can be heard in the distance.

"I'm so glad I got to experience this one more time," I say, "with you. Now we're sharing everything, all the way down to the word."

I close my eyes. Open them. I'm in a dream it's impossible to wake up from. Everything is collapsing around us, but it feels so unreal, like something I ought to write about.

I look at my husband and ask:

"How far along are you?"

I don't need to be more specific. He understands immediately. He answers:

"My book is finished."

P.S.:
Everything I've written is true
apart from what I've invented

Thank you to

Siri Holtung
Nikolaj Frobenius
Anne and Knut, Jacki and Claude
Hilde Stubhaug, Kari Marstein, Irene Engelstad

And everyone who has lent me their
eyes, so I could see better . . .

Born in 1975, EDY POPPY is a Norwegian author and former model. In addition to her work in the theatre and as a writer of short stories, poems, and essays, her debut novel ANATOMI. MONOTONI won the Gylendal Prize in 2005.

Born and raised in Norway, MAY-BRIT AKERHOLT now lives in Australia, where she is a recipient of a Fellowship from the Theatre Board of Australia Council. She has lectured on theater at the National Institute of Dramatic Art, worked as a Dramaturg and Literary Manager at Sydney Theatre Company, and has translated numerous plays.

SELECTED DALKEY ARCHIVE TITLES

MICHAL AJVAZ, *The Golden Age.*
The Other City.
PIERRE ALBERT-BIROT, *Grabinoulor.*
YUZ ALESHKOVSKY, *Kangaroo.*
SVETLANA ALEXIEVICH, *Voices from Chernobyl.*
FELIPE ALFAU, *Chromos.*
Locos.
JOAO ALMINO, *Enigmas of Spring.*
IVAN ÂNGELO, *The Celebration.*
The Tower of Glass.
ANTÓNIO LOBO ANTUNES, *Knowledge of Hell.*
The Splendor of Portugal.
ALAIN ARIAS-MISSON, *Theatre of Incest.*
JOHN ASHBERY & JAMES SCHUYLER, *A Nest of Ninnies.*
GABRIELA AVIGUR-ROTEM, *Heatwave and Crazy Birds.*
DJUNA BARNES, *Ladies Almanack.*
Ryder.
JOHN BARTH, *Letters.*
Sabbatical.
Collected Stories.
DONALD BARTHELME, *The King.*
Paradise.
SVETISLAV BASARA, *Chinese Letter.*
Fata Morgana.
In Search of the Grail.
MIQUEL BAUÇÀ, *The Siege in the Room.*
RENÉ BELLETTO, *Dying.*
MAREK BIENCZYK, *Transparency.*
ANDREI BITOV, *Pushkin House.*
ANDREJ BLATNIK, *You Do Understand.*
Law of Desire.
LOUIS PAUL BOON, *Chapel Road.*
My Little War.
Summer in Termuren.
ROGER BOYLAN, *Killoyle.*
IGNÁCIO DE LOYOLA BRANDÃO, *Anonymous Celebrity.*
Zero.
BRIGID BROPHY, *In Transit.*
The Prancing Novelist.

GABRIELLE BURTON, *Heartbreak Hotel.*
MICHEL BUTOR, *Degrees.*
Mobile.
G. CABRERA INFANTE, *Infante's Inferno.*
Three Trapped Tigers.
JULIETA CAMPOS, *The Fear of Losing Eurydice.*
ANNE CARSON, *Eros the Bittersweet.*
ORLY CASTEL-BLOOM, *Dolly City.*
LOUIS-FERDINAND CÉLINE, *North.*
Conversations with Professor Y.
London Bridge.
HUGO CHARTERIS, *The Tide Is Right.*
ERIC CHEVILLARD, *Demolishing Nisard.*
The Author and Me.
MARC CHOLODENKO, *Mordechai Schamz.*
EMILY HOLMES COLEMAN, *The Shutter of Snow.*
ERIC CHEVILLARD, *The Author and Me.*
LUIS CHITARRONI, *The No Variations.*
CH'OE YUN, *Mannequin.*
ROBERT COOVER, *A Night at the Movies.*
STANLEY CRAWFORD, *Log of the S.S.*
The Mrs Unguentine.
Some Instructions to My Wife.
RALPH CUSACK, *Cadenza.*
NICHOLAS DELBANCO, *Sherbrookes.*
The Count of Concord.
NIGEL DENNIS, *Cards of Identity.*
PETER DIMOCK, *A Short Rhetoric for Leaving the Family.*
ARIEL DORFMAN, *Konfidenz.*
COLEMAN DOWELL, *Island People.*
Too Much Flesh and Jabez.
RIKKI DUCORNET, *Phosphor in Dreamland.*
The Complete Butcher's Tales.
RIKKI DUCORNET (cont.), *The Jade Cabinet.*
The Fountains of Neptune.
WILLIAM EASTLAKE, *Castle Keep.*
Lyric of the Circle Heart.
JEAN ECHENOZ, *Chopin's Move.*

STANLEY ELKIN, *A Bad Man.*
The Dick Gibson Show.
The Franchiser.
FRANÇOIS EMMANUEL, *Invitation to a Voyage.*
SALVADOR ESPRIU, *Ariadne in the Grotesque Labyrinth.*
LESLIE A. FIEDLER, *Love and Death in the American Novel.*
JUAN FILLOY, *Op Oloop.*
GUSTAVE FLAUBERT, *Bouvard and Pécuchet.*
JON FOSSE, *Aliss at the Fire.*
Melancholy.
Trilogy.
FORD MADOX FORD, *The March of Literature.*
MAX FRISCH, *I'm Not Stiller.*
Man in the Holocene.
CARLOS FUENTES, *Christopher Unborn.*
Distant Relations.
Terra Nostra.
Where the Air Is Clear.
Nietzsche on His Balcony.
WILLIAM GADDIS, JR., *The Recognitions.*
JR.
JANICE GALLOWAY, *Foreign Parts.*
The Trick Is to Keep Breathing.
WILLIAM H. GASS, *Life Sentences.*
The Tunnel.
The World Within the Word.
Willie Masters' Lonesome Wife.
GÉRARD GAVARRY, *Hoppla! 1 2 3.*
ETIENNE GILSON, *The Arts of the Beautiful.*
Forms and Substances in the Arts.
C. S. GISCOMBE, *Giscome Road.*
Here.
DOUGLAS GLOVER, *Bad News of the Heart.*
WITOLD GOMBROWICZ, *A Kind of Testament.*
PAULO EMÍLIO SALES GOMES, *P's Three Women.*
GEORGI GOSPODINOV, *Natural Novel.*

JUAN GOYTISOLO, *Juan the Landless.*
Makbara.
Marks of Identity.
JACK GREEN, *Fire the Bastards!*
JIŘÍ GRUŠA, *The Questionnaire.*
MELA HARTWIG, *Am I a Redundant Human Being?*
JOHN HAWKES, *The Passion Artist.*
Whistlejacket.
ELIZABETH HEIGHWAY, ED., *Contemporary Georgian Fiction.*
AIDAN HIGGINS, *Balcony of Europe.*
Blind Man's Bluff.
Bornholm Night-Ferry.
Langrishe, Go Down.
Scenes from a Receding Past.
ALDOUS HUXLEY, *Antic Hay.*
Point Counter Point.
Those Barren Leaves.
Time Must Have a Stop.
JANG JUNG-IL, *When Adam Opens His Eyes*
DRAGO JANČAR, *The Tree with No Name.*
I Saw Her That Night.
Galley Slave.
MIKHEIL JAVAKHISHVILI, *Kvachi.*
GERT JONKE, *The Distant Sound.*
Homage to Czerny.
The System of Vienna.
JACQUES JOUET, *Mountain R.*
Savage.
Upstaged.
JUNG YOUNG-MOON, *A Contrived World.*
MIEKO KANAI, *The Word Book.*
YORAM KANIUK, *Life on Sandpaper.*
ZURAB KARUMIDZE, *Dagny.*
PABLO KATCHADJIAN, *What to Do.*
JOHN KELLY, *From Out of the City.*
HUGH KENNER, *Flaubert, Joyce and Beckett: The Stoic Comedians.*
Joyce's Voices.
DANILO KIŠ, *The Attic.*
The Lute and the Scars.
Psalm 44.
A Tomb for Boris Davidovich.
ANITA KONKKA, *A Fool's Paradise.*

GEORGE KONRÁD, *The City Builder.*
TADEUSZ KONWICKI, *A Minor Apocalypse.*
The Polish Complex.
ELAINE KRAF, *The Princess of 72nd Street.*
JIM KRUSOE, *Iceland.*
AYSE KULIN, *Farewell: A Mansion in Occupied Istanbul.*
EMILIO LASCANO TEGUI, *On Elegance While Sleeping.*
ERIC LAURRENT, *Do Not Touch.*
VIOLETTE LEDUC, *La Bâtarde.*
LEE KI-HO, *At Least We Can Apologize.*
EDOUARD LEVÉ, *Autoportrait.*
Suicide.
MARIO LEVI, *Istanbul Was a Fairy Tale.*
DEBORAH LEVY, *Billy and Girl.*
JOSÉ LEZAMA LIMA, *Paradiso.*
OSMAN LINS, *Avalovara.*
The Queen of the Prisons of Greece.
ALF MACLOCHLAINN, *Out of Focus.*
Past Habitual.
RON LOEWINSOHN, *Magnetic Field(s).*
YURI LOTMAN, *Non-Memoirs.*
D. KEITH MANO, *Take Five.*
MINA LOY, *Stories and Essays of Mina Loy.*
MICHELINE AHARONIAN MARCOM, *The Mirror in the Well.*
BEN MARCUS, *The Age of Wire and String.*
WALLACE MARKFIELD, *Teitlebaum's Window.*
To an Early Grave.
DAVID MARKSON, *Reader's Block.*
Wittgenstein's Mistress.
CAROLE MASO, *AVA.*
HISAKI MATSUURA, *Triangle.*
LADISLAV MATEJKA & KRYSTYNA POMORSKA, EDS., *Readings in Russian Poetics: Formalist & Structuralist Views.*
HARRY MATHEWS, *Cigarettes.*
The Conversions.
The Human Country.
The Journalist.
My Life in CIA.

Singular Pleasures.
The Sinking of the Odradek.
Stadium.
Tlooth.
JOSEPH MCELROY, *Night Soul and Other Stories.*
ABDELWAHAB MEDDEB, *Talismano.*
GERHARD MEIER, *Isle of the Dead.*
HERMAN MELVILLE, *The Confidence-Man.*
AMANDA MICHALOPOULOU, *I'd Like.*
STEVEN MILLHAUSER, *The Barnum Museum.*
In the Penny Arcade.
RALPH J. MILLS, JR., *Essays on Poetry.*
CHRISTINE MONTALBETTI, *The Origin of Man.*
Western.
NICHOLAS MOSLEY, *Accident.*
Assassins.
Catastrophe Practice.
Hopeful Monsters.
Imago Bird.
Natalie Natalia.
Serpent.
WARREN MOTTE, *Fiction Now: The French Novel in the 21st Century.*
Oulipo: A Primer of Potential Literature.
GERALD MURNANE, *Barley Patch.*
Inland.
YVES NAVARRE, *Our Share of Time.*
Sweet Tooth.
DOROTHY NELSON, *In Night's City.*
Tar and Feathers.
WILFRIDO D. NOLLEDO, *But for the Lovers.*
BORIS A. NOVAK, *The Master of Insomnia.*
FLANN O'BRIEN, *At Swim-Two-Birds.*
The Best of Myles.
The Dalkey Archive.
The Hard Life.
The Poor Mouth.
The Third Policeman.
CLAUDE OLLIER, *The Mise-en-Scène.*
Wert and the Life Without End.

PATRIK OUŘEDNÍK, *Europeana*.
The Opportune Moment, 1855.
BORIS PAHOR, *Necropolis*.
FERNANDO DEL PASO, *News from the Empire*.
Palinuro of Mexico.
ROBERT PINGET, *The Inquisitory*.
Mahu or The Material.
Trio.
MANUEL PUIG, *Betrayed by Rita Hayworth*.
The Buenos Aires Affair.
Heartbreak Tango.
RAYMOND QUENEAU, *The Last Days*.
Odile.
Pierrot Mon Ami.
Saint Glinglin.
ANN QUIN, *Berg*.
Passages.
Three.
Tripticks.
ISHMAEL REED, *The Free-Lance Pallbearers*.
The Last Days of Louisiana Red.
Ishmael Reed: The Plays.
Juice!
The Terrible Threes.
The Terrible Twos.
Yellow Back Radio Broke-Down.
RAINER MARIA RILKE, *The Notebooks of Malte Laurids Brigge*.
JULIÁN RÍOS, *The House of Ulysses*.
Larva: A Midsummer Night's Babel.
Poundemonium.
ALAIN ROBBE-GRILLET, *Project for a Revolution in New York*.
A Sentimental Novel.
AUGUSTO ROA BASTOS, *I the Supreme*.
DANIËL ROBBERECHTS, *Arriving in Avignon*.
JEAN ROLIN, *The Explosion of the Radiator Hose*.
OLIVIER ROLIN, *Hotel Crystal*.
ALIX CLEO ROUBAUD, *Alix's Journal*.
JACQUES ROUBAUD, *The Form of a City Changes Faster, Alas, Than the Human Heart*.

The Great Fire of London.
Hortense in Exile.
Hortense Is Abducted.
Mathematics: The Plurality of Worlds of Lewis.
Some Thing Black.
RAYMOND ROUSSEL, *Impressions of Africa*.
VEDRANA RUDAN, *Night*.
GERMAN SADULAEV, *The Maya Pill*.
TOMAŽ ŠALAMUN, *Soy Realidad*.
LYDIE SALVAYRE, *The Company of Ghosts*.
LUIS RAFAEL SÁNCHEZ, *Macho Camacho's Beat*.
SEVERO SARDUY, *Cobra & Maitreya*.
NATHALIE SARRAUTE, *Do You Hear Them?*
Martereau.
The Planetarium.
STIG SÆTERBAKKEN, *Siamese*.
Self-Control.
Through the Night.
ARNO SCHMIDT, *Collected Novellas*.
Collected Stories.
Nobodaddy's Children.
Two Novels.
ASAF SCHURR, *Motti*.
GAIL SCOTT, *My Paris*.
JUNE AKERS SEESE, *Is This What Other Women Feel Too?*
BERNARD SHARE, *Inish*.
Transit.
VIKTOR SHKLOVSKY, *Bowstring*.
Literature and Cinematography.
Theory of Prose.
Third Factory.
Zoo, or Letters Not about Love.
PIERRE SINIAC, *The Collaborators*.
KJERSTI A. SKOMSVOLD, *The Faster I Walk, the Smaller I Am*.
JOSEF ŠKVORECKÝ, *The Engineer of Human Souls*.
GILBERT SORRENTINO, *Aberration of Starlight*.
Blue Pastoral.
Crystal Vision.

Imaginative Qualities of Actual Things.
Mulligan Stew.
Red the Fiend.
Steelwork.
Under the Shadow.
ANDRZEJ STASIUK, *Dukla.*
Fado.
GERTRUDE STEIN, *The Making of Americans.*
A Novel of Thank You.
PIOTR SZEWC, *Annihilation.*
GONÇALO M. TAVARES, *A Man: Klaus Klump.*
Jerusalem.
Learning to Pray in the Age of Technique.
LUCIAN DAN TEODOROVICI, *Our Circus Presents . . .*
NIKANOR TERATOLOGEN, *Assisted Living.*
STEFAN THEMERSON, *Hobson's Island.*
The Mystery of the Sardine.
Tom Harris.
JOHN TOOMEY, *Sleepwalker.*
Huddleston Road.
Slipping.
DUMITRU TSEPENEAG, *Hotel Europa.*
The Necessary Marriage.
Pigeon Post.
Vain Art of the Fugue.
La Belle Roumaine.
Waiting: Stories.
ESTHER TUSQUETS, *Stranded.*
DUBRAVKA UGRESIC, *Lend Me Your Character.*
Thank You for Not Reading.
TOR ULVEN, *Replacement.*
MATI UNT, *Brecht at Night.*
Diary of a Blood Donor.
Things in the Night.
ÁLVARO URIBE & OLIVIA SEARS, EDS., *Best of Contemporary Mexican Fiction.*
ELOY URROZ, *Friction.*
The Obstacles.
LUISA VALENZUELA, *Dark Desires and the Others.*
He Who Searches.

PAUL VERHAEGHEN, *Omega Minor.*
BORIS VIAN, *Heartsnatcher.*
TOOMAS VINT, *An Unending Landscape.*
ORNELA VORPSI, *The Country Where No One Ever Dies.*
AUSTRYN WAINHOUSE, *Hedyphagetica.*
MARKUS WERNER, *Cold Shoulder.*
Zundel's Exit.
CURTIS WHITE, *The Idea of Home.*
Memories of My Father Watching TV.
Requiem.
DIANE WILLIAMS, *Excitability: Selected Stories.*
DOUGLAS WOOLF, *Wall to Wall.*
Ya! & John-Juan.
JAY WRIGHT, *Polynomials and Pollen.*
The Presentable Art of Reading Absence.
PHILIP WYLIE, *Generation of Vipers.*
MARGUERITE YOUNG, *Angel in the Forest.*
Miss MacIntosh, My Darling.
REYOUNG, *Unbabbling.*
ZORAN ŽIVKOVIĆ , *Hidden Camera.*
LOUIS ZUKOFSKY, *Collected Fiction.*
VITOMIL ZUPAN, *Minuet for Guitar.*
SCOTT ZWIREN, *God Head.*

AND MORE . . .